Stars Over Texas

Other Books by Beverly C. Warren

CASTLE OF SHADOWS
SAPPHIRE LEGACY
THE WILD VINES
THAT GENTLE TOUCH
INVITATION TO A WALTZ

Stars Over Texas

BEVERLY C. WARREN

Doubleday

NEW YORK

1988

RAP /87 3944

All of the characters in this book
are fictitious, and any resemblance
to actual persons, living or dead,
is purely coincidental.

Library of Congress Cataloging-in-Publication Data

Warren, Beverly C.
Stars over Texas.

I. Title.
PS3573.A769S74   1988   813'.54   87–20171
ISBN 0-385-24339-1

Stars Over Texas

1

Though on the surface Danielle Wexford was apparently calm, inside her stomach was churning with nervous anxiety. She had never been as uptight as she was as that moment. It was her first foray into the big leagues, and she was still stunned by the fact she had gotten this far. To be one of three to be called in for a personal interview with the reknowned Nicholas Hunt was a coup she hadn't expected. This was the first time she had ever bid on new construction and one of the largest contracts she had ever tried for. If she landed it, made good, and met the deadline, she would be firmly established in the kitchen-design and cabinetry business.

She gave her name to the attractive secretary, who gave her an oblique, appraising glance before telling her to take a seat; it would be a while, she said, before Mr. Hunt could see her.

With a somewhat trembling hand, Danielle smoothed out her new, navy-blue silk skirt as she sat in the air-conditioned waiting room of the high-rise office building. She placed her slim leather attaché case on the floor by her feet. She had spent a small fortune on the new suit and tailored, pale blue silk blouse in the hopes they would create an image of professionalism and success. Besides, the outfit complemented her blue eyes and her short, wavy, red-gold hair, which circled around her head like a halo of clouds at sunset. Being a novice at bidding for multi-unit kitchens, she felt she needed every advantage to create a favorable impression on Hunt Contractors, Incorporated.

As she sat there, her back rigid with growing tension, she tried not to let her mind dwell on the matter at hand, for it only served to increase her nervousness and make her unsure of herself. She forced her thoughts back to the early years of her working life and mentally recalled the events that had brought her this far in the business.

Born into a middle-income family in Iowa, Dani was a great disappointment to her family when she declined to go to college, even though her grandparents had left a sizable trust fund for that purpose. One week after graduating from high school, Dani got a job not far from home answering the telephone for a company that dealt in kitchen cabinets and related items. Two years later she was designing kitchens and ordering the cabinetry for them herself. When the company moved to Houston, Texas, Dani decided to go with them, much to the frustration of her parents.

It had taken Dani a while to get used to Texas, where distances were so vast that the land appeared to be endless. On one level a languorous aura seemed to cloak Texas like polyurethane, while underneath all the gloss there was a frenetic pace to life. The highways were so choked with Mercedes, Cadillacs, Jaguars, and BMWs, that no one gave them any more thought than eggs at a grocery store. Stores were crammed with the latest in fashion, jewelry, furniture—merchandise that radiated pure wealth. One could almost smell money in the Texas air. But being born and raised in Iowa, her tastes and wants were simple. At first she found the transition from one lifestyle to another demanding, but it also offered a challenge.

After two years with the Shaw Company in Houston, Dani became restless. Her duties with the company were no longer challenging. They had become rote, and she felt her talents weren't being used to their fullest capacity. At a small house party, someone suggested she go into business for herself. At the time Dani laughed, as did most everyone else at the party. Later, on reflection, the idea began to foment in her brain until it became an obsession. The obsession became reality, and she resigned from the Andrew Shaw Company.

She recalled how, with heart beating like the wings of a humming-bird, she packed her Buick, got on Interstate 45, and headed for Dallas, and how her excitement grew as its skyline came into view. She could almost feel the vibrancy of the city, as sleek glass and metal structures thrust themselves into the sky like images from a science fiction movie, fantasies of shimmering gold and silver flashing in the sun. Before she even stopped the car, Dani knew she was going to love Dallas.

The first thing Dani did after settling in a motel was to find a real estate agent and, with some of the money from her trust fund, make a large down payment on a house about ten miles outside the city limits, keeping enough money in reserve to see her through the lean periods. But the real estate agent, Janice Gordon, soon became a close friend and sent her a number of potential clients. Though the first year was touch and go, once her ability was established in the kitchen remodeling business and word of mouth spread regarding her excellent work, her little business began to grow. Her special inducement, which no other company in the area offered, was a rendering, in color, of the client's projected new kitchen, giving her customers a preview of the design they desired. It was a feature of her service that captivated her clients.

After five years in Dallas, her business became so brisk, she hired a young woman to assist her. Sandra Parks' task was to answer the telephone, help with the paperwork, and keep the books. Dani had found she was losing customers because she was missing too many telephone calls while she was out in the field measuring kitchens. The association proved to be beneficial, and she got along with Sandy exceedingly well.

Now she was waiting for the real coup of her little business, a chance to break into the big leagues and big money with a bid on doing the kitchens for three hundred and fifty units in a high-rise condominium on the fringe of Dallas proper. A choice plum for a twenty-seven-year-old woman. The Hunt Corporation had narrowed the bids down to three, and hers was one of them.

Dani quickly snapped out of her musings when the door to Mr. Hunt's office opened and a well-dressed man came out smiling confidently. Her heart sank—he looked too confident. He stopped and chatted with the secretary, with whom he was on a first-name basis. They appeared to know each other quite well. I don't stand a chance, thought Dani. The Hunt firm has probably been doing business with this guy for years and will give the contract to him rather than take a chance on a newcomer. And why not? Her high hopes and spirit were beginning to deflate. But when the secretary told her to go in, a ray of hope glimmered in her blue eyes. Dani stood, attaché case in hand, took a deep breath, then let it out noiselessly as she approached the door. She turned the knob with a clammy hand, thrust it open, and walked in with head high.

A dark head, its owner evidently deep in concentration, was bent over some papers on the wide black desk. To Dani it seemed like an eternity before he spoke.

"Take a seat," said the man behind the desk in a resonant voice and with a directional wave of his hand. "I'll be with you in a moment."

Dani sat primly in the indicated chair and waited patiently. From the angle at which she sat, she couldn't quite see his face, but noticed he was much younger than she expected. Late thirties, she guessed. There wasn't a trace of gray in his thick, straight, black hair. Impatiently, she watched him shuffle papers around on his desk until he finally found the ones he wanted.

"Well Dan . . . this looks pretty good. I like the way you've laid the kitchens out. You've managed to get a good deal of cabinetry into a confined space but at a reasonable per-unit cost. I assume it includes countertops and delivery," he said, never once looking up.

"It does," she replied, her expectations surging.

He looked up sharply at the sound of her voice and his dark brown eyes narrowed as he studied her face. He leaned back in his upholstered, black leather chair with its glittering chrome legs. A slow, wry smile began to curve his full, well-formed lips. "You are a woman."

"So I've been told." Don't get flip, she warned herself. There is too much riding on this interview.

His smile broadened. "When I saw Dan Wexford on the layout sheets, I assumed I would be dealing with a man."

"Actually it's Dani . . . short for Danielle."

He leaned forward and peered down at his desk. "Yes . . . I see now . . . Dani. I didn't notice the *i* before. I take it you are Wexford Kitchens," he said, sitting back and looking at her again.

"I am. I hope you have no objections to working with a woman," she said with an undaunted air.

"I don't know. I've never worked with one before." He eyed her cooly, then steepled his two forefingers and lightly placed them on his lips. "You're rather young to be in this line of work, aren't you?"

"It's my belief that age has nothing to do with experience. My background consists of a good seven years in the kitchen business. I started out with the Andrew Shaw Company in Houston. I'm sure they'll apprise you of my qualifications if you wish to call them, Mr. Hunt. It is Mr. Hunt, isn't it?"

"Yes. Nicholas Hunt. I'm sorry if I didn't introduce myself properly, Miss Wexford. Or is it Mrs.?"

"Miss Wexford."

"I've heard of Shaw. It's a good outfit but a little on the high side when it comes to costing out a job. I know they only hired the best in the field, as your layouts prove. They are quite professional. Your layouts, I mean."

Dani was a little surprised that so young a man was the sole head of a corporation which had made quite a name for itself in Dallas. Nicholas Hunt was somewhat of a celebrity who enjoyed making the rounds of exclusive parties and charity balls. He was one of the most prominent entrepreneurs in all of Dallas, and one of its most eligible bachelors.

He had a high-bridged Roman nose set between very dark brown eyes, over which black eyebrows arched high. His face was wide-set and seemed to be in a constant battle against a five-o'clock shadow. He wore a dark brown pinstripe suit and a beige shirt, the latter covered by a vest, with a dark brown tie. His sartorial perfection was due to good taste and extremely expensive tailors. But even if he had been dressed in rags, he would still have been a handsome and dynamic man.

"Thank you for the compliment," said Dani.

"I believe in giving credit where credit is due. However I'm a little hesitant. Your bid was quite low, and I'm a little doubtful about you're being able to deliver cabinets and counters at the per-unit cost you have submitted." His dark eyes slowly assessed the rest of her.

"I wouldn't have submitted the bid at that figure if I wasn't sure I could deliver." She wasn't greedy. She took a lower percentage from the cabinet and countertop companies than most. Even with a lower commission, she would stand to make a good profit because of the volume. All she had to do was the paperwork, and she didn't have the huge overhead that her competitors had.

"How much lead time would you need?" he asked.

"Six weeks."

He looked at her steadily for several seconds, then asked, "Do you live here in Dallas, Miss Wexford?"

"I have a house about ten miles outside the city limits," she answered, wondering what the question had to do with the matter at hand.

"North? South? East? West?"

"North of Dallas."

"Oh? Property values are really soaring up that way. How long ago did you buy your house?"

"About five years ago."

"Then it's probably increased its value tenfold."

"I suppose it has." She was becoming increasingly annoyed by this unrelated line of questioning. Where she lived had nothing to do with the condominium contract.

"If you've been in the business for the past five years, I'm surprised I haven't heard of Wexford Kitchens before. I make it a point to keep

track of those businesses related to the field of construction. Where is
your office located?"

"My office is in my home. Up to now my work has been limited to
remodeling kitchens in private homes. This is my first bid on new construction," she replied honestly.

"I see."

She wanted to scream, Do I get the job or don't I? Besides, his
unfaltering gaze was undermining her endeavor to maintain a cool,
professional attitude. There was something in his eyes that unnerved
her. She had the sensation he was visually undressing her, and it made
her uncomfortable.

"Do you have any brochures on the cabinets I would be getting at
this price?" he asked.

"Certainly. You would have your choice of three," she replied, reaching for her case, placing it on her lap and opening it. "One is a high-
pressure laminate, easy to maintain, in almond or white. Another is a
dark wood veneer; and the third is a light wood veneer." She took the
two-page brochures, each one picturing the cabinets mentioned with
detailed specifications, from her case, snapped it shut, and placed it
back on the floor before rising to put the brochures on his desk.

"And which would you recommend?" he asked after perusing the
colorful, glossy brochures for several seconds.

"The high-pressure laminate. It has a better box and double-track
drawers. A quality cabinet at a reasonable price. I would also recommend it for another reason. People who purchase condos tend to be
professional people who have neither the time nor the inclination for
extensive housekeeping. The laminated cabinets clean with a wipe of a
sponge. The wood veneer cabinets require more attention and care," she
said, proud of her clear and succinct explanation.

"You are indeed knowledgeable, Miss Wexford."

"It's all part of the job, Mr. Hunt."

"Can you leave these brochures with me?"

"Certainly. My name, telephone number, and address are stamped on
the back of each brochure."

"I'm sure you are aware your bid wasn't the only low one. I have one
other gentleman to see before I make any decision. At least I believe he
is a man. I must admit it threw me a bit off base to discover Dan
Wexford was a woman. But I don't think many women would adopt the

name Wilbur." He flashed a wide smile—white, even teeth glinting between those full lips, then stood and came around the desk.

Automatically, Dani rose when he did and picked up her attaché case.

"It's been a great pleasure to meet you, Miss Wexford," he said, extending his hand.

Dani grasped it firmly for a single shake. She was surprised to find he wasn't much taller then she was. But then she had three-inch heels on, whereas in her stocking feet she was only five foot four. He was a heavyset man with the physique of a well-trained athlete.

"I hope we can do business, Mr. Hunt," she said, flourishing her best smile.

"I should have an answer for you in a few days." He followed her to the door, opened it, then quietly closed it behind her.

Dani gave a quick smile to the secretary and started to walk out of the waiting room. Her peripheral vision spied a well-dressed man in his late forties or early fifties sitting in the chair she had previously occupied. His expression was so distraught she didn't think he even saw her. Next victim, she thought with some amusement.

She looked at her watch and groaned as she got into her car. Rush hour! It would take her decades to get home. She hoped Sandra Parks would realize she was caught in traffic and not wait for her. Sandra Parks had proved to be a gem assisting Dani. She had a pleasant manner on the phone, was a whiz with figures, and thoroughly dependable, if somewhat lacking in a sense of humor.

Dani had turned the game room of her seven-room house into an office. One could come in the front door and go directly into the game room without having to go through the formal dining room, living room, or the spacious kitchen with its small dinette. She thought it ideal for her purposes and, at the time, she couldn't afford to rent an office. Over the years it had worked out well. And Sandy also found it convenient, as she could fix her lunch there and not have to go out to eat. On the walls of the game room, Dani displayed door samples of the various cabinets she handled. Yes. Dani was more than pleased with the arrangement. It worked out so well she knew she would never be bothered renting office space. It would be a superfluous and unnecessary expense.

It had taken her twenty minutes to negotiate the section of the three lane highway that normally took slightly less than ten minutes. Sh always tried to schedule her appointments so she wouldn't be on any

the main arteries around Dallas during the rush hour. But the time of this appointment had been set by Nicholas Hunt, not her.

In the monotony of bumper to bumper driving, her thoughts strayed to the man she had just met. With the exception of his arresting brown eyes, she didn't think his facial features were particularly ideal; yet his face as a whole was handsome, and there was a undeniable appeal about the man. A masculinity that refused to be subdued and was forcefully compelling. She wondered what it would be like to work with such a man, seeing him on a fairly frequent basis. She didn't find the thought objectionable, even though she had the feeling Nicholas Hunt didn't approve of women in any phase of the construction business. Still, to work with him was an intriguing notion. The name Hunt Contractors was posted on large signs at almost every construction site in and around Dallas. To have a contract with the corporation would make her little Wexford Kitchens a notable company in Dallas. Why she might expand! Build her own empire!

With these thoughts of grandeur whirling in her head, Dani almost missed her service road exit, which would have annoyed her greatly. She was late enough as it was, and she was hungry.

Fifteen minutes later she was pulling into the driveway of her two-story, red brick house. She was surprised to find Sandy's car still in the driveway and even more surprised to see an unadorned yellow pickup truck there. It was at least ten years old, with pronounced traces of rust and an odd assortment of dents. The truck was totally unfamiliar to her.

Entering the small foyer, Dani heard Sandy's laughter echoing from the game room. It piqued Dani's curiosity, for Sandy was not quick to laugh. She had a tendency to stare vacantly whenever the punch line of a joke was told. Whoever was in the game room must be a master of humor, she thought, and strode into her office in a sure, steady gait.

A lanky man was sprawled on her maroon leather couch, a battered, beige cowboy hat resting on one of the cushions alongside him. Seeing her, he jumped to his feet, a broad grin on his wide, thin lips. A widow's peak invaded his thick brown hair, which waved carelessly about his head and ended slightly curled over the collar of his blue chambray shirt. He had a broad, high forehead, and his brilliant blue-gray eyes seemed to be in a perpetual squint above his high cheekbones, while his cheeks themselves hollowed down to a square bony jaw. His nose was aristocratically thin and straight, while his smile caused cobwebby lines

to crinkle about his eyes and mouth on his suntanned face. Even though Dani was wearing her three-inch heels, he towered above her like a gargantuan sculpture. His frame was lean, with exceptionally broad shoulders, then narrowed down to slim hips. Tight, faded blue jeans clung to muscled legs, and his feet were encased in heeled, well-pointed, brown lizard boots that bore traces of long and hard wear.

"Howdy, little lady," he greeted in a soft Texan drawl as he extended his hand.

"Hello," said Dani putting her hand in his, to have it dwarfed while he vigorously shook it.

"You must be Miss Wexford. Sandy here has been telling me all about your little company and what a real fine job you do with kitchens. She's quite a little saleswoman, that secretary of yours," he said, still flourishing a smile which gave him a boyish look that defied time.

"Sandy is my office manager, not my secretary," corrected Dani. "And who might you be?" she asked pleasantly, removing her hand from his.

"Scott Rowland, at your service ma'am."

"Scottie's been telling me some of the funniest stories I've ever heard," said Sandy, as she started to collect her things.

"It was good of you to stay and hold down the fort until I got back, Sandy," said Dani going to the desk. "Any messages?"

"Janice Gordon called and wanted you to meet her for lunch at the Anatole tomorrow. I said you'd get back to her. The rest of the messages are on the pad. How did it go this afternoon?" asked Sandy.

Dani flipped her hand back and forth in the air, a gesture of indecision. "He said he'd let me know in a few days."

Sandy shrugged as she moved from behind the desk to make room for Dani. "Then there's still a ray of hope."

"Only a slim one, if you ask me," said Dani.

"It's been a pleasure meeting you, Scottie," said Sandy, giving the man a bright smile.

"It's been my pleasure, little lady."

"See you on Monday, Dani," called Sandy as she left the office.

"Sorry about the business talk. I didn't mean to ignore you, but Sandy had stayed much later than she should have. I wanted to get the essentials done so she could leave," explained Dani.

"Shoot! I'm not going anywhere." Scott Rowland resumed his seat on the couch as if he was content to remain there indefinitely. "Nice place you have here. Comfy and homey like. Not one of those stark, impersonal offices."

"Thank you. I like it. Now . . . what can I do for you, Mr. Rowland?" asked Dani, giving him her full attention.

"Call me Scottie. Everyone does. I don't reckon I'd even turn my head if someone called for Mr. Rowland. I'm not one for formality. I'm here about doing a kitchen, little lady."

Recalling the none-too-spruce pickup truck in her driveway and the fact that he looked like a laborer, she assumed he was looking for work. "I'm sorry, Mr. Rowland, but . . ."

"Scottie," he interrupted.

"Scottie . . . I already have installers. I've used the same outfit for the past three years and find them quite satisfactory. I can give you their name. Perhaps they could use extra help."

"Whoa! You have me all wrong. I'm not looking for work. I want you to do a kitchen for me. My momma's. Her and Daddy have been married for over forty years and she's still rambling around in that forty-year-old kitchen. Darn if she doesn't still have a pantry. I thought it high time Momma had a modern kitchen with all the newfangled things that go with it. You came highly recommended, and I was told you draw and paint a picture of how the kitchen will look when it's finished. Momma would like that," he said.

"A new kitchen with all the modern conveniences could well run into quite a bit of money," warned Dani.

"Shoot! What's money for if you don't spend it?" He gave her a sly, crooked grin.

"My terms are one-third down with the acceptance of the contract, one third when the material is delivered to the job site, and the balance on completion," stated Dani in her best businesslike voice. There was something about the handsome man that made her uneasy, but she couldn't put her finger on it.

"Whatever you say, little lady. When can you get started?"

Dani thumbed through the desk calendar. "I can come out next week, say Wednesday, to measure your mother's kitchen. Could you give me directions to your parents' home?"

"I'll do better than that. I'll pick you up Wednesday morning and take you there myself."

"That won't be necessary. I work alone. Besides I usually try to accomplish other things when I'm in a certain area. It saves time," she said with a smile.

"You're so darn pretty when you smile like that. You must have all the fellas in Dallas knocking at your door. Have you got yourself a steady beau?"

Dani flushed slightly at the man's impertinence. "My personal life is none of your affair, Mr. Rowland."

"There you go again with that Mr. Rowland business. What do I have to do to make you call me Scottie?" Lines crinkled about his squinting eyes as he smiled that crooked and seemingly indigenous smile.

"For one thing, you can stop calling me 'little lady.' " She tried to say it without rancor, but a trace of annoyance slipped into her tone.

"I seem to be riling you every which way." He grabbed his cowboy hat and placed it on his head, the wide brim almost shading his eyes, and stood. He peered down at her through those narrowed blue-gray eyes, the smile gone. "I'd best be getting along before I ruffle your pretty feathers beyond placating."

"Are you still interested in having me remodel your parents' kitchen?" So she loses a remodeling job. It's not the end of the world. Besides she wasn't sure she wanted to work for this Scott Rowland. She always tried to keep her relationship with a client on a professional level, and this cowboy seemed determined to promote a relationship of familiarity.

"Of course. Like I said, I'll pick you up and take you out to the spread myself." He turned to go, hesitated, then faced her again. "By the way, that's a mighty pretty suit you have on. Makes you look mighty regal. Bye for now, ma'am."

Dani watched his long legs carry him from the room. She shook her head, sighed, then leaned back in the chair. Something deep inside her warned her not to take this Rowland job.

Sleep was elusive as she lay in bed. For the past five years, she dated various men on a fairly frequent basis. She had been to parties, meetings, and scores of gatherings with mixed groups. Some of the men she met, she liked, to some she was indifferent, while others were totally abhorrent to her. But not one of them had captured her attention like the two men she met in one day, two men so completely different from each other. First, a shrewd successful businessman with impeccable tastes. Short, but solidly built, Nicholas Hunt was a charismatic tycoon with a sharp eye and a quick brain for business. He was dark and handsome, and, though reluctantly, she admitted to herself that she was attracted to him.

Then she finds this rangy cowboy on her couch, and despite her initial disapproval of him, there was something formidable about him that stirred her interest. What really troubled her was the fact she knew it was more than a casual interest. His deep voice and boyish good looks struck an unfamiliar chord in her, one that apparently had been silent for some time. She tossed and turned, but the long day finally took its toll and she fell asleep.

The Anatole was a hotel on the grand scale. But then everything in Dallas was on a grand scale. The hotel's red facade was crowned with blue pyramid roofs. The luxurious interior was dotted with shops that catered to the very wealthy. Restaurants sparkled under the sunlight that brazenly filtered through the glass dome several stories above. It had the aura of an old Roman atrium which, sent through time, became modernized and displayed an opulence that more than rivaled the glory that was Rome.

Wearing a boxy yellow dress of madras cotton with a gold-tone chain cinching her waist, Dani walked into the Anatole to find Janice Gordon waiting for her.

"I hope I haven't kept you waiting, Jan," said Dani, who always prided herself on her punctuality.

"No, I just arrived myself. Let's get a table before they get too crowded," urged Janice, who wore a lightweight, bright purple suit with a pale lavender blouse. She had straight black hair of medium length that had been teased to fluff about her face, a striking, good-looking face. She was thirty-one and worked for a prestigious real estate firm in Dallas. She was quick, bright, and had an exceptional sense of humor. Her only conspicuous fault was her tendency to dominate a conversation.

But Janice Gordon was not the exception; neither was Dani. The atrium of the Anatole was filled with quick, bright, young professionals, some with briefcases and some without. To watch them walking through the restaurants and milling about was like seeing an exclusive showing of the latest in high fashion.

Seated, their cocktails on the table and their order of salads placed,

Janice asked with exuberance, "Well, what was the fabulous Nicholas Hunt really like? Is he all every woman dreams about?"

"I suppose so. I wasn't with him for very long, and it was strictly business," replied Dani.

"Oh come now, Dani. Don't tell me you didn't have some sort of reaction to the great Nicholas Hunt. For a man to reach his prominence, he must have a very definite type of personality," declared Janice.

"I'm telling you we talked business. I was more interested in getting a contract from him than analyzing his personality."

"You must have noticed if he was handsome, tall, short . . ." persisted Janice.

"I suppose you're not going to leave it alone until I give you some sort of answer," claimed Dani with a smile.

"Right."

"Well . . . he's quite handsome, rather on the short side but a very charming man who is very sexy and who I hope gives me the contract to do the kitchens for his condominiums."

"If he does, will you drop the remodeling end of it and do only new construction?"

"No. I really enjoy the remodeling. New construction is pure icing on the cake. With all the new construction around, you should be doing well," said Dani, changing the subject.

"Doing well? Dani . . . I'm on a roll. There don't seem to be enough homes to meet the demand, no matter what they cost. Even a lot the size of a postage stamp is going for a small fortune. I've managed to pick up a couple of properties for myself on spec. The payments are horrendous but if the boom continues, I'll have them paid off in no time, then buy more. You might do well to think about getting a lot or two yourself," suggested Janice.

"I have no intention of becoming a land baron."

"Dani honey, that's where the real money is here in Dallas. Land . . . and more land. If you get the contract with Hunt, you'll be floating in dough. What are you going to do with it all? Stuff it in your mattress? Invest it, Dani, invest it in real estate. I could keep an eye open for an excellent investment property for you. There's a prime piece I know will be coming onto the market any day now. I could give you first crack at it," said Janice leaning forward over the table in a conspiratorial tone only to lean back when the waiter brought their salads.

Dani laughed. "You are persistent, Jan."

"In my business one has to be. Seriously, Dani, promise me you'll think about it. It could start a whole new life for you. I'll tell you one thing, in another year, I'm starting my own real estate company. I have the connections now to make it succeed. Of course I wouldn't want my plans known. It's just between you and me. Okay?"

"Of course, Jan. Between you, me, and the dry martinis. The salad is quite good today."

"Food's food."

"That's the trouble with you, Jan. You never stop to enjoy anything," declared Dani.

"And you do, I suppose, working ten or more hours a day, driving around in a six-year-old Buick. Come on, Dani. You're a worse workaholic than I am."

"I work hard five days a week. Saturday and Sunday I do as I please and I don't think about kitchens. You're hustling every waking minute and don't you dare deny it. And for your information, I like my old Buick," said Dani good-naturedly.

"Keep your old Buick, then and I'll trade my Cadillac in every two years for a new one. What are you going to do, Dani? Wait for some Prince Charming to come into your life and make you princess of the universe? Believe me, it won't happen. There are no Prince Charmings out there. Only hustlers like you and me. That's all there is in Dallas—hustlers."

"Don't be so cynical, Jan," said Dani, her blue eyes sparkling, her lips smiling. "Maybe there are some Prince Charmings left in this world after all."

Janice eyed her friend suspiciously. "So Hunt did get to you after all. Watch out for that one. From what I've heard, women are mere commodities to him. Never takes any one of them seriously. I guess he thinks they're out for his money and power."

"I wasn't thinking of Nicholas Hunt," said Dani, and oddly enough she wasn't. For some peculiar reason unknown to her, Scott Rowland had fleetingly popped into her mind.

"Who then?" asked Janice, her eyebrows arching in curiosity.

"No one in particular. Are you showing any property today?"

"I wrapped up a deal this morning, so I decided to treat myself and take the afternoon off. Want to go into town and do a bit of shopping? I could use a new dress for the party at Jane's tonight. You're going, aren't you? She always asks the most delicious men."

"Of course I'm going. And shopping sounds like a good idea. It'll take my mind off the uncertainty of the Hunt contract."

"The contract or the man?" teased Janice.

"The contract," replied Dani firmly, but underneath she had doubts.

2

Dani turned over in bed and muttered, "Go away." But the chimes of her doorbell were persistent. She slowly opened one eye and peered at the alarm clock. Nine in the morning! Who in heaven's name was at her door at this hour on a Sunday morning? She wasn't expecting anyone. She grabbed her pillow and snuggled it over her head. Maybe they'd go away if she ignored them. The doorbell chimed as though it were embarking on an endless symphony.

"What's the use?" she cried aloud and got out of bed reluctantly, her mood malevolent as she slipped into her beige, cotton-and-nylon robe with its fiery dragon embroidered on the back. She stalked to the door with sleep still hazing her eyes and vengeance grumbling in her heart. She flung the door open and her jaw sagged; the clever admonitions she had been practicing vanished from her mind.

"Good morning, Miss Wexford," greeted Scott Rowland with a boyish grin.

"Do you realize it's nine o'clock in the morning? What the devil are you doing here?" she asked, one hand still on the doorknob, the other braced against the jamb, preventing his entrance.

"The day is so beautiful, I got to thinking that nice Miss Wexford might like to take a ride out to my daddy's place and measure up that kitchen. So I saddled up my pickup truck and came on over." He handed her the voluminous Sunday paper encased in its plastic home.

"I don't work on Sunday," she said tersely, then snatched the newspaper from him.

"You don't have to work. Tell me what to measure and I'll do all the work. Besides, it's a real pretty drive. Say, you look like you could use a good cup of coffee. I make one of the best doggone pots of coffee in all of Texas," he boasted.

Her shoulders sagged. He was trying so hard to be friendly, and here she was being rude and thoroughly obnoxious. He even made a point of not calling her little lady. She swung the door open and motioned for him to come in.

"Come in," she said. "I apologize for my brusqueness, but I was sound asleep when you started ringing the doorbell. I'm still a little asleep."

"Have a bad night?"

"No. A late one." Jane's party last night was as always. A lot of talk, a lot of food, a lot of cocktails—all of it inconsequential. Dani was never sure whether she enjoyed herself or not. As a rule, the guests were nice and she liked meeting new people and talking to everyone. Though she made it a rule never to have more than two cocktails at any of these affairs, others didn't restrict themselves, and the entire affair ended up with everyone talking too much and too loud and not listening to anyone else. The party had been in full swing when she left at two in the morning.

"Where's the kitchen?" he asked.

She led him into the kitchen. "There's the coffee maker and the coffee . . ."

"I'm sure I'll find what I need," he interrupted.

"Then you won't mind if I take a shower and get dressed," she said with a sleepy voice.

"Not at all, little . . . Miss Wexford," he corrected himself. "I'll just make myself at home. Wear some jeans or slacks and sturdy shoes."

"Are we going to walk to your parent's home?"

"No," he replied with a crooked smile. "But we might do some walking around when we get there, unless you can ride a horse."

"Never had the inclination to learn."

She hurried up the stairs, looking forward to a cool shower that would bring her body and mind fully awake. As she dressed in jeans, sneakers, and a white sleeveless cotton blouse, her mind cleared, and she realized how carelessly she had acted. She had let this Scott Rowland into her house without really knowing the man, then blithely took a shower without locking any of the doors. For all she knew he could be loading his pickup with her furnishings and the few valuables she possessed. But when she opened her bedroom door, she knew the man was busy with other things, for the smell of bacon frying assailed her nostrils with its tantalizing aroma, and the delicious scent of coffee brewing teased her palate. She quickly went down to the kitchen, where the table was set for two.

"You didn't have to go to all this trouble. Just coffee would have been fine," she said, a little overwhelmed by his attention to detail. Napkins, cutlery properly placed, grapefruit all sectioned with a maraschino cherry on top. "Can I help?"

"Sit yourself down. I'm quite an expert in the kitchen, though I don't get to indulge in the practice of the culinary arts very often," he said, slipping the bacon and buttered toast in the oven to keep it warm while he joined her at the table, bringing the coffeepot with him. He poured a cup for each of them. Cream and sugar were already on the table.

"Where is your parents' place?" she asked, then took a swallow of the coffee before tackling her grapefruit.

"About fifty miles east of here, Miss Wexford."

"The name is Danielle. Most people call me Dani."

"Danielle." He spoke the name as though he was savoring it. "French, isn't it?"

"My mother always wanted to go to Paris. She was enamored of everything French. Hence . . . Danielle," she explained.

"Any brothers or sisters?"

"Two brothers back in Iowa."

"Were you born in Iowa?"

"Born and raised there. And you, Scott?" she asked.

"Born right here in Texas. Have a sister living in California." He removed their finished grapefruit and took the dishes to the sink. "How do you like your eggs?"

"Over easy. Have you ever visited your sister?"

He nodded as he broke two eggs into the frying pan. "Been out to see her a couple of times. Her and her husband have a real nice place a little south of Los Angeles. They also have two fine children."

"I'm surprised you're not married."

"Why?" he asked concentrating on the eggs.

Dani shrugged. "I don't know. I guess you seem like the family type."

"I suppose I am basically. Just never found the little lady who could win my heart."

"What do you do for a living?"

"Oh . . . a little bit of everything," he replied.

"Like a handy man?"

"You might say that. I don't go for the nine-to-five routine. I like to vary what I do and be outside when I can. Makes life more interesting." He brought the eggs to the table, then went back for the bacon and toast.

They ate in comfortable silence. Once in a while Dani would lift her head to see those blue-gray eyes gazing at her and Scott would flash a quick grin, like a child who had been caught with his hand in the cookie jar. Dani found it pleasing and flattering. She felt at ease with the lanky cowboy and wasn't the least bit self-conscious about not having put any makeup on.

He poured more coffee for them, then leaned back in the chair and stretched. "Real nice place you have here, Dani. Too bad you don't have a swimming pool."

"The lot is too small for one. Do you like to swim, Scott?"

"Swim and ride horses . . . my two great vices. And you?"

"Swim, yes. I was on the girl's swimming team in high school. It's the only sport I really care for. Haven't been swimming in ages though."

"Too busy working?"

"It seems that way," replied Dani, piling up the dishes and taking them to the sink.

"Want some help with those?" asked Scott.

"No. I'll put them in the sink to soak, then load the dishwasher when I get back. I'll go put my face on—then we can leave."

"I'd rather you didn't. To me you're as pretty as a picture without it," he said.

"Then I'll just get my case with the things I'll need to do your mother's kitchen." She went into the game-room-turned-office. She felt lightheaded, sensing he had made the remark about no makeup with sincerity, not ingratiatingly to flatter her.

On the ride to his parents' home, the old pickup emphasized every rut and bump in the road. Dani felt like a milk shake in the hands of an erratic mechanical shaker gone mad. But Scott's mellifluous, soft voice with its Texan drawl, was soothing as he discoursed on the wonders of Texas. It was clear to Dani the man loved the land and was proud to be a Texan.

They drove up a long, dirt road where a white, two-story, wood-framed house shone golden under the morning sun as it rose stark against the vast plain. An old-fashioned porch wrapped itself around the house protectively. Here and there, near the house, trees proudly spread their branches and stood tall against an azure sky. Fields stretched out as far as the eye could see without another house to intrude upon the visible horizon. With the exception of power lines, the scene lacked the accoutrements of modernity, no golden arches denoting fast food, no television antennas protruding in the air like metal skeletons. The rustic scene made Dani feel as though she had entered the twilight zone, when Indians roamed the range and settlers stood alone against the rustlers and evil men. The glitter, dazzle, and affluence of Dallas seemed to belong to a dream world she had left behind and found hard to remember. Her mind sped back to the simplicity of Iowa, causing her to wonder which world she really belonged to.

The pickup choked to a halt and Dani heard the slam of an old wooden screen door. She looked to the white porch to see an older couple standing there expectantly, cheery smiles on their pleasant faces. They reminded her of her own mother and father. Before she knew it, Scott had opened the truck door and was offering her a hand down. For some strange reason, she felt like a prospective bride about to be paraded before the groom's parents for their approval.

After introductions she was ushered inside, Mrs. Rowland's arm tucked through hers, while Scott followed with his father. She thought it somewhat incongruous that the turn-of-the-century farmhouse boasted central air-conditioning, but was glad it did. The ride had been hot and dusty. She glanced around at the furnishings, which were in good taste, neither very old nor modern, but homey and comfortable.

"We've been looking forward to your visit, Miss Wexford," said Agnes Rowland.

"Didn't Scott tell you this isn't really a visit? I've come to measure your kitchen so I can design a new one for you, Mrs. Rowland," said Dani.

"Oh yes, he told us. But we see so little of him that when he does show up we always make a visit of it. And do call me Agnes. Mrs.

Rowland sounds so stuffy. Besides, you being such a good friend of
Scottie's, I feel we should be on a first-name basis."

Dani smiled and thought, I hardly know the man. Yet the woman
was so kindly, she wasn't about to argue the point. "Everyone calls me
Dani, short for Danielle."

"What a pretty name! I suppose you'd like to see the kitchen first so
we can get the business out of the way and have a nice visit for the rest
of the day," said Agnes.

"Fine with me." Dani was a bit surprised. She hadn't expected to
spend the entire day at the Rowlands'. On the other hand, she didn't
have any commitments at home and except for movies, restaurants, and
a few flea markets, Dallas was virtually closed down on a Sunday.

"Momma—Daddy and I are going out to the barn," called Scott
from one of the other rooms.

"All right son," Agnes called back. Then to Dani she said, "Here we
are. It's pretty out of date, I suppose. There's only Dad and I now. We
don't really need a big, fancy kitchen. But Scottie insisted. He said it
would make my work much easier and that I'd find it a real pleasure to
cook in a modernized kitchen."

"I think he's right," said Dani, scanning the kitchen with a knowledgeable eye. It was certainly a spacious kitchen, with a refrigerator off
to one side, an old gas stove some distance from both the antiquated
cast-iron sink and the refrigerator. There was very little cabinetry and
hardly any counter space. Most of the work seemed to be performed on
the bare oak table in the middle of the floor. "Where do you keep all
your canned goods, Agnes?" asked Dani.

"In the pantry. Come. I'll show you," said Agnes, steering Dani
around the corner from the refrigerator to a windowless, cramped,
closetlike room. Agnes pulled a string that lighted a single bare bulb.
Shelves circled around the pantry above a narrow counter, under which
were stored miscellaneous pots and pans and roasters.

"You must be on your feet a lot and do a tremendous amount of
walking to prepare a meal, Agnes. A new kitchen would eliminate a lot
of tiresome trotting around for things," commented Dani.

"One gets used to doing things a certain way, and after a while
doesn't give it a second thought," said Agnes. "Can I make you a cup of
coffee or tea?"

"I'd like to get my measurements first. I'd appreciate a cup of coffee when I'm through, if you don't mind. Your son makes excellent coffee," said Dani.

"Oh, he's quite a cook. Loves to dabble in the kitchen. He makes a bowl of chili that makes your fingernails itch. The only trouble is he hates to clean up after himself."

"You said you don't see much of him. I thought he lived here," said Dani placing her trim case on the oak table and opening it up.

"He keeps himself quite busy in Dallas, and thereabouts, so that he keeps a small apartment in Dallas," said Agnes, sitting down in one of the padded wooden chairs at the table.

With her steel measuring tape, layout pad, and pencil, Dani went around the kitchen with expertise, jotting down numbers and notes. Within a half hour, she had everything she needed to design the Rowland's new kitchen.

"I could use that coffee now," said Dani, returning her material to her case and smiling fondly at Agnes.

"All ready for you, Dani."

Dani had been so engrossed in her work, she hadn't noticed the slight woman bustling about making coffee and setting the table with cups and saucers. She sat down at the table while Agnes poured. "I have some brochures of the various types of cabinets available. I'll leave them with you so you can decide what type of cabinetry you prefer." From her case Dani took out glossy photographs of the better, custom line of cabinets she could obtain. She also removed a chain of laminate samples for the countertops and put it on the table.

"This is just like Christmas," exclaimed Agnes, her warm gray eyes smiling with delight.

"Will you want a dishwasher?"

"Scottie said to get everything there was going," replied Agnes as she studied the brochures.

"Microwave oven too?"

"I suppose so. But I don't want an electric stove. I like my gas for cooking."

It didn't take Agnes long to pick out the style and type of cabinet she wanted, but the choice of laminates was so generous she couldn't make up her mind. She asked Dani if she might keep the chain for a few days so she could go over it with Tom, her husband. Between the two of them perhaps she could come to a decision. Dani told her she could keep them for as long as she wished, as she had plenty of them at the office.

"Now I know where Scott learned to make such good coffee. This is excellent. I'm afraid my coffee leaves a lot to be desired," said Dani, as Agnes poured another cup for each of them. Her heart gave a little jump when she heard the screen door bang shut. What was the matter with her? she wondered. Scott Rowland was just another man.

"Got any more of that brew of yours, Momma?" asked Scott, as he and his father came into the kitchen and tooks seats at the table.

"Sure have," replied Agnes, then saw to their needs.

"All finished Dani?" asked Scott, swooping the cowboy hat from his head and hooking it on the spindle of the chair.

"Yes. I managed to do it all on my own, even though I remember someone offering to do it for me," Dani teased.

"I had a notion that you'd prefer to do it for yourself and wouldn't be wanting some dolt fooling around with your pad and pencil," said Scott, his eyes and lips smiling at her fondly. "When we finish our coffee, you'll have to come outside and see Daddy's new mare. Fine animal."

"You raise horses, Mr. Rowland?" asked Dani.

"That I do, little lady. Riding horses and quarter horses." Tom Rowland was tall and lean like his son, only his face was far more weather-worn, lines more deeply etched in a handsome face.

"Daddy raises some of the best quarter horses in all of Texas," claimed Scott proudly.

"Now son . . . don't go exaggerating," chided Tom Rowland.

"You do and you know it, Tom Rowland," insisted Agnes.

"Is there much demand for horses these days, Mr. Rowland?" asked Dani.

"In Texas there is always a demand for a good horse. And call me Tom, little lady. We don't go in for formalities around here. Scottie will have to take you riding. I have some real gentle mares."

"Dani doesn't ride, Daddy," informed Scott.

"Then teach her, boy, teach her," said Tom.

"I've never been around horses," said Dani a little apprehensively.

"Well then, it's high time you were. Can't live in Texas and not know your way around horses. Finish your coffee, Scottie, and take the little lady out to the barn and show her what gentle creatures they are."

"Don't stray too far, Scottie. We'll be eating in an hour or so," warned his mother.

"We won't," said Scott, pushing his chair back and draining his cup at the same time. He plucked his hat from the chair and put it on. "Ready Dani?"

"Yes." She snapped her case shut. "I'll put this in the truck if you don't mind. I don't want to forget it."

When she stepped outside onto the porch, the full force of the summer's heat hit her in the face. No matter how long she had lived in Texas, the contrast between air-conditioning and the hot, dry winds of Texas never ceased to stun her. Scott opened the door of the truck and she tossed her case on the seat.

In a leisurely gait, they strolled toward the long horse barn and went inside, where it was surprisingly cooler.

"Your folks are very nice," said Dani.

"They're good people. A little old-fashioned at times, and Momma has a strong tendency to be unnecessarily frugal. I had a heck of a time talking her into a new kitchen. That old kitchen will wear her right down to a nub."

"It is outmoded." A horse whinnied and Dani literally jumped to clutch at Scott's arm.

"Take it easy, sugar," said Scott, putting his arm around her shoulders. "He knows you are new around here and is giving you his hearty welcome." He led her down the barn to a stall where a large stallion busily shook his head up and down.

"Good Lord! He's huge!" exclaimed Dani, highly aware of his arm over her shoulders. It felt good. It made her feel warm inside and definitely feminine. His body brushing against hers caused sensations that were extremely pleasant.

"He's a big one, all right. One of daddy's best studs. Let's go down to the end stall. There's something there that I think will erase your fear of horses."

When they reached the stall, Dani let out a sigh of admiration at the sight of a mare and her newborn foal. "When was it born?"

"Yesterday," replied Scott, removing his arm from her shoulders as though he had just realized it was there. "Daddy already has a buyer for the little fella."

"Don't they wait until the animal grows up so they can see what they look like before buying them?" she asked, smiling as she watched the little colt scamper about the stall.

"Not always. It's a matter of bloodlines, wanting a particular stud for breeding purposes. Sometimes too much inbreeding can make a horse too skittish, too hard to handle."

"Well he's adorable just as he is now. It's when they grow up that I become afraid of them."

"You shouldn't be. They're quite docile and friendly if you give them half a chance. Of course, now and then a rogue will come along, and no one can do anything with the critter."

Dani continued to watch the newborn animal with amusement at its antics, clumsily tossing its neck and matchstick legs. After a while she sensed Scott's heated stare, and she could feel the fine hairs on the nape of her neck quiver. She had been stared at before, and it never bothered her. But this cowboy's steady gaze was having a disquieting effect on her. The long, cool horse barn was closing in on her, strangling her with its confinement. She had to get outside, with only the sky for a canopy.

"Where are all the other horses?" she asked, turning to face him.

"Out to pasture. There's some in a field not too far away. Would you like to see them?"

"Yes," she replied quickly. She wanted to go anywhere that he would be not quite so close to her.

He shoved his hands into the back pockets of his old, faded jeans, and they walked outside to follow a dirt lane that stretched between fences like a reddish-brown ribbon. Dani looked around her and breathed deeply of the sweet, fresh air. There was a purity to the air, a smell of lush grass, that wasn't present in Dallas. She had a strong impression of freedom as they silently trod along the dirt road, freedom from the stress of business, from having to smile when she wasn't in the mood, from the din of a city bursting with life.

"There they are," said Scott, going to the fence and putting one booted foot on the lower lath of the fence, then resting his arms on the top rail. "There's about six of them in that field."

"Oh, they are beautiful," she commented, watching the sleek animals prance about the field, some at a gallop with their manes flying like pennants in a strong wind. "How many does your father have all to-gether?"

"About thirty." He stared out over the field, his eyes squinting in the bright sun even though his broad-brimmed hat shaded his face. He was quiet for sometime as he continued to gaze over the field, then asked abruptly, without turning to look at her, "What were you thinking about as we were walking down here?"

"Oh . . . nothing much . . . how peaceful and quiet it is here. Seems like we're a thousand miles from Dallas. It's like another country."

"If you think this is quiet, you should see West Texas, especially west of the Pecos," he said. "Have you seen much of Texas?"

"Just Houston and Dallas. Of course I got some glimpses from the highway when I drove from Houston to Dallas. Didn't see too much though. Too busy driving."

"There's a lot more to Texas than Houston and Dallas. Out west there is a desert of some four thousand acres whose windswept dunes rival those of the Sahara. Big Bend National Park, with its purple-hazed mountains, canyons becoming gold when rays from the sun curl down into them, would leave you breathless. The contrasts down there are spectacular as they leap from desert to lush flood plains to the cool woodlands of the eerie Chisos Mountains. Sometimes I think it would take a lifetime to really see all of Texas."

"Have you seen all of Texas?" asked Dani, looking up at him, her hand shading her eyes.

He finally looked down at her and smiled. "You really should get yourself a wide-brimmed hat, sugar. This sun can be disastrous to a skin as fair as yours. To answer your question, I have seen most of Texas, but there is always something new to discover even in familiar surroundings."

"Where else have you been besides Texas?"

"Been to Oklahoma and California. Always glad to get back here, though." Off in the distance a clanging of iron objects sliced through the quiet air with irresistible urgency. "That'll be the dinner bell. Hope you have a good appetite."

"After the breakfast you made?"

"Momma will expect you to eat as though you've come back from a six-month trail drive with a bad cook."

Dani laughed, and they made their way back to the house. The table was set in the formal dining room with linen tablecloth and linen napkins. The best china and silverware were gracing the table when they sat down. A platter laden with fried chicken was passed around, along with bowls of roasted potatoes, green string beans, and julienned buttered beets. Homemade hot biscuits were a special treat to Dani. She hadn't had any like them since she left home. She ate more than she thought possible, much to the delight of Agnes.

When her help in clearing the table was refused, Dani sat contentedly listening to the two men discuss horses, with Tom Rowland occasionally asking her how she liked the place and what she thought of his stock.

A beaming Agnes came back into the dining room carrying a large, deep-dish apple pie, which she proudly placed on the table before scurrying back into the kitchen for the coffee.

"Here you go, Dani," said Agnes, after she resumed her place at the table and handed Dani a plate with a large slice of pie on it.

"Oh dear, I don't think I can eat another thing. The meal was so delicious I ate more than I should have," said Dani, placing a splayed hand on her flat stomach.

"You have to have a piece of Mother's pie," insisted Tom Rowland with a big grin. "You need some meat on those bones, little lady."

With a weak smile and a faint sigh, Dani took the proffered pie with reluctance. She wondered what her stomach would do when that first piece of pie hit it. She was pleasantly surprised and relieved to find it savored the excellent pie.

After a second cup of coffee and empty plates, Scott announced their departure, over Dani's protests that she should help Agnes clean up. But Agnes declined any offer of assistance, and Dani thanked them both for their hospitality with sincerity, promising to have the kitchen designed as quickly as possible.

Scott started the truck with a rattling roar and Dani expected him to leave the same way they came in. But the truck leaped forward to go around the barn and bump its way along the dirt road they had walked along earlier.

"Where are we going?" she asked.

"There's something I want to show you. I think it's one of the dog-gone prettiest spots in all of East Texas. I didn't want you going home without seeing it."

They drove for what seemed like hours until Dani finally asked, "Are we still on your father's land?"

"Yep."

"He must own half of East Texas," commented Dani.

Scott laughed. "Hardly, sugar. There's only about a thousand acres here. Real pretty acres though." He stopped the truck, saying, "We'll have to walk from here."

He helped her down from the pickup. Then, shoving his hands in his back pockets again, started through the meadows generously dotted with trees. Dani tried to match his long, loping gait without success and had to used hurried steps to keep up with him. The tall grasses swayed in the warm breeze as bluebonnets, buttercups, and fiery red Indian paintbrushes began to surrender their waning blossoms to the onset of summer.

"There," said Scott with a directional sweep of his arm. "Isn't that the prettiest sight you've ever seen?"

Dani looked up and beheld the clear river sparkling like silver as it cut a snaky path through the verdant land. "It is. It's quite beautiful," she replied as they moved closer to the embankment.

"The river is the southern boundary to Daddy's land. As you can see from the bank, it is a little lower than it was in early spring. It gets much lower in the middle of the summer, but one good thing about it, it never completely dries up. Always runs at a couple of feet unless there has been a severe and prolonged drought. Let's walk up the bank a ways. There's some shorter grass and a big shade tree where we can sit for a spell." He took her hand in his and they trudged along the embankment.

With Scott holding her hand, Dani felt like a girl of sixteen out on her first date. It seemed like centuries since a man had held her hand as they walked along. It was a novelty, a sweet novelty. Coming to the desired location, he motioned for her to sit down. Then he sat down alongside her, his long legs pulled up with his arms loosely embracing them.

"Now I know why you wanted me to wear sturdy shoes," said Dani.

"If you knew how to ride a horse, the trek wouldn't have been arduous at all. Now that you're here, do you think the walk was worth it?"

"Definitely!" she exclaimed, her eyes taking in the entire scene with awe and delight. "I'm surprised your parents didn't build their home here. It's a veritable paradise."

"Too far from the main road, and to bring utilities in this far would have marred the beauty of all the fields."

"I never thought of that."

"Why don't you let me teach you how to ride? Daddy has a mare that a three-year-old could ride with ease, safety, and confidence. I know you'd enjoy it once you've learned how. There are trails all over Daddy's spread where the countryside is really beautiful, especially in the spring and fall," he suggested.

"I don't think so. I'm much too afraid of the animals, and I doubt if anyone could teach me to ride."

"You're only afraid because you're not used to horses. Believe me, I'd be a good instructor."

"I'm sure you would be, but I really don't have the time," she added, as more opposition to the idea.

"Shoot! One can always find the time. You don't work on Sundays, you told me so yourself, and there must be days through the week when you don't have to be working every minute. Being self-employed, I'm sure you could juggle things around to get an afternoon off," he argued.

Dani shrugged as if to refute his suggestions as her mind struggled to think of a more absolute reason to refuse, but she was hard pressed. Of course the simplest answer was to say plain no, but a trickle of excitement rumbled through her at the thought of spending some time with the handsome, lanky cowboy. She knew very well she could rearrange her schedule to take some time off without affecting her business for the worse.

"We'll see," she said at last, thinking indecision was the best decision for the time being.

"Never mind 'we'll see,' little lady. We'll start this week. You name the day," he insisted, as Dani started to laugh. "What's so funny?"

"I can see 'little lady' is a long-standing tradition in your family."

He smiled wryly and looked at her obliquely. "That term sticks in your craw, doesn't it? I don't know why it should. You are little and you are a lady. But I'll confess it is a habit picked up from you know who. Would you prefer 'darlin',' or 'sugar'?"

"How about plain old Dani?" she asked with some amusement.

"You're as sweet as sugar and a darlin' woman. Why rebel against them so?"

"They make me feel like a nonentity, as though you could be talking to anyone and not recognizing me as a person, an individual with a distinct personality and a certain amount of self-pride," she explained.

He took her hand in his and covered it with his other hand. "I could never think of you as a nonentity, as you put it. You have a very definite personality, Dani, and I'm highly aware of it, believe me. To me you're a very special lady, and one I would never mix up with someone else, never."

Their eyes linked for several moments, and Dani sensed a headiness beginning to invade her entire being. She tried to convince herself the scenery was creating an idyllic mood conducive to fanciful romantic notions.

"I was under the impression you lived at home, but your mother told me you have an apartment in Dallas," said Dani, pulling her hand from his to lessen the giddiness rising in her.

"I occasionally stay at a place in Garland, not too far from Plano and the LBJ Freeway. Nothing fancy, but it comes in handy from time to time."

"Has your family always been in Texas?"

"As far back as I can remember. I've heard tales of how my great-grandaddy fought the Comanches and the Apaches. He told of how elite Comanche warriors were invested with the power of the wolf. Scouts from a raiding party would disguise themselves as wolves by wearing the pelts of the animal. They would carry strips of wolfskin with them into battle so they could tie themselves to sturdy pegs in the ground, to prevent them from retreating in battle. They prided themselves on dying in battle. Now the Apaches, they were trained from their youth in guerilla warfare. They could run for miles with a mouthful of water and never swallow a drop. I hear Great-grandaddy could sure tell some tales. Even my grandaddy is no pussyfoot when it comes to telling tales of the Indians. Though they'd never admit it publicly, I think each of them, in their own way, had a little admiration for the Comanche and the Apache."

"You seem to know a good deal about the Indians," said Dani.

"I once made a study of them and their different cultures. Did you know an Apache showed his respect for his mother-in-law by never speaking to her?"

"It certainly must have prevented a good many arguments," observed Dani with impish humor in her blue eyes. "If your great-grandfather was from East Texas, how did he run across the Apaches and Comanches? I thought they were in New Mexico and Arizona."

"They were nomadic tribes and roamed the entire Southwest. And Great-grandaddy lived in West Texas between the Pecos River and the Mustang Draw River. Grandaddy still lives there. Cantankerous old coot. But I guess being well over eighty and seen and been through what he has, has earned him some privileges."

"What made your father move to East Texas?" asked Dani.

"He didn't. Momma did. It's her father that lives in West Texas. She came to Dallas to attend SMU—Southern Methodist University—to get a teaching degree. She taught third grade in Dallas for four years before meeting Daddy and getting married," explained Scott.

"Was your father a teacher too?"

"No. He was a geologist until he retired early to run the horse ranch."

"Has your mother ever been back to West Texas?"

"Sugar, you sure can ask questions. You'll know more about me than I do if you keep it up. Momma and Daddy go out to see Grandaddy fairly often. I go about three or four times a year. Grandaddy can still ride and rope with all the verve of a top-notch wrangler. He's something to watch in action."

"He sounds like a fascinating old man."

"He is! And he'd like you. Always admired anyone who could make his own way in the world. I'll have to take you out there one of these days, if you'll promise not to let him sweet-talk you. After all, I found you first," declared Scott.

Dani smiled at him coyly. "I think I'd better get back to town. I'm anxious to start on your mother's kitchen. It offers quite a challenge." And she wanted to get away from this cowboy who seemed to be taking a lot of things for granted. Riding lessons and now West Texas.

"Can't I talk you into taking a while longer? Where else can you find a spot like this on a day like this?"

"I'd really like to go back now."

He hopped to his feet and offered her his hand, which she warily took. The thought of him keeping it in his both excited and alarmed her. The attraction she felt toward him was growing stronger than any emotion she had had for a man. It frightened and allured her at the same time. He didn't release her hand until they were in the truck.

He regaled her with more tales of Indian lore all the way back to her house on the outskirts of Dallas. When she asked him in for a cup of coffee, he declined, and she wasn't sure if she was relieved or disappointed.

After a light and late supper, Dani went into her office and began to draw the basic plan for the new Rowland kitchen. But ideas were slow in coming. Her mind kept drifting back to the horse ranch. Visions of her sitting next to the tall, lean cowboy, watching the flow of the crystal river, flashed unexpectedly across her eyes. The more she thought about the day, the more impossible it became for her to work and concentrate. Finally she gave up and, after snapping on the television set in the living room, went to settle herself on the couch. Her laughter was tinged with irony when the screen lit up to another rerun of a spaghetti western with Clint Eastwood. In a way he reminded her of Scott Rowland. She watched the film to the end, her eyes never leaving the screen.

3

It was late afternoon. Every time the telephone rang, Dani's pencil hovered in midair and her spine stiffened. She glanced at Sandy when the latter replaced the receiver.

"Well?" asked Dani anxiously.

"Just a confirmation of the cabinet delivery date for the Winston job," responded Sandy, shaking her head despondently. "I should think Hunt would have made up his mind by now. I thought he was known for quick decisions and judgments."

"Maybe his fingers are broken and he can't dial the phone," quipped Dani.

"His secretary could call for him," said Sandy seriously, oblivious to the attempt at humor.

Dani's eyes raised as though she were trying to count her eyelashes, then returned to the sheet where she was costing out the Rowland kitchen. The cost of that kitchen was beginning to reach rather enormous proportions, and she hadn't even added the charges that would be made by the plumber and electrician, which she knew would be sizable. She leaned back in her chair behind the drawing board and sighed. Scott Rowland, jack of all minor trades, would never be able to afford this, she mused with a certain amount of sadness. She liked the Rowlands and was especially moved to see the light of expectation glow in Agnes Rowland's eyes at the prospect of a new, modern kitchen. On a more personal level, she wondered if it would be the end of any more contact with the handsome, rangy cowboy. She found the notion an unpleasant one.

The doorbell rang and the door opened simultaneously. Dani's heart leapt in the hope it might be Scott Rowland. But the high-pitched voice of Janice Gordon shattered her illusions.

"It's quitting time, you two. Time for wine and roses," announced Janice, waving a bottle in the air. "I don't think that good old Benedictine monk realizes what a precious gift he gave to the world—champagne, ladies. A full, uncorked bottle of Dom Pérignon!"

"You're coming up in the world, aren't you? What's the occasion, Jan?" asked Dani rising from her chair and giving a lazy stretch.

"Coming up in the world? I'm soaring! I closed on two houses this morning and a condo this afternoon. And for the icing on the cake, I have five more closings this week—all in the hundred- to two-hundred-thousand-dollar bracket. You are looking at a woman of means who is set on celebrating. Follow me, ladies, and I shall make you so envious you'll flush as green as the shamrock," said Janice, flouncing her way into the kitchen, Dani and Sandy in tow. "Glasses, Dani."

"These will have to do. I don't have any regular champagne glasses," said Dani, taking three cocktail glasses from one of the cabinets and placing them on the table, while Janice, with a flourish, popped open the bottle and poured.

"Ladies . . . a toast . . . to the Gordon Real Estate Agency," said Janice, lifting her glass to clink with the others. After they all took a sip, Janice continued. "Let them now 'cry havoc and let loose the dogs of war.' I'm ready for them."

Sandy looked startled and took another sip of the champagne, then sat down at the kitchen table.

Dani smiled. "Well . . . you're finally going to take the plunge. Aren't you a bit ahead of schedule?"

"Perhaps. But the commissions from this week alone will keep me going for some time and also allow me to rent an office, advertise—the whole ball of wax. The coup d'état came when I was approached by the builders of Ridgefield Homes. He wanted to know if I might be interested in being the sole agent for his houses with the possibility of becoming the exclusive representative for Valleymark Condominiums, to be constructed fairly soon in Plano, Irving, and Garland. How's that for salted peanuts?"

"Why you?" asked Sandy, her face wrinkled with puzzlement.

"Weldon Real Estate Agency, whom I used to work for"—she looked at her watch—"about a half an hour ago, is the best in this area, and he heard I was their best agent. But he had a quarrel with Tom Weldon that created insurmountable differences. In short, they hate each other. He's dangling the carrot in front of me, hoping I'll leave Weldon, thus depriving old Tom of his best agent. Little did he know I was preparing to make the move on my own. I would have left Weldon by the end of the summer anyway, lure or no lure. So his offer was most opportune, to say the least," explained Janice.

"Here's to the unconquerable, intrepid, dynamic Janice Gordon. Long may she reign as queen of Dallas real estate," toasted Dani, and they all drained their glasses.

"I do hope it all goes well for you, Jan," stated Sandy. She covered her glass with her hand when Janice gestured to refill it. "None for me. I'm heading for home."

When the telephone rang, Dani automatically reached for it. She took a deep breath before saying, "Wexford Kitchens." After a moment she handed the phone to Sandy. "It's for you."

"The boyfriend?" asked Janice when Sandy hung up.

"Yes. He wants me to meet him at El Chico's at six-thirty," replied Sandy, getting up to leave.

"Big night on the town, Sandy?" asked Janice somewhat sarcastically.

"No. Just dinner and maybe a movie. Bye all."

When the door shut, Janice's eyebrows raised. "Good Lord, Dani! When is Sandy going to dump that parasite? She's an intelligent, good-looking young woman. What does she need him for? He's a leech and will suck her dry. I'll bet you another bottle of champagne she pays for the movie," grumbled Janice. "Hmph! El Chico's—the Tex-Mex Mac-Donald's!"

Dani shrugged. "She's also a grown woman, and I don't feel it is my place to interfere."

"Well someone should put a bug in her ear. With all the men there are in Dallas, she should play the field and not limit herself to a guy who makes Scrooge look like the greatest philanthropist that ever lived."

"Maybe she loves him and can't help herself."

"You can love a man with scads of money, one who is eager to spend it, just as easily as you can love a poor or stingy man."

"I don't think you can pick and choose with whom you fall in love. It just happens, and there is damn little you can do about it," said Dani defensively, though she didn't know why she felt so protective about her views on love.

"Why, Dani, you sound as though you've been smitten," exclaimed Janice with a sly look at her companion.

"Don't be silly, Jan."

"Don't try to con me. I'm a master of the game. I saw the look of apprehension on your face when the phone rang. I thought you'd rip it off the wall."

"Granted, when that phone rings, my skin crawls. But not for the reason you think. I've been waiting to hear whether or not I got those kitchens for the Hunt condos," explained Dani.

Janice looked at her wristwatch. "Well . . . I guess you'll have to wait until tomorrow now. It's after five. By the way, where were you yesterday? I called several times but there was no answer."

"I went to measure a kitchen."

"On Sunday? That's not like you, Dani, working on a Sunday. What was it? Something special?" asked Janice.

"In a way. It was more like a visit than work. And Sunday seemed to be the only day my client had the time."

"An old friend?"

"A new friend, you might say."

"Male or female?"

"Male. Are you practicing for the Spanish Inquisition, Jan? What were you calling me for?"

"A meeting of builders and realtors to get an overview of the market. What's moving and what isn't. It was more of a party than a meeting. I thought you'd might like to go and spread the word of Wexford Kitchens among the builders."

"Was Hunt there by any chance?" asked Dani.

"If he was, I would have known it. I make it a point to know everyone at these shindigs. By the way, I met a man there, another realtor who could melt ice in Antarctica in the dead of winter. I'm having dinner with him tonight. A walking, talking doll! I do believe this could become serious. Something clicked between us. It seems like this is my week to shine."

"I can't picture you becoming serious about any man, especially a competitor."

"Don't be a cynic, Dani, it doesn't become you. Besides you haven't seen him. Tall, a mane of white hair, a Herculean build, the face of Adonis, a voice that could charm angels—a real man's man. I think I'm going to let myself fall in love with him," said Janice, her light brown eyes tinged with a glow.

"Sounds like the epitome of mankind. But, by your own criteria, is he rich?" teased Dani.

"A poor man doesn't wear Italian, hand-tailored, silk suits," exclaimed Janice.

"He could have picked it up at a second-hand store." A devilish glint sparkled in Dani's eyes.

"Oh Dani!"

"White hair? How old is he?"

"Late forties or early fifties, I guess. I didn't ask him his age."

"If he's so impressive, how come you haven't noticed him before? I thought you knew every realtor in Dallas," claimed Dani.

"He's just come down from Chicago. He read about the meeting in the paper and thought it would be the fastest and best way to get acquainted with everyone in the business here. I'm really looking forward to dinner tonight."

Dani laughed.

"What's so funny?" asked Janice.

"I had a thought and it struck me funny. That's all."

"What?"

"Oh . . . only that I'd like to see the look on your face if he took you to El Chico's or MacDonald's."

"It'll never happen," declared Janice indignantly.

"It was just a thought I found amusing. What time is he picking you up?"

"Eight o'clock. I'd better be getting home. I'm going to luxuriate in a hot, bubbly tub and take my time dressing. Lately I seem to be in a constant mad dash. I deserve some R & R and I really want to look my best this evening." Janice rose and started for the small foyer with Dani behind her.

"Oh!" cried Dani. "Your champagne."

"You keep it. I have a feeling from here on out there is going to plenty of the good bubbly stuff."

With Janice gone, Dani went back to the drawing board in the office, took the cost sheets she had been working on for the Rowland kitchen, and put them on the desk. She went over all her figures again, quickly punching numbers into the calculator. She then thumbed through the appliance catalogs, copying model numbers and the cost of the various appliances she had decided on for the Rowland kitchen. After adding the installation price, the total package came to a hefty sum, and it didn't include the plumber or electrician. She shook her head ruefully, thinking the cowboy could never afford it and that she had been wasting her time. She decided she'd better call him before she went any further with the kitchen.

She skimmed through the Rowland file only to find she had neither his address nor his phone number. The only address and phone number she had was that of his parents. She released a long, low sigh of self-recrimination. She had always been very careful about getting names, addresses, and telephone numbers when she was doing a job. How could she have been so careless this time? Scott Rowland had a debilitating effect on her. She knew when she was with him that her mind was more on the man than on the job.

Reaching for the phone, she hesitated. She certainly wouldn't want to give the Rowlands the cost of the kitchen, as it appeared to be a gift from their son and she didn't want to spoil it. She could call them for Scott's number but wondered if it would sound too forward of her, or make her out to be a totally negligent person for someone in business.

Her hand dropped back to the desk. Her mind wandered back to the river and the marvelous sensations she felt sitting next to the tall, lanky man, especially the way he held her hand in his. So comforting, so warm, so blissful. It was difficult for her to admit she wanted to hear his voice again and be with him. She even harbored a vague hope that when she called him he would come over and review the kitchen with her.

Desire overcame better judgement, and she dialed the Rowland ranch.

"Hello?"

"Hello, Agnes. This is Dani Wexford."

"Why hello, Dani. When is that son of ours going to bring you out to visit us again?" asked Agnes cheerfully.

"I don't know," replied Dani, feeling herself redden. "I'm ashamed to say I forgot to get his telephone number and wondered if you'd mind giving it to me."

"Of course not . . . you just hold on a minute . . . it's right here in the desk." She fumbled in the desk for a second, then read the number to Dani. "Have you thought about our kitchen yet?"

"I've been working on it for the greater part of the day. There are a few points I would like to clear up with Scott."

"Well . . . both Tom and I hope you will be out here real soon. We enjoyed the little visit with you and Scottie," said Agnes.

"I enjoyed it too. And the meal was excellent. Again, let me thank you."

"Don't think anything of it. We were happy to have you. Well, goodbye for now and hope to see you soon, you hear."

"Goodbye," said Dani hanging up the receiver and staring at Scott's number. She couldn't understand why she was so nervous as she lifted the receiver again and dialed his number. After all, it was only a business call. She let it ring ten times before she hung up. She would try again in twenty minutes.

She got up and went into the kitchen. She opened the refrigerator, trying to decide what to have for supper as she scanned the contents. Leftover spaghetti, cold chicken, a small piece of ham—none of which really appealed to her. She looked at the half-full bottle of champagne and smiled. Jan and her men! she thought. Jan always started off with such enthusiasm about the new man in her life. Invariably he was the one she had been waiting to become serious about. Then, bit by bit, Jan began to find little faults, faults that she gradually exaggerated until she felt she couldn't possibly go with the man any longer. Dani believed that, in reality, Janice dreaded making any hard and fast commitment to any man.

As she reached for the telephone in the kitchen to try and reach Scott Rowland again, it rang. She snatched the phone from its cradle and gave a tight "Hello."

"Miss Wexford?" asked an unfamiliar male voice.

"Yes. Who is this?"

"Nicholas Hunt. I know this is rather short notice, but will you have dinner with me this evening? Before you say no, I want you to know you have the contract. Dinner will be a mixture of business and celebration."

Dani could feel her entire body grow taut with excitement and elation. She had the contract for the condos! She wanted to laugh and cry at the same time. A big bubble of joy was about to burst inside her. It constricted her throat and fired roman candles in her brain.

"Hello? Are you still there?" asked Nicholas Hunt.

Dani put her hand on her throat as if it had curative powers and emitted a weak "Yes."

"Well . . . can you make it for dinner tonight?"

"Yes. What time?" she managed to choke out.

"I'll pick you up at eight."

Dani heard the click of the receiver on the other end but sat there listening to the dial tone as though in a deep hypnotic trance. For a fleeting moment she wondered if the call had been illusory; heavy wishful thinking could play tricks on the mind. Slowly she replaced the receiver, leaned back in the chair, and stared at the telephone as a smile widened on her lips. She *had* heard Nicholas Hunt's voice, and she *did* have the contract! Janice's luck was rubbing off on her. She took a deep breath and let it out slowly before she suddenly realized it was almost seven o'clock and the man was going to pick her up at eight.

Showered, her short hair shampooed and blow-dried, she ruffled through her closet for a suitable dress. She drew forth a rust-colored, scooped-neck dress she had bought last year. Its classic lines and dolman sleeves gave it an aura of timelessness. She examined it for a moment or two, then quickly slipped into it. She studied herself in the mirror and was pleased with the effect the dress afforded her figure. It also complemented the color of her hair. She wondered if she had chosen it subconsciously, knowing that Nicholas Hunt was not a tall man and that the shoes that went with the dress had only a one-inch heel. With makeup carefully applied and a trace of perfume, she went downstairs to wait.

The doorbell rang precisely at eight. After nominal greetings, she locked the door behind her and let herself be led to the large white Cadillac parked in her driveway.

"Did you have any trouble finding the house, Mr. Hunt?" asked Dani, as they sped down the highway.

"None whatsoever. All I need is an address. I have detailed maps of Dallas and its surrounding areas. I also have explicit maps of Houston," he replied, his handsome profile flickering light and dark as the lights on the highway caught it.

"Do you plan to do some construction work in Houston?"

"Thinking of it. Condos are springing up down there like weeds in the desert after a rainstorm." He glanced at her and smiled, then turned his eyes back to the stream of fast-moving traffic. "Do I detect a note of interest in your voice?"

"Where there is a possibility of doing kitchens, I am always interested. By the way I'd like to bring my standard contract to your office tomorrow morning for you to sign if you'll be in."

"Make it around twenty to twelve. That'll give us twenty minutes or so to go over everything before I take you to lunch."

"That won't be necessary."

"I've already planned on it. I had my secretary shuffle things around so I'd have two free hours for our luncheon appointment. I won't take no for an answer."

"Do you ever take no for an answer?" Dani was a little irritated by his presumption. She was selling kitchens, not her private life.

"Not if I can help it. I wouldn't be where I am if I let people say no when I need an affirmative reply to push ahead. I don't imagine you like to have your plans thwarted either, Miss Wexford."

"No. I don't suppose so," said Dani with a smile in her eyes.

At the restaurant the maître d' was more than agreeable; he was solicitous to the point of distraction as he ushered them to a quiet table for two where a candle flickered its amber light on the pristine linen tablecloth.

The appetizer of pieces of shrimp, crabmeat, and lobster nestled among various sauces was followed by soup, a savory cream of mushroom and broccoli. The waiter precisely poured a delicate white wine at the slightest hint their glasses might be empty. After the Caesar salad, he switched to a robust red wine as he served their entrées. Dani's petit filet mignon, which lay girded in bacon, was done to perfection. Her eyebrows arched when the waiter placed on their table the steak Nicholas Hunt had ordered; it looked like a small roast of beef. Dani declined dessert, as did Nicholas.

When the table was cleared and coffee served, Dani asked, "Are you originally from Texas, Mr. Hunt?"

"No. I was born and raised in New Jersey. My father is a contractor there. And you? A native?"

"No. Iowa. I moved here when the Shaw Company did. I'm surprised you didn't stay in New Jersey and work with your father."

"I have two older brothers who went into business with him. I wanted to get out on my own. The contracting business looked good in Houston and Dallas so I thought I'd try my hand down here. As you've probably gathered by now, I've done quite well."

"Why did you choose Dallas over Houston?" Dani asked before taking a sip of her coffee, her eyes meeting his over the rim of the cup. He was indeed a handsome man and quite appealing. Dani had to lower her eyes to keep from being mesmerized by those magnetic black orbs of his.

"I wish I could give you a solid business reason, but it was pure chance that caused me to make Dallas my base. Perhaps instinct told me Dallas would boom. Why didn't you stay in Houston with the Shaw Company or build your own business there?"

"The Shaw Company was good to me. I didn't want to compete with them. I thought it best to break new territory, a place where I could grow on my own. Dallas appealed to me," she said with a slight shrug.

"I think we both made very wise decisions. I came here when I was twenty-five, thirteen years ago now. Dallas was still pretty much of an embryonic city, circumscribed by flat, rolling, and unending prairie. Now it is reaching the proportions of a world-class city. If one works hard, there is money to be made here," said Nicholas.

"I agree with you. But one has to have enthusiasm and stamina to get to the top. The first year I ate my lunch in the car, on the phone, over my desk or drawing board. There were no set hours to work—just all day long," said Dani.

"No young professional in Dallas lingers over lunch. Eat and get back to the business at hand, for if you don't there is always someone behind you on the ladder to push you off or climb right over you on their way to the top." He had a smile on his face, but there was a hint of doubtful suspicion in his eyes which didn't go unnoticed by Dani.

"You still have misgivings about working with a woman, don't you?" she asked.

"We'll see." His smile widened to show even white teeth.

"If you are so uncertain, why did you select my bid?"

"Frankly, you had the best price and the best selection of cabinetry. We'll have to wait and see if you can deliver on time."

Dani resented his lack of confidence in her abilities based solely on her sex, and the coolness in her tone reflected it. "When the time comes, I'll have to take field measurements to make sure your blueprints are accurate. As I said I need six weeks lead time, so I would appreciate a few days notice so I can take those measurements and have the order placed with the factory in time."

"Touched a nerve, haven't I?" he asked, an expression of wry amusement on his face.

"I don't like having my abilities questioned."

His dark eyebrows arched above ebony eyes and he stared at her. "You'll have to understand this is the first time I have dealt with your company and the first time any of my principle suppliers has been a woman. Old habits are hard to break. If you can deliver at those prices, on time and without snags, it could mean a number of future contracts for you and bidding maneuverability for me. If you were in my position, you'd be cautious too. I have a deadline to meet. There are financial penalties if I don't deliver a finished building on time." He glanced down at his watch then looked up and said, "I had planned to take you dancing, but something came up at the last minute and I have to meet a plane at the airport. I hope you'll give me a raincheck for another evening, Miss Wexford."

Saying nothing, Dani pushed her chair back and rose, which prompted Nicholas to do the same. He escorted her to the canopied entrance where, in moments, his car was brought around. On the short distance back to Dani's house, their conversation was desultory. An unnamed tension hovered in the confines of the large car. Dani felt a sense of relief when she entered her house and closed the door behind her, deadening the sound of the powerful Cadillac as it roared off. Though she looked forward to getting the contracts signed, she was apprehensive about having lunch with the formidable Nicholas Hunt. He disturbed her emotionally, making her feel skeptical of her abilities and yet, at the same time, making her feel very much a woman, a vulnerable one at that. There was a superiority about him that she found both compelling and repelling.

The next morning Dani said nothing to Sandy about getting the Hunt contract. She wanted to watch her expression when she showed her the signed papers. Before leaving for the Hunt office, she tried to reach Scott Rowland several times to no avail. She told Sandy to keep trying the number and, if she reached the elusive cowboy, to apprise him of the cost of his mother's kitchen and find out if he wanted to go ahead with it.

There was no waiting in the air-conditioned outer office of Nicholas

Hunt. She was ushered in immediately. With a warm smile, Nicholas rose from his desk and came around to greet her.

"Miss Wexford . . . you're prompt. I like that. I want you to meet Jack Sanders, my attorney. If you'll be good enough to give him your contracts, he'll go over them and we can conclude the formalities," said Nicholas.

After preliminary greetings and a firm shake of the hand with the attorney, Dani placed her case on one edge of the large desk, opened it, took out her contracts, and handed them to the lawyer. Jack Sanders took a seat behind the desk while Nicholas extended his hand, signaling Dani to take a seat. Dangling one leg over the edge of the desk, Nicholas sat down facing Dani.

"As soon as we've had our lunch, I'll take you over to the site, where you can see for yourself the progress made on the condos. I want you to know the site and feel free to visit it anytime you wish," said Nicholas.

"I can't stress too strongly the fact I need six weeks lead time. I'm determined to have those cabinets there on time," she said.

"And counters," added Nicholas.

"And counters," she agreed, thinking there was something different about the sartorial, elegant Mr. Hunt this morning. He appeared more relaxed, more amiable. She wondered if it had anything to do with his late-night appointment at the airport. An old ladyfriend from back east perhaps?

"Things are beginning to move along rapidly now. I think you might want to place that order with the factory next week. But you'll see for yourself when we get to the site."

"Everything seems to be in order, Nick," said Jack Sanders. "It's a good contract. Every base has been touched."

Nicholas stood and went to take the chair instantly vacated by the attorney. He signed the duplicate contracts along with the original. "Miss Wexford?" he asked holding his pen in the air for her to take.

Dani came around the desk and leaned over to put her signature on the contracts. She became very much aware of her proximity to the man. His warm breath breezed over her neck; the scent of his expensive cologne teased her nostrils. Leaving one copy on his desk, she scooped up the others and put them back in her case.

"I'll see you later, Jack," said Nicholas rising from his chair, then taking Dani's arm. "Ready for some lunch?"

"Yes." Dani felt a warm, joyful glow consume her, but she wasn't sure if it was because she had obtained the signed contracts for the kitchens or because Nicholas Hunt's hand encircled her bare arm.

4

A rare rain pelted Dallas. The moaning rumble of thunder snaked its way through the glass monoliths, in and northward of the city. Reunion Tower, lunging its globe almost three hundred feet into the air, while rectangular glass buildings clustered about the base in a struggle to reach its heights, appeared as an ultramodern impressionistic cityscape painting in the gray rain, dominating the flat plain like a futuristic Oz. Even from Danielle Wexford's home in the suburbs, one could feel the lure of Dallas, its challenge that promised success in exchange for hard work. Dani had met that challenge, and now her fingertips were beginning to curl about that elusive substance called success.

She sat in the kitchenette savoring an early morning cup of coffee. A smile of self-satisfaction graced her lips. The cabinet company had been so impressed with her order, and the possibility of more large orders like that, they had given her an extra one-percent commission. And she had two more remodeling jobs on the drawing board. Joining the garden club two years ago had really paid off. Word had spread from member to member and beyond, bringing a good volume of business her way. She heard the front door open and slam shut.

"It's raining out," said Sandra Parks, announcing the obvious as she marched into the kitchen.

"Help yourself to some hot coffee," offered Dani. "The rain won't last long. It never does."

Sandy, with a mug of coffee in her hand, took a seat at the table. "Have you been able to get a hold of that Scottie Rowland yet?"

"No. I'm beginning to wonder if he really existed. Maybe he was a spectre from the Twilight Zone," said Dani with a twinkle in her eye but a strange sense of emptiness in her heart.

"Of course he was here. I saw and spoke to him, Dani." Sandy wore a pained expression, as though insulted by Dani's absurd suggestion. "It's funny we haven't heard from him. He seemed so set on getting a new kitchen for his mother."

"I think it's a question of money. He probably realized it was going to be beyond his means and decided to back out before getting too involved."

"Well . . . I still am surprised he didn't at least call to find out what it would cost. He didn't seem like a deadbeat to me," argued Sandy.

"You're right about one thing. Most people who want new kitchens usually wait until they hear what it is going to cost before they drop it."

"Are you going out to measure anything today?"

"No. I want to finish these watercolors of those two new projected kitchen jobs. Why?"

"I thought I'd leave early today if you were going to be around. I'm moving into a new apartment this weekend, and I want to be all settled by Sunday," explained Sandy.

"Sure. In fact why don't you leave at noontime? Friday is always a slow day, and I'll be right here to handle any calls."

"Oh that would be great!" exclaimed Sandy. "I'll get right at the paperwork."

By midmorning the hot Texas sun of early summer had made its appearance and caused air to vibrate above the concrete. The soft hum of the central air-conditioning went unnoticed by the two women working diligently in the office of the red brick house. When Sandy left at noon, Dani turned the radio on, grabbed a quick sandwich, then went back to work on her watercolor sketches. The ink drawings, all in accurate perspective, had been completed and, by the time she finished her sandwich were dry and ready for the application of color.

As the six o'clock news came on the radio, Dani leaned back in her chair and stretched her bones, which had stiffened from sitting so long in one position. Regardless of her aching back muscles, she was pleased with her accomplishment. She had completed the paintings for both kitchens. Tomorrow she would frame them, and on Monday she would present them to her clients. Wiggling her torso to ease the tension in her muscles, she walked to the desk and thumbed through the appointment calendar. The big day was still a few weeks away—the day for the cabinets and counters to be delivered to the Hunt job. She flipped back the pages to a week from today and made a note to call the factory and the countertop maker to make sure the delivery of the items would be on time. As she laid her pencil down, her doorbell chimed. With a frown of puzzlement, she went to the door and opened it.

"Howdy!"

Dani's jaw fell full agape when she saw Scott Rowland standing there in his tight, faded jeans, old lizard boots, and a pale yellow dress shirt with sleeves rolled up to just below the elbows. His battered cowboy hat was pushed back on his high-browed forehead, while in each muscled arm rested a bag of groceries.

"Aren't you going to ask me in?" His smile cut a wide path across his bronzed face; his bluish-gray eyes sparkled mischievously.

She stepped aside while running a splayed hand through her short hair, then followed him into the kitchen. "Where the devil have you been?" she asked. "I've been trying to call you."

He placed the grocery bags on the counter, then turned to face her. "I had to go see my grandaddy. If I had known you were so anxious to see me, I would have stopped by, picked you up, and taken you with me, sugar."

With lips compressed, Dani gave a sigh of impatience. "I wanted to talk to you about your mother's kitchen."

"You haven't gone ahead with that yet?" he asked, genuinely surprised.

"I don't go ahead with anything until I get approval on the cost and one-third down with a signed contract. Your mother's kitchen is a large one and mounted to quite a piece of change. I didn't know if you wanted to go that high," explained Dani, her heart thumping at the sight of the rangy, rough, good-looking cowboy before her. "It's been a while since I heard from you, and I thought you might have forgotten about the kitchen."

"I seldom forget a thing." He looked at her hard, like a hungry man who was gazing into a fabulous restaurant where food was displayed in abundance. "I'd never forget you, sugar."

Dani felt her cheeks grow hot. There was something about him that drained her, leaving her weak and a little giddy. "Aren't you curious about the price?"

"Whatever the cost, you just go right ahead, sugar."

"I think it's much higher than you anticipated."

He smiled, leaned against the counter, and folded his arms over his chest. "I can see you're bound and determined to spit some numbers at me, Dani. Go ahead . . . let's get this business out of the way so we can get on with the evening."

She gave him the figure and added, "That's installed and with all new appliances. It also includes rough estimates from the plumber and the electrician. They won't give me a final figure until they see the job," she said hurriedly.

"Fine. Go ahead. I'll bring you the money on Monday. Go get those contracts and I'll sign them now."

Dani complied and placed them on the kitchen table. She handed him a pen and their fingers touched, causing the fine hair on her arms to stand at attention. His eyes held hers for a moment and his expression turned serious. Dani stepped back.

"Sign at the bottom. The duplicate copy is yours," she informed him.

He signed with a flourish. "Make sure you do a real pretty picture for Momma." He handed her the original and, folding his copy up, placed it in his shirt pocket. "Now . . . can we get down to serious business?"

"What are you talking about?" she asked mechanically, a little stunned by his quick and unquestioning acceptance of the whole deal.

Scott turned back to the two bags on the counter and began to empty the contents on the counter. "I'm going to cook up a bowl of real Texas chili that'll set your toes to tapping and your stomach begging for more. French bread, iced tea, salad fixings, cherry pie, whipped cream," he said naming each item as he took it out of the bag.

Dani had to laugh. The entire scene and conversation became utterly ludicrous to her. His claim that chili takes precedence over thousands of dollars was suddenly very funny. And the mixure of foodstuffs!

"What's so funny? Don't you think I can cook? Why I'm the best cook you're ever going to know, little lady. I might concede Momma has a slight edge. But for good old Texian cooking—you'll not find anyone to match me."

"I can see modesty is not one of your stronger attributes," remarked Dani, with humor still in her blue eyes.

Scott grinned. "While I'm fixing dinner for us, why don't you go do whatever it is women do before they go out for an evening of hard and fast dancing."

"And what makes you think I'm free this evening? I may have other plans that don't include you, Scott Rowland," she said with a trace of indignation.

"Do you?"

There was such a look of sadness and hurt in his eyes, she knew it would be impossible for her to say no to him. Besides, she thought, she would like to go out with him.

"Well?" His eyes narrowed to a squint as he stared at her.

"No."

"Good. It's settled. Off with you while I work. I wouldn't be able to cook a thing with you standing around looking so beautiful. And don't put on anything fancy," he called, as she headed for the stairs.

Even though she resented being taken for granted by him, she knew she could never be really angry with him. He had a way about him that was soft and gentle. His resonant voice made an order sound like a request, and his stern look was always tempered by amusement and kindness in his eyes.

Showered and dressed in a sleeveless, scooped-neck dress of powder blue whose tight bodice gave way to a full skirt, Dani entered the kitchen. "Is this all right?"

Scott turned from the stove to gaze at her and, without smiling, said, "You'll be the prettiest little gal there."

"Where are we going?"

"To a place where they play good ol' foot-stomping music. I want to show you off. Why don't you set the table? This is almost ready."

Dani had to admit the meal was excellent, if a strange assortment. With happy expectations, she let Scott assist her into the old yellow pickup and they were soon plunging and chugging down the highway.

The music was loud and all country, as elbows furiously pumped up and down rapidly, drawing the bow across the fiddle; fingers strummed, plucked, and picked away madly on the strings of guitars. The thump of feet bounding on the wooden floor never seemed to miss a beat. The slight aroma of beer wafted in the smoky, dimly lighted room. Laughing, talking, humming, singing voices were occasionally punctuated by a loud, happy cry of "Yahoo!" The dancers looked like Irish step dancers gone mad, feet flying in rapid cadence to the music. The atmosphere was one of wild gaiety, reminiscent of the early western saloon without the proverbial gamblers, dance-hall girls, and shiny, mahogany, mirrored bar.

Scott and Dani sat at a small table where a candle in a red glass globe cast a crimson glow over the red-checkered tablecloth. When the cute little waitress, dressed in black pants and white shirt with a black bow tie came to their table, Scott ordered nachos with cheese and chili peppers, potato skins, pretzels, and a pitcher of iced tea.

"Iced tea?" asked Dani.

"They don't serve cocktails or hard liquor here."

"I took you for a beer drinker."

"I don't drink. Not even soda. Momma's lemonade, hot coffee, and iced tea are about the only things I drink. I hope you aren't disappointed by the lack of cocktails."

"Not at all."

"Would you prefer beer?"

"I don't drink beer," said Dani.

"Then the iced tea is a happy choice."

"Anything cool after your chili would be a happy choice. I think my taste buds have been obliterated. The membranes of my throat are scorched to ashes, and my stomach is a replica of Dante's Inferno," declared Dani, her eyes laughing.

"I knew you'd love it."

"I suppose it could grow on one. What was the dressing you used on the salad? I never tasted anything like it."

"Did you like it?"

"The best I ever tasted," confessed Dani.

"Good! I've got a hold on you now. A dubious one, I'll admit, but nonetheless, a hold." He reached for her hand and folded it over his. "Shall we dance?"

"I'd like to wait for that iced tea first," said Dani, warmed by the pressure of his hand.

As if driven by ESP, the waitress brought their order and placed it on the table before flouncing away. Scott poured them each a glass, then, with amusement, watched Dani take a deep, long swallow.

"Scottie!" boomed an approaching voice.

"Smokey!" greeted Scott.

"Woweee! Now I can see why you've been scarcer than a June bug in January. Who is this pretty little lady?" asked the huge barrel of a bearded man as he turned a chair backwards and straddled it, his burly arms resting on the back rung.

"Smokey MacDonald meet Danielle Wexford. Dani . . . Smokey. We call him Smokey 'cause he looks so much like Smokey the Bear. But don't let him sweet talk you, sugar. He's the only Scotsman to swallow the Blarney stone whole," said Scott.

"Scottie, boy, you wouldn't be trying to keep the little lady all to yourself, now would you?"

"The lady has a mind of her own, I assure you."

"Mighty pretty lady, mighty pretty. How did you ever get yourself hooked up with this old buzzard, Miss Wexford?" asked Smokey.

"I'm not hooked up with him, as you put it," said Dani with a gracious smile.

"Dani's a kitchen designer and is going to redo Momma's kitchen for me," explained Scott.

"I knew it had to be something like that." The big man focused his attention on Dani. "Scottie here don't much cotton to taking on lady friends. Not that the ladies don't cotton to him. Shoot! All he has to do is snap his fingers and the little ol' gals in all of Texas would come running. Ain't that true, Scottie?"

"You talk too much, Smokey."

"Then if you don't mind, I'll just be taking our Miss Wexford and give her a spin around the floor. That okay with you, little lady?"

"Why not?" Slowly, Dani was becoming resigned to being called little lady. It seemed to be the sine qua non of the male species indigenous to Texas.

For a big, heavy man, Smokey moved with the grace and lightness of a ballet master. Several times he lifted Dani right off the floor as he whirled her in a high-stepping dance. The rigorous dance left little time for conversation, not to mention breathing. By the time they returned to the table, Dani was breathing hard and crumpled into her seat. With gratitude, she watched Scott fill up her glass with iced tea, which she quickly drank with zeal. She was about to reach for a nachos, only to find the plate empty.

"No wonder the little lady is so tiny, Scottie. You hog down all the food before she can get to it." Smokey raised his hand for the waitress. "Thank you for the dance, Miss Wexford. It was truly a great pleasure. Why you're as light as a roadrunner's feather."

"I enjoyed it," said Dani, a little surprised to find she really did.

Soon the waitress placed a pitcher of beer, a pitcher of iced tea, and a double order of nachos on the table. By then Smokey had devoured the potato skins, and he had to order more. With amazement Dani watched Smokey consume a large mug of beer in one gulp, then quickly refill his

glass mug. She chomped on the nachos with chili peppers, hardly noticing the fiery taste after Scott's chili beans.

"Scottie . . . why don't we go looking at new pickup trucks tomorrow. Let's give those dealers a hard time," suggested Smokey.

"Going to Galveston tomorrow," declared Scott.

"Your grandaddy acting up again?" asked Smokey.

"Grandaddy is always acting up," replied Scott.

"Trouble?" asked Smokey.

"Not really. You know Grandaddy."

"Best rider, best roper, best shot, and best cusser in all of West Texas.
How is the old coot?" asked Smokey.

"Why don't you ride out there and see for yourself?" said Scott.

"Guess I'll have to one of these days. Miss Wexford, have you ever
met Scott's grandaddy?" asked Smokey.

"No."

"Make Scottie take you out there. It's an experience that comes once
in a lifetime."

"I understand he has a bagful of stories about the Indians," ventured
Dani.

"Stories? Tall tales is more like it," said Smokey.

"Great-Grandaddy wrote it all down. Grandaddy doesn't tell tall
tales," said Scott defensively.

"Don't be working up your saddle sores, Scottie. You know I love the
old man. I'm only teasing you. Really, Miss Wexford, to meet and listen
to that old man is an education in the history of the American West. Try
and talk ol' Scottie here into taking you out there," said Smokey, finishing off the pitcher of beer and the second platter of potato skins. "Well,
I can't be lollygagging around here for the night. I still have to find the
lady of my dreams tonight. She must be here somewhere. It's been a
real pleasure to have met you, Miss Wexford," said Smokey, getting up
and setting the chair straight.

"Thank you for the dance, Smokey," said Dani.

"As I said, my pleasure, little lady. And it's been real nice meeting
you." And he melted into the crowd.

"He seems like a nice man," said Dani.

"He's a good ol' boy. I can always depend on him in a pinch. Never
lets me down."

"What does he do for a living?" asked Dani, assuming the big, burly man was in some sort of construction work. She pictured him wielding those big cranes that dotted the Dallas landscape.

"Believe it or not, he's a top-notch computer man. A programmer, an analyst, designs both software and hardware. He knows more about computers than all the big companies put together."

"That's hard to believe. He looks like a man who does hard physical labor."

"He may look it. But Smokey has the quick, sure, delicate hands of a surgeon. You can never really tell what or who a person is by the wrappings," said Scott.

"I suppose not. I certainly never would have guessed that Smokey was into computers."

"And who or what do you think I am?" asked Scott with a crooked smile.

"I have the advantage there. You've already told me you do odd jobs. A jack-of-all-trades."

"If I hadn't told you, then what?"

"Oh . . . a lonely cowboy riding point on some dusty trail, dreaming of the day when he'll own his own ranch. But your dreams will come true," declared Dani.

"Oh? How so?"

"Someday you'll inherit your father's horse ranch. Are you looking forward to it?"

He shrugged his wide shoulders. "Doesn't much matter. I like the life I lead now. I'm my own master. I can come and go as I please without being tied down."

"Is that why you never married? A distaste for being tied down?" There was devilment in her eyes as she gazed at him with a lift of her chin.

"Marriage is a lifelong commitment to me, and up till now, I never met a woman I wanted to give that commitment to." He returned her mischievous look, adding a broad smile. "Are you sufficiently rested to try another dance?"

Dani nodded. He clutched her hand and led her onto the floor. He danced as though he'd been stomping to western music all his life. They danced two fast-stepping dances in a row until the musicians finally took pity on everyone and launched into a slow western ballad, with a male singer warbling plaintive words of a lost love. Dani was caught unaware when both his arms went around her and drew her entire body against his. She put her hands on his shoulders and looked up at him with a mixture of uncertainty and anxiety in her blue eyes.

"Put your arms around my neck, sugar, and relax. I'm not going to bite you," said Scott with a crooked grin on his face, while a grimness invaded his eyes.

Dani looked around the floor and observed it seemed to be the normal Texas way of dancing to a slow tune. She let her hands creep over his shoulders, feeling a little awkward about the sudden intimacy. What was the matter with her? She had danced with men before . . . and quite closely. Yet . . . somehow, this was different. Sensations and feelings she never realized she possessed were awakening, the intensity of which frightened her.

"Will you relax," he whispered down into her ear.

Though her mind fought it, her body obeyed and melted against him. She laid her head on his hard chest and let her arms wrap around his neck. She could hear the steady beat of his heart and the sound lulled her brain into neutral. She let pure sensation dominate her. When he laid his cheek on top of her head, a blaze flowed through her like a fiery river. She looked up at him, her eyes awash with confusion while he gazed down at her unsmiling, his eyes cool as the depths of a mountain pool.

"Want to go back to the table?" he asked hoarsely.

"No," was all she could say. A tremor rested somewhere in her throat. She laid her head back on his chest hoping the rhythmic beat of his heart would soothe her ruffled emotions.

He continued to hold her when the small country band stopped playing for a moment. Dani didn't object to being in his arms and standing still. In fact, she never wanted to move. She felt perfectly happy and content where she was, and when another slow western love song was played, she smiled inwardly. This time a young woman, dressed in flashy cowgirl garb, sang the sad words of a lost love while the fiddles bowed mournfully.

Dani's body seemed to merge with Scott's as they slowly moved about the floor like a single fluid column. The scent of him and the heat from his body penetrated all her senses, captivating her like no other man ever had. Was she falling in love? Or was it the atmosphere? The mood of the moment? She had absolutely nothing in common with this roustabout cowboy, yet . . .

The music stopped and Scott led her back to the table wordlessly, only to find Smokey sitting there working on another pitcher of beer. Dani noticed Scott's eyes narrow to his habitual squint.

"Hope you folks don't mind. The ladies who were interested in me, I found uninteresting. The ones I found to my liking, found me a clod. So here I am with the only friends I have in the world," said Smokey, his words a bit garbled.

Scott shook his head ruefully as he sprawled in a chair, Dani taking a seat next to him. "You've always got Marguerite."

"Ah yes, Marguerite . . . the only one who is constantly faithful and adoring," muttered Smokey.

"Who is Marguerite?" asked Dani.

"My cat," Smokey informed them, causing Dani to laugh. "What's so funny, little lady?"

"I find it hard to picture you with a cat, Smokey."

"She's a sweet, pretty little thing. Won't let anyone pet her except me. Won't even sit on anyone else's lap."

"Are you originally from Texas, Smokey?" asked Dani.

"Born and bred in Lubbock."

"How did you and Scott meet?" Her curiosity was unbounded when it came to the two totally mismatched men and what they could possibly have in common.

"Well, Scott needed . . ."

"I needed a place to sit and eat my lunch in a crowded restaurant. Smokey let me share his table," interrupted Scott, preferring to keep his true vocation from Dani.

Smokey nodded his head, his eyes bleary, with a tendency to close often.

"I think I'd better take you home, Smokey," said Scott then, turning to Dani. "Mind if we leave now? I would like to get him home while he can still maneuver. As dead weight, he's too much for me."

"It's time I did get home. It is getting late," agreed Dani. "What about his car?"

"Oh, someone will drive him over in the morning to pick it up. He's not as friendless as he pretends," said Scott.

Dani sat between the two men in the front of Scott's pickup, and by the time they had reached Dani's house, Smokey had fallen sound asleep against the truck door.

"Slide out my side," said Scott, his hands circling her waist as she flung her legs toward the running board. He released her, then walked her to the door of the red brick house.

"I'd ask you in for coffee, but I can see you have your hands full. I had a lovely time. Thank you, not only for the night out but for the great dinner you prepared," said Dani, leaning against her front door and looking up at him.

"We'll have to do it more often. It's been a while since I've danced so much."

"I'll start the sketch for your mother's kitchen tomorrow."

"You won't have time."

"What do you mean? I don't have any set plans for tomorrow."

"Good. Then you have no excuse not to go to Galveston with me for the weekend," said Scott, smiling down at her.

"What?" she cried, astonished by the inference.

"I said you're coming with me to Galveston for the weekend."

"Over my dead body. I don't spend weekends with strange men. I mean I don't spend my weekends going away with any man. How dare you even suggest such a thing when we hardly know one another? You have a nerve, Scott Rowland. I've never been so insulted in my life. What kind of woman do you take me for anyway?" Her cheeks were hot, and her stomach churned with anger and indignation. Love? She loathed him for implying she was an easy mark. He was a crude, arrogant cowboy who thought every woman was his for the asking. His good looks and beguiling charm had gone to his head, she thought. She never should have weakened and let herself go dancing with him.

"Whoa! Don't go getting your dander up, sugar," he pleaded.

"Don't call me sugar!" She spun around and fumbled for her key, its whereabouts in her purse elusive. His hand settled on her shoulder firmly but gently and made her turn to face him.

"You've got me all wrong, Dani. I'm not suggesting a quick, clandestine, sordid affair. You mentioned you never saw the Gulf of Mexico. I thought we could have a swim and see the sights, as I have to go down on some business anyway. Believe me, Dani, I have no intention of taking advantage of you in any way except to try and show you a good time. I'll stay the night at the other end of the island if you want me to. I need a little break from the rat race, and I suspect it would do you a world of good too. Please come with me, Dani. I promise to keep my distance—and my hands in my pockets all the time."

Dani sighed, knowing she was weakening. It would be a pleasant divertissement and a complete change for her. She hadn't taken a vacation since she started in business for herself. But what really decided her was the fact she believed him. And, more importantly, she had complete faith and trust in him. There wasn't a hint of dishonesty in those blue-gray eyes.

"Please," he implored again.

"All right. But remember, I'll hold you to your word."

"Hands in pockets. Promise."

"What time?"

"I'll pick you up at eight o'clock." He placed a crooked finger under her chin and lifted her face. His head lowered, and his lips brushed hers lightly. "Thank you for trusting me. I won't forget it, Dani. Good night."

"Good night," she murmured. She stood there and watched the yellow pickup drive off, then traced a finger over her lips, which were burning more ferociously than the hottest chili pepper made.

5

Though it was a Saturday, the traffic in and around Dallas seemed to be as congested as ever. It took the yellow pickup almost an hour to reach the small municipal airport in Dallas. Dani swung her large canvas bag over her shoulder as they walked to a small, single-engine airplane.

"Yours?" asked Dani with surprise.

"No. It belongs to a friend of mine," replied Scott.

"I hope you can fly the thing."

Scott laughed. "Now would I be jeopardizing your life and mine?"

"It was a stupid statement. Forgive me."

"You know I'd forgive you anything." All humor drained from his face.

"You promised me you wouldn't get serious. This is supposed to be a weekend of sheer relaxation for both of us," warned Dani, more fearful of being able to control her own emotions than she was of him.

"Here, let me throw that in the back," said Scott, reaching for her shoulder bag and swinging the door to the plane open. "Got your bathing suit?"

"Of course. I want to be able to brag to everyone how I swam in the Gulf of Mexico."

He helped her into the aircraft and was soon at the controls. After a brief conversation with the tower, Scott pointed the light plane down the runway and gathered speed quickly. Once airborne, Dani's eyes scanned the ground as though she had never seen it before.

"Have you ever been in a small plane before?" asked Scott.

"Yes. Some of the bigger fairs in Iowa had airplane rides. I went on them whenever I could. Why do you ask?"

"The way you were looking down at the ground."

"It never ceases to fascinate me. It's a whole different world down there when you see it from this perspective. You don't realize how flat everything is until you see it from the air. Rivers look like coiling silver lanes, not sections of water," Dani claimed.

In his soft Texas drawl, Scott gave a descriptive account of the areas as they flew over them. Time passed as swiftly as the plane flew, and he was soon nosing down to a grassy field in which black oil pumps pecked at the ground like mechanical chickens.

"Isn't there an airport in Galveston?" asked Dani.

"Yes. Schole's Field. But I have a friend here who'll lend me a car. Can't see all the sights on foot, now can we?" he replied. Scott landed the plane and then taxied to a large corrugated metal building. When the plane was at a complete stop, he hopped out, came around the plane, and helped Dani out.

"Scottie!" called a man emerging from the building and rushing toward them.

"Have you a car for me, Sam?" asked Scott after briefly introducing Dani.

"Sure do. Over there." He gave a directional nod of his head.

"Thanks a lot, Sam." He led Dani over to the old station wagon that seemed to cringe at the thought of actually being driven. After she seated herself on the passenger side, he closed the door and said, "I forgot to tell Sam something, sugar. I'll be right back."

Dani couldn't help but watch him walk off. Those long legs striding in an easy lope, the slim hips giving way to wide, square shoulders. She looked away and focused her attention on some gulls screeching their presence as they soared loftily around the clear blue sky. As the minutes passed, she glanced over toward the building, expecting to see Scott and his friend outside, but they were nowhere to be seen. A full twenty minutes went by before Scott returned to the time-worn station wagon and climbed in.

"Sorry to keep you waiting like that, especially in this heat. It couldn't be helped, but I'll make it up to you, sugar," apologized Scott.

"I turned the windows down and caught a breeze now and then. I can hardly wait to get into the water."

"It won't be long now."

He drove down the fairly empty road to Port Bolivar where they had a short wait to get onto the ferry that would take them to the island city of Galveston. Once on Galveston, Dani's eyes brightened at the sight of the seemingly endless beach, as the car made its way down Seawall Boulevard. Then Scott turned down one street, then another and another, until Dani thought she was in a maze. He finally pulled into the driveway of a red brick house whose fairly spacious grounds were girded with a black wrought-iron fence.

"This looks rather private. Are you sure you have the right place?" asked Dani peering at the grand house that was a little short of a mansion in comparison to the houses she saw when they left Seawall Boulevard.

"Trust me, sugar. It belongs to a friend of mine," he said, bringing the car to a halt.

"You seem to have an awful lot of friends," she stated, somewhat suspiciously.

"I'm a real friendly fella. Haven't you noticed?" He smiled and got out of the car. As he did, the front door opened and a woman in her early sixties came to stand outside, while an older man brushed past her.

"Mr. Rowland . . . how good to see you. Anything I can help you with?" asked the man.

"No, I think we can manage. Dani, I'd like you to meet Jim Ryan, and this is his wife, Amy," introduced Scott as the beaming woman came over to greet them.

Dani smiled and nodded, yet all the while she wondered what was going on. Scott led her into the house with the Ryan couple following.

"Hungry?" Scott asked Dani.

"Starved. And thirsty."

"I'll take you up to your room and have Amy rustle up some grub for us."

"Who are they?" she asked in a whisper.

"Caretakers. My friend doesn't used the place much in the summertime. He keeps the Ryans on to look after the place and take care of any of his friends who might want to stay the night in Galveston," he explained, as he steered her up the luxurious staircase. They moved down the hall before Scott opened one of the doors. "Like it?"

Dani's head slowly swiveled as she scanned the airy, dainty room. "It's lovely. I haven't seen a fourposter like that before." She went to the bed and fingered the delicately carved cherrywood. "Really beautiful."

"Make yourself at home while I see about getting us something to eat," he said, closing the door behind him.

Dani marveled at the ultrafeminine room that boasted of another era. Though neither an expert nor an aficionado, she was reasonably sure the room contained genuine antiques, perhaps valuable ones. There was a private bath with shower, not modern but completely functional. She washed her hands and face, brushed her hair, and went down stairs. She wandered into the spacious living room and soon realized the furniture and decor were also of another period in time. The deep-pile Oriental carpet masked Scott's steps, and Dani swung around when his hands came down on her shoulders.

"Quite a house, isn't it? A little on the old-fashioned side, but comfortable." He dropped his hands, stood alongside her, and offered a crooked arm. "Shall we go to lunch?"

"Definitely." She ran her hand through his arm and they went into the formal dining room, where solid mahogany furniture gleamed richly.

The beach was sparsely populated as they spread out the blanket. Dani, a short beach jacket covering her one-piece bathing suit, sat down and, with her hand shading her eyes, looked up at Scott. "Aren't you going in the water?"

"Sure am."

"But you're fully dressed."

"Have my suit on under my clothes. After that whopper of a lunch

we tucked away, I thought we ought to sit a while and enjoy the view."
He sat down beside her, knees drawn up and his arms loosely embracing them. "It's been a long time since I've been to the seashore.
Grandaddy used to take me to Corpus Christi when I was a boy. Sure
had myself a good time then, splashing about in the water like a fool.
Then I learned to swim, and Grandaddy had a hard time getting me out
of the water."

"If you love it so much, why have you stayed away so long?" asked
Dani, still shading her eyes from the sun.

"When are you going to get yourself a hat, sugar? One of these days
that little ol' sun is going to get to you." He gazed at her with concerned fondness, then sighed. "To answer your question, I left child-
hood and entered manhood and found there was more work than play
in that stage of my life. And do get yourself a hat."

She smiled and shook her head. "You sound like a mother hen." She
looked out at the gulf and watched some far-off ships ply their way
through the water. Their distance on the horizon was blurred, making
them ghostly apparitions. "I noticed a lot of the places along Seawall
Boulevard are called Treasure Island this or Treasure Island that. Is
there any particular reason?"

"Sure is. In the early nineteenth century, 1817, I think, the notorious
pirate Jean Lafitte and his followers established a settlement here. Ru-
mor has it he buried a vast fortune on Galveston, though it has never
been found. So this is still Treasure Island, with a few hoping to discover his fabulous cache. And in more ways than one it is an island of
treasure. Galveston was the first city in Texas to have electric lights; it
had the first telegraph, the first brewery, the first medical college and
the first Roman Catholic convent. St. Mary's Cathedral was the first
Catholic cathedral to be built in Texas. There are some fine old
churches here in Galveston. We'll take a look around tomorrow."

"You seem to know your history, Scott."

"Only if it has to do with Texas. Now Grandaddy has a way of
weaving history into a story that makes for real fascinating listening."

"You're quite fond of your grandfather, aren't you?"

"We're pretty close. The only trouble is he can read me like an open
book." He shucked off his boots and socks, then put his old Stetson on
the blanket before standing to remove his shirt and jeans. "Ready for
that swim?"

Dani stood and let her beach robe fall to the blanket, revealing her well-rounded, petite figure swathed in an aqua swimsuit; its design exposed the flesh of her side by means of crossstrap webbing. Scott's approving glance did not go unnoticed by Dani, and she did some admiring of her own. With clothes on, Scott presented an almost skinny image, but in a swimsuit it was apparent he was all muscle, sinewy and hard, a well-proportioned man for his height. He had the virile physique that exuded strength and male sexuality. Dani was more than impressed; she was a little awed.

"I'll race you," she cried, dashing toward the water.

They hit the gently rolling waters at the same time and swam through the warm liquid side by side and horizontal to the beach. Simultaneously, they turned in the water and sliced their way back. They stood waist high and let the waves lap at their bodies.

"The water is so warm," exclaimed Dani pushing her wet, auburn hair back from her face.

"You're not a bad swimmer," commented Scott.

"You do all right yourself." Suddenly, with a loud cry, Dani threw herself into Scott's arms.

"What is it?" he asked, his face clouded with concern.

"Something bit my toe," she said, trembling with an unknown fear.

He lifted her up off the sandy floor and held her close, her hands resting on his shoulders. "Take it easy, sugar. Nothing but a little crab who thought your toe was a tempting morsel." His voice was resonant and soothing.

Their eyes caught and held. Silver flecks glinted in his eyes as his chest heaved with increasingly deep breaths. Dani was transfixed, and the veins in her neck pulsated erratically. All her instincts told her to pull away as the undulating waters pushed flesh against flesh, but all she could do was stare into those blue-gray eyes that held her captive and made her skin tingle with inexplicable joy. She lowered her eyes, hoping to break the spell.

Keeping one arm firmly about her tiny waist, Scott cupped her chin and lifted it. "Dani," he whispered, before his lips touched hers. When her hands slipped over his wet back to encompass the thick cords of his neck, Scott dropped his hand from her chin to firmly circle around her back. His mouth moved over hers with increasing passion, increasing urgency, increasing demand, yet with a slow, steady gentleness.

If Dani had any resistance, it flowed out her toes to dissipate into the water. She clung to him, meeting his ardor with growing desire and totally unaware they were in a public place. Her senses were being provoked to a new awareness, a sharp yearning that was propelling her into a realm where only velvety pleasure reigned.

A resounding wave crashed against them, the undercurrent tugging their feet from the sandy bottom and causing them to lose their balance.

When Dani's head bobbed up, she laughed.

"The gods are against me," said Scott, joining in her laughter. "Let's take another swim."

The afternoon spun away like cotton candy as they swam, lay in the sun, and walked the fine line between sand and surf with hands entwined. They browsed through the various shops that lined Seawall Boulevard, stopping only to indulge in a double-decker ice cream cone. They held hands more often than not but refrained from talking of the incident in the water or anything that involved their personal emotions.

After a shower and shampoo, Dani put on the one dress she had brought with her. The material was a crinkle cotton with a dash of synthetic threads woven in, causing it to look crisp no matter how crumpled it became. It was a gray, boxlike dress with a vee neck and loose three-quarter sleeves. A wide maroon leather belt cinched it in at the waist. Gray-toned nylons and maroon pumps completed her ensemble, as she descended the staircase to the admiring eyes of Scott, who was waiting in the foyer for her.

"You sure are a marvel, Dani. Looking so pretty and sweet after a day in the sun and salt," said Scott, dressed in tight tan slacks and a white shirt.

"Thank you. You look pretty good yourself," she countered, letting him guide her into the dining room where he gallantly held her chair.

"I feel a little guilty putting the Ryans to so much trouble," said Dani, watching Scott take his seat at the table. "Don't you feel like you're imposing?"

"Nope. They enjoy it. Amy loves to show off her culinary skills and doesn't get the opportunity to do so very often. Having company to fuss over is a novelty for them. Keeps them from getting into a rut. The people that own the place hardly come down any more. The Ryans depend on their friends to use the place."

"If your friend doesn't use this place all that much, why doesn't he sell it? He could always stay at a hotel when he wanted to visit Galveston. I should think it would be a cheaper," said Dani.

"I guess he's fond of this old place. Besides, where would the Ryans go at their age?"

Dani shrugged, then concentrated on the aromatic dish of tomato soup laced with onions and garlic. The salad which followed was crisp, with a hot, spicy dressing dribbled over it. The main course, giant baked shrimp stuffed with crabmeat that had been marinated in a sauce liberally touched with tabasco, was accompanied by a rice that was pungently flavored with green peppers, onions, garlic, and bright red chili peppers. Fresh string beans, swimming in butter, were placed on the table in individual serving dishes. Dessert was a light airy lemon chiffon pie.

"That was wonderful! Mrs. Ryan certainly has the restaurants beat by a mile," declared Dani, settling back in her chair as coffee was served.

"Then you approve of the dishes?" asked Scott.

"Definitely."

Scott grinned boyishly. "These are my recipes. I gave them to Mrs. Ryan when we first arrived."

"My compliments to you." Dani raised her coffee cup in mock salute. "The dishes were unusual and very tasty. I'd appreciate it if you would share your recipes with me."

"Any time, sugar. Whatever I have is yours for the asking."

Dani let that remark slide by and asked instead, "Perhaps you can tell me why, when the weather is so hot down here, the food is so hot and spicy? I could understand it if we were in a cold climate."

Scott sat back in his chair and looked at her. "I never really thought about it. I suppose one might reason if you're hot enough inside you won't notice how hot it is outside." He drained his cup, then smiled at her. "If you're finished, I'll show you some of the city."

He parked the station wagon in the business district, where the old and the new resided in harmony. They walked along the Strand, where the nineteenth-century commercial buildings had been restored and the ancient gaslights readapted to the twentieth century. Specialty shops, art galleries, pubs, restaurants, delicatessens, and an old-fashioned candy factory now filled the buildings which were once known as the Wall Street of the Southwest.

They strolled slowly, peering in windows, going into a shop or art gallery to browse. When her enthusiasm for the business district waned,

Scott steered her down Twenty-second Street to the Galveston ship channel and the piers.

Dani's eyes widened at the sight of an old merchant ship whose three masts towered one hundred and three feet above the water line. The four-hundred-ton square rigger had been completely restored and sat in the channel with the air of a proud, vain lady.

"She's one of the oldest merchant ships afloat," informed Scott, draping his arm over Dani's shoulder as they both stared at the ship. "Built in Scotland in 1877 and called the *Elissa*. I'm afraid we're too late for the tour."

"Beautiful," exclaimed Dani. "Does it ever set sail?"

"Sometimes it leaves its mooring for a sail up the channel. I don't know exactly when, though."

"What are those ships?" asked Dani, pointing off to her right.

"That's the shrimp fleet. There are also some fishing boats for hire there too. Galveston is quite a port. Along with the shrimp fleet, international ships and banana boats pull up to these piers."

Their pace down Port Industrial Boulevard was leisurely when suddenly the clear skies were routed by churning black clouds.

"A squall," announced Scott. "We'd better get back to the car." He pulled his brimmed hat down and, holding onto it with one hand while his other arm gathered Dani to him, he urged her head to his chest.

A wind of gale proportions swirled sand in the air like fine shards of glass. The fine granules stung and bit into the flesh, settled in hair, eyes, ears, nose and mouth. Dani found it difficult to breathe as the sand-laden air clogged her nostrils and clung to the dampness of her lips. She gratefully sheltered her head on Scott's hard chest as they tried to walk rapidly against the deterring wind. The sky was becoming more menacing and inky as she tried to keep the stride set by Scott's long legs. Large globules of rain began to spot the gray cement, causing the whirling sand to weaken its assault, promising the more ominous portent of a torrential rain.

"We'd better make a run for it," said Scott, taking her hand.

"Wait a minute," implored Dani. She reached down and slipped the high heels from her feet and, holding them in her free hand, said, "Let's go."

Before they were halfway to the car, the sky opened up as though a sharp knife had sliced open a gargantuan plastic garbage bag filled with an ocean of water. Within moments both of them were thoroughly soaked. Scott stopped running, causing Dani to halt.

"What's the use? We can't get any wetter than we are now." He lazily smiled down at her, rain pouring in rivulets from the front and back of his old Stetson.

Dani returned his smile. "I think you're right. Besides, I don't think I can keep up this pace all the way to the car."

With measured steps they made their way back in silence to the forlorn-looking car, Scott never relinquishing her hand. They sat in the station wagon and he coaxed the recalcitrant automobile to start. The windshield wipers waved furiously as Scott cautiously drove the vehicle through a labyrinth of streets.

"I hope your pretty outfit isn't ruined," said Scott, his eyes squinting as they tried to discern the area before him.

"Everything is washable. I feel like a fish dragged onto shore. Clammy and waterlogged."

"Amy can put everything through the washer to get rid of the sand, then run them through the drier. I'm sure there are plenty of robes kicking around the house. Dry clothes and a good, hot cup of cocoa will set everything to rights."

"I'm going to need a shower again. I'm loaded with sand. I feel like I've been swimming in it. It all happened so fast. Is it always like that down here?"

"Not always, but sudden squalls are not unusual."

"I wonder if it did any damage anywhere," mused Dani.

"I doubt it. Ever since the great hurricane of 1900, Galveston knows how to gear for disaster. These little squalls are like a tap on the cheek compared to the force of a full-blown hurricane. That 1900 hurricane caused flooding that inundated the entire island, causing the deaths of five to seven thousand people. The city fathers began the construction of the seawall soon afterward. It's proved its worth more than once," said Scott.

"Does it run the entire length of the island?"

"No. Only for ten miles. The public beaches run for thirty-two miles along the edge of the island. Ah! Here we are."

Dani stood under the shower and scrubbed her head vigorously, removing all traces of sand from her hair and ears. Now she understood why cowboys wore neckerchiefs all the time. Dust and sandstorms could whip up at any time, especially in the more arid sections of West Texas. She assumed Mrs. Ryan had left the navy-blue robe on the bed for her and gratefully slipped into it when she had finished her shower. She towel-dried her hair as best she could while wishing she had her blower.

Scott was waiting for her in the living room, a tray with mugs of hot cocoa and plates with wedges of cherry pie on the coffee table resting before the sofa.

"My . . . you are a pretty lady no matter what you have on," Scott exclaimed, patting the sofa's cushion next to him. "Sit down and get something hot into you."

"That was quite an experience. I doubt if I'll ever forget it," said Dani, sitting down on the cushion next to him. She clutched the mug and took a deep swallow. "Oh . . . that tastes good."

"Wait until you taste the pie."

"If I keep on eating like this, I'll look like a beached whale," said Dani, reaching for the pie.

"Not you, sugar. But speaking of whales, tomorrow we'll go to Sea-Arama Marineworld—after I show you a palace."

"Palaces here in Galveston?"

"Why not?"

When she finished the pie, Dani leaned back in the softness of the sofa, mug clasped with two hands. She was disappointed when Scott moved down to the edge of the sofa, his back half hinged on the arm rest. She thought the evening might lean toward the romantic, for the setting was perfect, and after his kiss on the beach and her eager acceptance of it, she felt in a warm, mellow mood. But Scott seemed indifferent to it all as he discoursed on the early history of Galveston Island. It was past ten in the evening, and Dani could no longer smother a yawn.

"Am I boring you, sugar?"

Dani shook her head with a wistful smile. "I'm not used to so much outdoor activity. I was up very early this morning, and this cocoa seems to be doing its job. I really enjoy and am interested in your narrative regarding Galveston, but I think I'd better get to bed and hear the rest of it tomorrow."

"Sure, sugar. I could do with a good night's sleep myself." He stood and offered her his hand. Dani put down her empty cocoa mug on the table, took his hand, and allowed herself to be drawn up. "Goodnight, Dani." He turned her hand palm up and kissed it.

"Goodnight, Scott." She smiled, her body filled with a warm glow.

The rays of the sun spilled into the room where Dani lay on the fourposter bed. She pulled the sheet up over her head, attempting to block out the annoying light, but the sun's brilliance was too powerful. It penetrated her closed eyelids to a degree that could not be ignored. She threw the sheet back and rolled onto her back. Her eyes blinked open and she smiled as she beheld the charming bedroom. Perhaps she would redecorate her own home when she received the check from Nicholas Hunt. Her mind wandered to the enigmatic Mr. Hunt but quickly snapped back when, after fumbling for her watch on the adjacent nightstand, she saw the time. After nine in the morning! She scrambled into the robe and dashed downstairs to what apparently was an empty house. Standing in the dining room, she wondered where the kitchen was, only to have Mrs. Ryan come bouncing in.

"Do sit down, Miss Wexford. I'll have your breakfast out in a jiffy," said a beaming Mrs. Ryan before she hurried back to her domain.

Dani sat at the dining table, curiously aware that it was set for one. A pot of coffee and grits were served first. By the time Mrs. Ryan brought toast, eggs, and bacon, Dani could no longer hold back the question foremost in her mind.

"Where is Mr. Rowland?" she asked with some trepidation. She didn't relish the idea of getting back to Dallas on her own, even though it was no big deal—a taxi to the municipal airport, where she could either wait for a plane going to Dallas or hire one, if necessary.

"He left very early this morning, but said you shouldn't worry as he'll be back as soon as he can, and that should be well before noon," replied Mrs. Ryan.

"I see." Dani was greatly relieved. She firmly believed Scott to be a man of his word.

"That was quite a storm last night," commented Mrs. Ryan.

"Yes, it was. And it came up so suddenly."

"Well . . . it's over now. I washed and dried your things. I'll put them up in your bedroom while you eat your breakfast."

"Thank you, Mrs. Ryan. In fact, thank you for everything," said Dani.

"It's been a pleasure for both me and Jim to have you here. It's always nice to have young people about the house." She gave Dani a warm smile, then left the dining room.

After eating a generous breakfast, Dani went upstairs to dress.

Remembering the sudden squall, she wore the same outfit she had traveled to Galveston in. She wasn't about to get caught in a dress and high heels again. Deep orange slacks, a white, shortsleeve blouse of cotton eyelet, and sandals were suitable enough, she thought, and packed her other things in the canvas tote bag. As she was about to open the bedroom door, she heard the front door open and close, then feet galloping up the stairs. She stepped into the hall to see Scott coming toward her, his expression instantly turning to one of elation.

"You're here," he said breathlessly.

"Where else would I be?"

"I was afraid you might take it into that pretty little head of yours to think that I deserted you when I wasn't here and go back to Dallas on your own."

"Mrs. Ryan said you'd be back."

He grinned at her sheepishly. "Is your bag all packed?"

"Yes."

"We'll put it in the station wagon. We won't be coming back here."

"Are we still going to Sea-Arama?" she asked as they descended the stairs.

"Yes, ma'm. First to see the palace, some lunch, then to Sea-Arama before winging back to Dallas," he replied happily.

He drove down Broadway, then turned down Fourteenth Street to park the car near the palace. The impressive structure, with its gables, towers, and minarets, had an exterior composed of white limestone, red sandstone, and granite. It did indeed have the appearance of a castle on the Rhine, only on a much smaller scale.

Dani listened intently as the tour guide led the small group through the interior of the minor palace. She marveled at the elegant, intricately handcarved grand staircase composed of rosewood, mahogany and satinwood. Its polished red glow curved upward on its journey to the second floor, displaying exquisite stained-glass windows. Crowned high above the staircase was a wondrous dome of stained glass. Scott slipped his arm around her waist and Dani forced herself to listen to the guide's explanations so the warmth of his hand would not fire her body in the air-conditioned mansion.

"This excellent example of Victorian architecture was designed for

Colonel and Mrs. Walter Gresham by Nicholas Crayton. It took seven years and $250,000 to build it, being finally completed in 1893. The chandelier you see before you is of Venetian crystal; the damask wall coverings are from London. During the great flood of 1900, the Greshams opened their house to hundreds of homeless victims. It was purchased by the Catholic diocese in 1923 and became the home of Bishop Byrne until 1950, thus the name Bishop's Palace. It is the state's only building to be on the list of one hundred outstanding buildings in the United States." The guide expertly went on to give a historical account of various items as they moved from room to room.

As Scott headed the station wagon back to Seawall Boulevard, Dani said, "I suppose the tour was a bit boring for you."

"Not at all, sugar. I've never been in the palace before. Real elegant it is. And don't worry about Sea-Arama. I've never been there before either. Never did have much time for sightseeing. I'm a tourist just like you."

They stopped at a small place to eat lunch, where Scott ordered a bowl of chili and Dani a hamburger, the large breakfast having curbed her appetite. After one spoonful of the chili, Scott called the waitress back and requested a bottle of hot sauce, which caused Dani to smile.

"I wouldn't be the least bit surprised if you mixed chili peppers with your grits," she said.

He gave her his lopsided grin. "I've never tried it but it sounds good. I do sprinkle cayenne pepper on my eggs in the morning. Does that count for anything?"

"Definitely. You get 'I' for inventive cookery. Really, Scott. Hot pepper on eggs?"

"Why not? It sets one alive in the morning. You ought to try it, sugar, before you sneer at it."

"Maybe I will." Dani drained her large glass of iced tea.

Like two children abandoning themselves to wonderland, Scott and Dani watched the dolphins and sea lions perform their aquatic acrobatics, applauding the magnificent efforts of the sea animals. The show put on by the tropical birds was equally entertaining. Holding hands, they wandered through the Oceanarium, where twenty killer sharks were displayed. They gazed through windows and marveled at the rare species of fish before taking in the park's turtles, alligators, river otters, African pygmy goats, and scores of wild birds, with a water-skiing show forming one of the highlights of Sea-Arama.

After a quick dinner of Chinese food, they were on their way back to the ferry that would take them to Port Bolivar and the mainland, where the plane was waiting for them.

"This isn't the way to my house," said Dani as the yellow pickup passed by Dallas's Interstate 75 North.

"I hope you don't mind, but I want to stop off at my apartment first. These boots are still damp and I want to change them before they drive me crazy," explained Scott.

"I don't mind in the least." She wanted to see his apartment and was delighted for the opportunity.

As they drove into the project, Dani was unimpressed. Two-story frame buildings were huddled together in rows like troop formations dressed in a drab gray. He pulled into a well-marked parking spot before a set of cement steps, flanked by plain iron railings.

"Want to come up?" asked Scott. "There's not much to see."

"I'd like to. I always like to look at kitchens designed by others."

She followed him up the steps to a landing where neglected newspapers had gathered. He scooped them up before opening the door and allowing her to precede him.

"Like I said, it's not much," reiterated Scott. "There should be a pitcher of iced tea in the frig. Help yourself."

The apartment startled Dani. Scott was right when he said there wasn't much to see. An old beanbag chair constituted the only living room furniture. A well-used table and two chairs sat forlorn in the dinette. Walking to the small galley-type kitchen, she peered down the truncated hall that had swallowed Scott up to see through the doorway into the single bedroom, which contained nothing more than a sleeping bag. After opening a few cabinet doors which revealed equally sparse contents, she finally found the one that hid the glasses—three in all and plastic. She took two of them, then went to the refrigerator, which spread its light on a bowl of eggs, a quart of milk, and the pitcher of iced tea. It was hardly worth having it plugged in, she thought, removing the pitcher and then a tray of ice cubes. She filled both glasses with the tea and ice cubes, then brought them to the table as Scott emerged from the hall.

"You do lead a Spartan life," she commented, as they sat down at the table.

He shrugged indifferently. "It's a place to eat and sleep. I don't require much more than that."

"Wouldn't it be more comfortable if you lived at home? It's really not that far to drive."

"I like being in the heart of the city. It gives me a better perspective on things. I take it you don't approve of my abode, sugar," said Scott, a glinting amusement in his eyes.

"If it's how you prefer to live, it's certainly none of my business. And if you are happy with it, then my opinion really doesn't matter."

"What do you think of the kitchen?"

"Very efficient."

"Could you have done better?"

Dani craned her neck to view the kitchen once again. "I don't think so. The space is so limited, one can only use a certain standard design." She finished her tea. "Shall we go?"

He nodded and drained his glass.

Scott drove the pickup through the back streets, avoiding the main highways. Dani was surprised to find that from his apartment it was only about a fifteen-minute drive to her house.

"Care to come in for some coffee or hot cocoa?" asked Dani after he walked her to the door.

"No thanks, sugar. I have a real early day tomorrow."

"I had a marvelous weekend, and I thank you very much for everything," said Dani, suddenly feeling like she was talking to a complete stranger.

"My pleasure." He bent down and kissed her lightly on the cheek. "I'll be in touch, Dani."

She unlocked the door and went into the house. Never before had she felt so utterly bewildered. The passionate way he kissed her while they stood in the waters of the Gulf of Mexico belied the brotherly attitude he assumed for the rest of the weekend. A kiss on the cheek no less! And here she was beginning to think she meant something to him. She knew he meant something to her, even though she wasn't quite sure what it was.

Early the next morning, a bonded messenger handed Dani a sealed envelope for which she had to sign. She closed the door absently and went back into the office. Her silence caused Sandy to look up from the desk.

"What is it?" asked Sandy.

"I don't know," replied Dani, reaching for the letter opener on the desk. She slit the envelope open and peeked inside to see crisp one-thousand-dollar bills neatly tucked in the envelope. She took them out and counted them. Ignoring Sandy's exclamation of surprise, she searched the envelope for a letter of explanation. All she found was a folded sheet of paper torn from a small pad. She removed it, folded it open to read, "Order Momma's kitchen————Scott." She tossed the note on the desk for Sandy to read.

"Wow!" exclaimed Sandy. "Do you want me to take that money to the bank right away?"

"No. I have some watercolors to deliver. I'll stop at the bank first," replied Dani, experiencing a sudden deflation of her spirit. No affectionate salutation. A cold impersonal business message. She had begun to like being called "sugar," especially the way Scott said it. Perhaps she shouldn't have returned his kiss with such anxious zeal. She took a deep breath and let it out slowly. Damn him anyway. She didn't need any poor cowboy coming in and messing up her life anyway.

"Sandy . . . please call the factory and order the kitchen for the Rowland job." Dani turned on her heel, shoved the money into her purse, picked up the case with the pictures, and stormed out of the house.

6

Dani shaded her eyes against the hot, bright Texas sun as she watched the three huge semis pull onto the Hunt condominium job site. She had hired a high school girl, who occasionally filled in for Sandy, for the day. Between Sandy, the competent young girl, and herself, they could check the contents of all three trucks simultaneously. Hunt's men took the cartons into the buildings as the three women checked them off against the original order, making sure that all cartons ordered had been shipped. Dani prayed the factory hadn't made too many mistakes. She liked all her jobs to go smoothly, and the majority of them did. But they were all single kitchen orders. This was her first venture into multiple kitchens, and she wasn't sure how well the factory would handle it. She had checked over her order to them so many times she thought her eyeballs would fall out. Now it was up to them.

It took the entire morning to unload the trucks. With a broad smile, Dani signed the trucker's bill of lading indicating all the cabinetry ordered was delivered. When the trucks left, she went to compare notes with her assistants.

"How did you make out, Marge?" Dani asked the obliging high school girl.

"All accounted for except for one twelve-inch base cabinet," replied Marge.

"Sandy?"

"A refer cabinet missing," replied Sandy.

Dani gave a quick sigh of relief. "That's not bad at all. At least those are small enough to be sent UPS. When you get back to the office, Sandy, you'd better call the factory and have them send those two cabinets out immediately. Meanwhile I'm taking you two to lunch as a small celebration."

"Aren't you coming back to the office with us, Dani?" asked Sandy.

"No. I'll be coming back here. The countertops are supposed to be delivered early this afternoon," replied Dani.

"I was wondering why you drove your own car," said Sandy.

"Can we go somewhere elegant for lunch?" asked Marge.

"You bet we can," said Dani, her face flushed with pride and good humor.

After lunch, Dani drove back to the job site, and it wasn't too long before her good humor deserted her. The countertops were over an hour late being delivered. It wasn't like John Kellner to be late. Horrible visions of overturned trucks with countertops smashed assailed her brain. She glanced at her watch, deciding to give him another hour before calling his shop. She was glad she decided to wait, for in less than twenty minutes the big, dark blue truck pulled up to the new building.

"What kept you?" she asked of the heavyset man.

"That truck." John Kellner shook his head ruefully. "If it isn't the spark plugs, it's the battery or some other idiotic mechanical failure."

"Well John, with contracts like this, you'll be able to buy a whole fleet of new trucks," consoled Dani, too relieved to be angry.

"You're not kidding. Do you think you'll be getting more work from Hunt?"

"I don't know. But if this goes well, I don't see why not. I can underbid most of them in the kitchen business, unless you're contemplating raising your price to me," she said good-naturedly.

"I can make a greater profit with volume than from individual kitchens, and I can buy the laminate much cheaper when I buy in large amounts. With this order, I put my men on an assembly line. Henry Ford of the countertop business they've been calling me," he said with a grin.

"Well, let's unload. This heat is getting to me."

Regardless of the weather, Dani viewed the unloading of the countertops with a practiced eye, scanning for chipped laminate and keeping an approximate count in her head. She knew John Kellner was reliable, and if there was any discrepancy, he'd make good.

She stood watching the last of the countertops being carried into the building, then spun around as a voice close by startled her.

"Do you always stay on the job with such devotion?"

"Mr. Hunt . . . I didn't expect you here."

"Why not? It's my project." Nicholas Hunt gave her a tight but warm smile.

"I assumed your foreman took care of all the site work," said Dani.

"He told me you've been here all day."

"I like to personally make sure the contents of the trucks contain what they are supposed to."

He stared at her hard, the sun flecking gold on his black hair. He appeared dynamic and commanding in a light, tan, vested suit with a dark brown shirt and beige tie. "You look like you could use a tall, cold drink."

"I could."

"Let me buy it for you." He cupped her elbow and began to steer her toward his long, white Cadillac.

"My car," she protested.

"I'll have one of my men drive it home for you."

The promise of a cold drink was too tempting for Dani to offer any serious objection. Besides, he might be working on another project and it wouldn't hurt to get in on the ground floor.

The Cadillac still retained a modicum of its air-conditioning, and Nicholas started the car immediately to ensure a comfortable temperature. "Where are your car keys?" he asked.

"In the car. I didn't think I'd be leaving the area," Dani replied.

He picked up the car phone and instructed the listener on the other end to take Dani's car to her house, then gave him her address which he made a point of remembering from the contract.

"You look worried, Miss Wexford," he said after replacing the receiver.

"I'm not. I'm sure your man is a good driver."

"Set your mind at rest, Miss Wexford. If anything happens to your car, I'll buy you a brand-new Cadillac."

Dani laughed. "That's a tempting offer. Perhaps you should call one of your men who has a *poor* driving record to take my car home."

He smiled as the car moved swiftly and silently along the access road before melting onto the highway. "I like a woman with a sense of humor. Too many people lose it in the scramble to get to the top. Their humor tends to be caustic and snide."

"There's no sense getting to the top if it takes one's ability to laugh, not only at the world but at one's self," declared Dani.

"Have you ever laughed at yourself, Miss Wexford?"

"Quite a bit." For the past few days she had really been laughing at herself for her gullibility, her stupidity in letting herself fall for a lanky cowboy. Oh yes, she had laughed at herself, loud and strong.

Nicholas Hunt was well known in the small, exclusive café, and they were immediately ushered to a secluded table in the dim cool room.

"What will you have, Miss Wexford?" Nicholas asked.

"A large glass of iced tea."

"An iced tea and a scotch," he said to the waitress, then turned back to Dani. "There's one thing I'd like to get straight, Miss Wexford, if we are to do any business in the future."

"And what is that, Mr. Hunt?"

"Stop all this damn Mr. Hunt–Miss Wexford business. My friends call me Nick, and I know you prefer Dani. Is it a deal?"

"A deal, Nick," said Dani eagerly eyeing the tall glass of iced tea the waitress placed before her. "You sound as if there is another project in the offering."

"I've got a shot at several developments on the fringes of Houston. Condos, duplexes, and single homes. A sizable package. Once I get the architectural plans, I'd be interested in seeing what you come up with for the kitchens."

"Sounds formidable." Juices of excitement flowed through her. From the way he talked, she might be in the running for a million-dollar contract. "When do you think you'll be getting the plans?"

"You sound eager."

"I am," Dani replied quickly.

"At least you're honest." His dark eyes searched hers intently. "Let me take you to dinner tonight. And I owe you a night of dancing. A new place has opened up downtown. I think you'll like it."

"I'm sorry but . . ."

"Please don't say no. I realize you've put in a long, tiring day. A night of relaxation would be just what the doctor ordered. I'll take you right home when you've finished your tea, and it will give you three hours to have a rest and get ready."

"You're very persuasive, Nick. What time?" she drained the cool drink.

"I'll pick you up at eight. But first I have to get you home." He quickly swallowed the rest of his scotch, stood, and threw some bills on the table.

Dani, who preferred a shower, ran a hot tub and liberally sprinkled in bath salts and bubble bath. She slipped in and put her brain in neutral. She quickly succumbed to the soothing effect of the water, letting her entire body be seduced by the perfumed bubbles. Time had no meaning as the stress of the day flowed from her body. By the time she had shampooed her short hair and rinsed off, she felt like a new woman, and was looking forward to a night in Dallas.

The royal blue silk dress enhanced the opalescence of her skin. Finely rolled straps held the snug bodice in place while the multi-gored skirt swirled in gentle folds that ended just below her knees. Her short hair fluffed about her oval face, the sun having gilded the auburn with coppery highlights. After struggling with the tiny clasp of the short, gold rope necklace, she deftly skewered her gold earrings through her earlobes.

Holding the thin-strapped, royal blue shoes in her hand, she debated if she should wear them or not. The heels were high and would bring her to almost the same height as Nick. She searched her closet in vain for a pair of low-heeled shoes but nothing matched the dress as well as the ones she had in her hand. With a shrug of resignation, she slipped them on her feet.

At the restaurant, the car valet greeted Nick by name as he took the

Cadillac at the canopied entrance. Inside the foyer, crowded with waiting customers, Nick signaled the maitre d' and was immediately led to one of the best tables.

Before opening the menu, Dani looked around at the period decor of the restaurant. It was definitely a replica of the grand restaurants so popular in the early Gay Nineties. The highly polished mahogany bar, with its sparkling array of various shaped glasses, proudly lined one entire wall with a floor-to-ceiling mirror as a backdrop. Twin baby grand pianos nestled back to back on a platform over the bar, the pianists playing both old and new songs.

But what fascinated Dani the most was the long, red velvet swing that hung directly over the middle of the bar. A young woman, in a red velvet costume, sat on the swing, then pumped herself back and forth until she was in a wide arc over the bar. At the farthest point, she would kick a bell suspended from the ceiling with her foot. On the return swing, she would hit a bell high on the opposite wall with her hand. Dani's head swayed back and forth as she watched the feat being performed over and over again.

"Haven't you ever been here before?" asked Nick.

"No."

"Five years in Dallas and you've never been here?" Nick asked. "I'm surprised. It's a very popular place, as you can see from the crowd. Saturday night it's almost impossible to get in."

"I'll bet you don't have any trouble getting a table."

"I entertain clients quite often. Most of the better establishments know me. I'm a generous tipper." He gave her a rascally smile.

"Well, it certainly seems to pay off." Dani scanned the menu.

"Are you ready to order?"

"I think so," she replied, putting the menu aside, then slicing a piece of swiss cheese from the large slab on the table. "Want some?"

"If you're doing the honors, please."

Their conversation was a mixture of business, Dallas, and personal opinions regarding the state of the nation. Dani found Nick to be a good conversationalist and far more personable than she had thought from their first meetings. He seemed to relax and open up.

"Do you care for classical music, Dani?" asked Nick as the waitress cleared their table, then set cups of coffee in front of them.

"Most of it. I've never been wild about Mahler. I would say my preferences lean toward the three *B*'s, Bach, Beethoven and Brahms," she replied.

"You have to let me take you to the symphony when it is playing. Your choices happen to be my favorites too. I'll watch for the schedule of performances. And the ballet?"

"Again the classical ones. Too bad the season is so short. It's as limiting as the opera season."

"You've been to the opera?"

"Many times. Both the ballet and the opera, if they are playing the ones I like," replied Dani.

"Our tastes seem to coincide. I'll bet your favorite ballet is *Swan Lake* and your favorite opera is *La Bohème.*"

"You win. Although *Tosca* runs a close second to *Bohème.*"

"I can see we are going to be quite busy this winter." When the waitress came by to offer more coffee, they refused. "Are you ready to go?"

Dani nodded, took her napkin from her lap, and placed it on the table before rising. Nick's arm circled her waist as he guided her through the still crowded restaurant. As they stepped outside, the valet dashed away, and in moments the white Cadillac was in front of them, the valet opening the door for Dani.

"I've never been in the place I'm taking you to, but from all reports it is quite a place and extremely popular with the young crowd," said Nick as he headed the car southeast across Dallas.

"You say 'young crowd' as though you belong to the rocking chair set," observed Dani.

Nick laughed a rich, deep laughter. "I'm thirty-eight, and when I say young I am usually referring to those in their twenties, like you."

"Well, thirty-eight doesn't exactly qualify you for social security."

"Maybe not. But when you consider the median age in Dallas is around twenty-eight, I feel I'm categorized in, shall we say, the more mature group," said Nick, still smiling.

Entering the favored night spot was like walking into a world where only light and sound had any meaning. Strobe lights pulsated in a rainbow of colors; multi-faceted, mirrored globes reflected the startling hues like eerie planets in space. The entire place throbbed with life as the recorded music, from the Bee Gees to Boy George, seemed to emanate from the very walls. Undulating bodies swarmed the dance floor; people clustered about the U-shaped bar as though attached to it by an umbilical cord. The few small tables scattered about could never hope to accommodate the horde that filled the huge, high-ceilinged room.

Nick spotted a couple leaving a table for the dance floor, and swiftly moved Dani toward it.

"Stay here and guard the fort. What would you like to drink?" asked Nick.

"A white wine cooler," replied Dani, then watched him instantly disappear among the bodies. She turned her attention to the swirling mass of people that became a kaleidoscope of color as the strobe lights flashed around.

"I thought I saw you come in," said Janice Gordon, collapsing into the empty seat at the table. "My feet are killing me."

"Jan! What a surprise!" exclaimed Dani.

"Please don't say 'what a small world.' That's all I've heard all night. Every time I run into someone I know, I get 'what a small world'. Was that Nicholas Hunt with you?" asked Jan.

"Yes. He took me to dinner, then we came here. Are you alone?"

"Are you kidding? I'm trying to get a hotshot realtor to come to work for me. He's a real go-getter."

"Is that the same one you met at the meeting a month or so ago?" asked Dani.

"Good Lord, no. For all his good looks and charming ways, he was nothing more than a user, pumping me all the time about the ins and outs of real estate here in Dallas. No. He wasn't for me. He was a real sleaze bag. I'm going out with an executive from Data Control Systems now. Quite a man, let me tell you. And absolutely gorgeous! Where is Hunt?"

"Getting drinks."

"I hear it won't be long before that big condo of his is finished. Put in a good word for me, Dani."

"He probably has a real estate agent already, one of long standing."

"Give it a shot anyway. Mind if I stick around till he comes back? I'd like to meet him," said Janice.

"Be my guest. Won't your friend mind, though?"

"He's kicking up his heels with some weird young thing on the dance floor. Is it getting serious between you and Hunt?"

"Don't be silly, Jan. This is only the second time I've been with him socially."

"You could do worse. He positively drips money."

"Almost everyone in Dallas drips money or can if they really put their mind to it," said Dani. "Here comes Nick now."

"Nick, is it?" Janice rolled her eyes, then smiled slyly as the well-dressed man elbowed his way through the crowd, carrying a tray.

"I'm back," said Nick, placing the tray on the table and smiling at Dani before glancing at Janice.

"Nick, I'd like you to meet my good friend, Janice Gordon. Jan, this is Nicholas Hunt," introduced Dani.

"Miss Gordon," said Nick with a nod of his head.

"I've heard a great deal about you, Mr. Hunt. And do call me Jan. I hate formality," said Janice.

"Has Dani been talking about me?" asked Nick with a quick, approving glance at Dani.

"Dani is not much of a talker about her private life. No. Your name is frequently mentioned in the trade. I'm a realtor. Perhaps you've heard of the Gordon Real Estate Agency. My company is the sole agent for Ridgefield Homes, among others. I understand you will have a number of condos to put on the market soon. I do hope you'll consider using my agency. I'm sure we could do a bang-up job for you. My ad campaigns are quite impressive, and I am always willing to discuss an equitable commission. On multiple units the size you'll be offering, I think you'll find I can be more than competitive when it comes to a commission." Janice stood and offered her hand, which Nick took. "It has been a pleasure to meet you, Nick. Dani knows how to reach me if you are interested." She picked up her purse from the table and said to Dani, "I hear the newly remodeled J. C. Penney has all sorts of goodies, and Sakowitz is having a full week of informal modeling of the new fall lines from Halston, Saint Laurent, Sarasola and Nipon. If nothing else there is always Neiman-Marcus at NorthPark. It's been weeks since we've been shopping together, Dani. I'll call you next week and we'll make a day of it."

Dani nodded as she desperately tried to control the laughter rising within her. Janice gave a little wave to Nick and was off.

A soft laughter finally erupted from Dani, causing Nick to look at her quizzically. Dani took a sip of the wine before she could speak. "That Jan. She wanted me to put in a good word for her with you. I don't think that's necessary now, do you?"

"I feel as though I've been run over by a steamroller."

"I'll admit Jan's a pusher, but she is a hard worker and, really, a very nice person under all that fluff. What are these?" asked Dani, noticing the plate of hors d'oeuvres.

"There were several plates on the bar, so I grabbed one," said Nick.

"How can you think of food after that dinner we had?" asked Dani, as she plucked a bacon-wrapped scallop from the plate and popped it in her mouth.

"I didn't, but evidently you did," he said, with a sidelong glance and humor in his eyes.

Their drinks and tidbits finished, Dani and Nick ventured onto the dance floor and executed the latest steps to the music of a host of leading rock bands and singers. Nick's dancing abilities amazed Dani. For a short, stocky man, Nick was exceptionally graceful and agile. By mutual agreement, and after a number of dances, they decided to quit the dance floor.

With a protective arm around her shoulders, they sliced through the mass of people to elbow some standing room at the bar. Dani got her wine cooler and Nick his scotch. Before long they were embroiled in conversations with a variety of garrulous patrons of the night spot. It was after midnight when Nick brought the Cadillac to a halt before her door.

"Would you care to come in for some coffee?" asked Dani, thinking he probably wouldn't.

"I'd be delighted."

"Go into the living room and make yourself at home. It'll only take me a minute to get the coffee ready," said Dani, closing the front door behind them. She went into the kitchen while Nick veered off into the living room. After starting the coffee maker, she loaded a tray with the necessary items, and in a few minutes she was marching into the living room, tray in hand.

Nick was standing by the bookcase atop a line of cabinets next to the fireplace, perusing the titles. "I see we have another thing in common, our reading habits."

"You've read those?" asked Dani, as she put the tray on the coffee table.

"A number of them. I can see you and I are very much alike, Dani. And from what I've seen of it, I like your home. I understand you keep your office here."

"Yes. As soon as you've finished your coffee, I'll show it to you, if you wish." She kicked off her shoes and sat down on the sofa, while Nick sat down in the overstuffed chair opposite her.

"Fine. At the state fair grounds they have a large flea market on Sunday. Would you be interested in going with me?"

Dani hesitated, as Scott Rowland flashed through her mind. He might pop up on Sunday. But what did she care? She couldn't regulate her life according to his whims. "Yes, I would. Are you a flea market addict?"

"Not really. But I collect coins, and once in a while I can find one I've been looking for at a reasonable price. It's a hobby I occasionally indulge in without fanaticism. Are you a collector of anything?"

"I never seem to have the time. And to tell the truth, I've never found anything in the way of collectibles that has caught my fancy," replied Dani.

"No hobbies at all?"

"Oh, once in a while I'll do a watercolor other than a kitchen."

"What kind?"

"Oh, flowers, a scene—something along those lines."

"Well—" he drained his cup "—how about that grand tour?"

"Sure." Dani led him through the entire lower floor, then returned to the living room. "More coffee?"

He nodded and held out his cup. "A lovely place you have here."

"Thank you. Do you live in a house or an apartment?" she asked, replenishing both cups with coffee.

"A condo. You'll have to see it some time. Nice place. Are your watercolors handy? Those other than kitchens, I mean. I'd like to see them."

"They're nothing special."

"Let me be the judge of that."

Dani shrugged slightly and went into the office to get her large, black portfolio, then returned to the living room with it. She opened the portfolio and watched Nick go through the paintings slowly, studying some longer than others. Dani gazed at his dark head and his clean-cut handsome features. A strange yearning trembled through her, and she experienced a new awareness of the man, an awareness of his potent sexuality.

"These are quite good. In fact, I'd like to buy this one from you," he said, holding up a scene of Reunion Tower, with its shimmering glass buildings around it.

"Consider it a gift."

"I couldn't do that. I want to pay you for it."

"Nonsense. I want to give it to you to commemorate my first multi-kitchen contract. Please. I insist."

"All right. But only this once." He leaned the painting against his chair and closed the portfolio.

"Let me have it framed for you," said Dani.

"No. The painting is enough." He looked at his watch, picked up the painting, and stood. "I must be going. It's later than I thought."

Dani trailed behind him as he walked to the door. "Thank you for dinner and the entire evening. I had a great time."

"So did I," he said with a smile. "Thanks for the painting. I'll pick you up around ten in the morning on Sunday."

"Fine. Good night, Nick."

"Good night, Dani."

She closed the door behind him, then carried the tray from the living room to the kitchen, where she left it, deciding to clean up in the morning. Her foot touched the first step of the staircase when her doorbell chimed. With an inquisitive frown, she went to the door and opened it, thinking perhaps Nick forgot something. His expression was solemn when he stepped in.

"Forgot something?" she asked with a smile.

"Yes."

He kicked the door shut at the same moment his arms reached out and pulled her to him. In an instant his mouth rapaciously covered hers. When her body relaxed against his, he held her tighter, while his kiss followed an inexorable path of deepening passion, a passion that shook Dani to the core and swept away any physical inhibitions she might have had. In moments she yielded to the dynamic force of his lips on hers and joined him in a delectable exploratory kiss. His mouth moved over hers, seeking new angles to savor the kiss while his hands ran up and down her back with an urgent pressure, causing her spine to set up shock waves throughout her system. When she felt herself slipping into a point of no return, she gently and breathlessly broke away from the kiss, but not the delightful contact with his body.

His dark eyes were glazed with emotion as he gazed deeply into hers. "I've been wanting to do that ever since I looked up from my desk and saw you standing there that first day in my office." His hand raised to cradle her head against his, his lips brushing her earlobes with tiny kisses. "You're not angry, are you?"

"No," she murmured feeling a bit light headed from the power of his kiss and physical presence. "But I think you'd better go."

"Must I?" One arm was still firm about her back while his hand on her head moved slightly, giving his lips greater access to her long, white throat.

Dani took a deep breath and pushed herself away. "I can't be rushed, Nick."

He released her, saying, "I'm sorry. But when I want something I tend to come on like a bulldozer run amuck." He tenderly placed his open hand on her cheek and smiled. "On the other hand, I can be a very patient man. Good night, Dani."

Dani returned his smile. "Good night, Nick."

"Sunday?"

"Sunday."

The next morning a messenger brought one dozen long-stemmed yellow roses. The card had no message, only "Nick" scrawled across it.

7

Three weeks had passed since Dani received Scott's money and cryptic note. She had had no other word or sign from him. It was as though he had fallen off the face of the earth. But the memory of him was insidiously being vanquished by the constant attention showered on her by Nick Hunt. A common ground of mutual preferences was drawing them closer together, and the physical attraction Dani felt for him was growing stronger.

Page after page of her calendar had little notes: "Nick, art show @ 4 P.M."; "Nick, dinner @ 6 P.M., then theater." She never failed to enjoy herself in his company, and his ardor when they were alone was quite persuasive and delightful. He was a master at knowing what pleased a woman. Nick was everything any woman could want, and Dani was highly aware of envious glances tossed her way by other women wherever they went. Then why did the image of Scott Rowland dart into her mind at the most unexpected moments? Her heart seemed to pump all the blood from her limbs whenever she thought about him. Her mind clouded and whirled if she thought she spied him when she was in the city. A tall man in a crowd with a battered cowboy hat always drew her total attention, her pulse racing until she learned it was not Scott but some stranger. She tried to rationalize the phenomenon away by telling herself it was because she had met both men on the same day. Yet she never really convinced herself of it.

"Mrs. Rowland would like to speak to you, Dani," said Sandy, covering the telephone's mouthpiece with her hand. "Shall I tell her you're busy?"

"No . . . no." Dani left her drawing board and walked to the desk and took the phone from Sandy. "Hello, Agnes. How are you?"

"Fine, Dani. And you?" asked Agnes.

"Busy, but well. What can I do for you?"

"I was wondering if you had any idea when they'll be putting in the new kitchen."

"By all accounts, the first week in September."

"Oh, good."

"In fact, I've been meaning to get out there with the drawing of your kitchen. Would tomorrow morning be convenient?" asked Dani.

"Oh, how wonderful! I'm anxious to see it. And do plan to stay for lunch."

"Thank you for the offer, but I don't think I can."

"Of course you can. We had such a nice visit last time. Tom and I are looking forward to another one. I won't take no for an answer," declared Agnes.

"Well . . . we'll see."

"Tomorrow morning, then."

"Yes. I'll see you then, Agnes."

"Bye-bye for now."

"Bye." Dani replaced the receiver in the cradle, knowing she probably would stay to lunch with the Rowlands. She couldn't let her frustration over Scott's silence affect her attitude toward his parents. They were clients, and she must be civil. Besides, she genuinely liked them.

"You finished the drawing for the Rowland kitchen some time ago, Dani. How come it's taken you so long to deliver it?" asked Sandy. Dani shrugged. "Been so busy it slipped my mind, I guess."

"Funny . . . that Scottie hasn't been around to see how things were progressing. After all, he has a tidy bundle invested in it. I know I'd want to make sure you got the money all right and was doing something about it," said Sandy sternly.

"I signed for the envelope, so he must know I received the money," said Dani, wishing Sandy would drop the subject. She didn't want to talk about Scott Rowland.

"Still . . . if I were him I would check up on it occasionally," Sandy persisted.

"Would you please call Jan's office and see if she's in?"

"And if she isn't?"

"Leave a message for her to call back," said Dani.

She was glad she wasn't seeing Nick tonight, but on the other hand, she didn't want to be alone. She and Janice could have dinner and browse through the shops until they closed. Janice had a way of taking her mind off pressing problems, and right now, Scott was a pressing problem—if only in her mind. The thought that he might be at the Rowland's spread tomorrow was already disconcerting her. Nervous bubbles were forming in her stomach. What if Scott *was* there tomorrow? How should she act? How *would* she act?

"Order the chicken divan," urged Janice as they sat in the restaurant. "The way they make it here is divine. I'm so glad you called and suggested this outing. I was feeling a bit down."

"That's unusual for you, isn't it Jan?" asked Dani closing her menu and putting it aside.

"That coporate executive I told you about, you know, the one from Data Control Systems. Anyway what a goon he turned out to be. 'I was made for marriage, home, and family,'" Janice mocked, one splayed hand on her chest. "And his idea of a family was at least eight children with mother there all the time to wipe their noses. He didn't approve of women working after they became a marriage partner. Can you imagine that? He doesn't want a wife. He wants a brood mare. Can you picture me with eight children, too buried in diapers to get to the hairdresser?"

"It's a possibility," said Dani, an impish grin on her lips.

"Danielle Wexford! How dare you even suggest such a gross obscenity." Jan sighed. "He was such a nice guy until he got on the marriage kick and began spouting all his Victorian notions that a woman's place is in the home—scrubbing, cleaning, cooking, and all that jazz. A throwback to the caveman days, that guy. One night I actually dreamed he was in an animal pelt and chased me with a big club in his hand. That did it! I told him in no uncertain terms the relationship was ended."

"Maybe you'd like domesticity," suggested Dani, then, along with Janice, gave her order of chicken divan to the waiter.

"Are you kidding? I don't see you rushing out to tie the noose."

"I thought it was knot."

"For you, maybe. For me it's a noose. Speaking of marriage, how are you and Nick coming along?"

"Famously."

"I hear it's more like inseparable. Any chance of an impending announcement? I'm dying for an excuse to throw a great big party," said Janice.

"Don't hold your breath. I'm still feeling my way through a labyrinth of emotions."

"Really, Dani, you can tell me. Is it serious between you and Nick?"

"I really don't know. Tell you what, Jan, when I find out, you'll be the first to know."

"Promise?"

"I promise."

"I'd hate to hear it from someone at the garden club."

"You won't. By the way, I never did ask you why you quit. Any special reason? I always thought it was a good source of clients and information for you," said Dani.

"I milked that dry. I'm thinking of joining an art appreciation group or a historical society. I haven't decided yet. Doesn't that look gorgeous," exclaimed Janice as the waiter placed their entrées on the table. "Was there anything in particular you wanted to shop for?" asked Janice, after they had savored several morsels of the chicken.

"No. Just browse and see what the latest is. Styles have a way of changing before I even get around to buying the last one. From what I've seen in the paper, some of the new fall lines are quite radical," said Dani.

"That's what I need. Something radical, A new suit or dress. Oh, how I wish all the malls were within walking distance. My sweet temples of conspicuous consumption. Malls . . . glorious shrines erected to enhance the art of spending money. I worship all of them," proclaimed Janice quite expansively.

The next morning, Dani dressed with care as the sun began to climb the Texas sky. She had no way near matched the purchases made by Janice, but she had weakened at the sight of a Halston-designed day dress of baby-blue linen. She reasoned the new, flattering dress would bolster her suddenly shaken confidence when she went to the Rowland house.

She spread out a map on the kitchen table, studying the route to the Rowland's. When she was sure she had it down pat, she grabbed the neatly wrapped painting and called a good-bye to Sandy.

As she approached the white, sprawling Rowland house, she had to consciously regulate her breathing. Then, as she moved up the driveway, her heart flew into high gear and remained there when she saw the old yellow pickup truck. Maybe he parked it there while he went somewhere else, she told herself. What was it the Earl of Shaftesbury said? "True courage is cool and calm." That's what I'll be—cool and calm.

She parked her car and walked up onto the porch, gripping the package so tightly her knuckles were white. Before she could ring the bell, the door began to open and her heart pounded with increasing fury.

"Dani, how good to see you again. Come in," urged Agnes Rowland. She took Dani by the arm and led her into the cool living room. "Tom and I have been looking forward to your visit."

"I hope you'll be pleased with the look of your kitchen," said Dani, opening the package and removing the glass-framed watercolor and handing it to Agnes.

"Oh! How beautiful! You really mean my new kitchen will look like this?" exclaimed Agnes.

"I certainly hope so," said Dani with a nervous smile. She had glanced around the house, which appeared to be empty save for her and Agnes. She came back to the business at hand quickly. "I must tell you, Agnes, that your kitchen will be, for all intents and purposes, utterly useless while the transition is being made. All cabinets must be emptied before the workmen can start. Will it be a problem for you?"

"No problem at all, my dear. Tom and I plan to take a little vacation while the work is being done. Wait until Tom sees this picture. He won't believe how beautiful the kitchen will be. Why, I can hardly believe it myself," said Agnes, gazing with wonder and excitement at the framed watercolor.

"Who would take care of the horses?" Dani wondered if Scott would be staying at the ranch to do the chores. As she always stopped in to check on the progress of a job, she might run into him on occasion. Oh, what for? she scolded herself. Why even think of the drifting cowboy when she had a good stable relationship with Nick? A relationship that was comfortable and intellectually satisfying.

"Tom has a few hired men now. They'll take care of everything on the ranch. Come into the kitchen with me, Dani. I want to hold up your conception of the new kitchen against the old," said Agnes, rising.

Dani went with her into the kitchen and listened to Agnes extol the virtues and looks of the new kitchen. They sat down to a glass of iced tea and discussed the changing face of Dallas. Agnes reminisced about the Dallas of the 1930s, when it was an incipient city boldly thrusting itself from the prairie in the middle of nowhere. How Dallas plucked the Texas Centennial Exposition from San Antonio in 1936. How the immigrants to Dallas were skilled and cultured English, Swiss, German, and French.

Finally Agnes could no longer contain herself. She had to show her husband the picture of their new kitchen. Excusing herself and telling Dani to make herself at home, she rushed out the back door. Dani took the empty glasses to the sink and looked out the window at the darting figure of Agnes disappearing into the barn.

Dani trembled when his arms slipped about her waist, drawing her back against his solid physique. She didn't have to turn around. She knew by the woodsy scent it was Scott. When his lips brushed against her neck, she could feel every drop of her blood drain to her toes and air began to rush in and out of her lungs.

"Miss me, sugar?" he whispered, his lips now lodging tiny kisses on her ear lobe.

Dani braced her hands on the sink and closed her eyes, then swallowed hard in an attempt to get her voice under control.

"I sure missed you," he continued. "All I could think about was your hair, your big blue eyes, the way you smiled—everything. Tell me you missed me just a little."

"I think you'd better let go of me. Your mother will be back soon." Why couldn't she bring herself to tell him she did miss him—terribly.

He turned her around, still keeping her in his arms. "You sound angry, Dani. Or is it indifference I hear in your voice?" he asked, his blue-gray eyes narrowing as they searched hers.

"I'm neither. Now please let me go."

Scott dropped his arms to his side and, with eyes still squinting, looked down at her. "Out of sight, out of mind. Is that how it is with you, Dani? I haven't forgotten one second of the time I spent with you."

"What do you want me to say? That I wrapped a cocoon around myself and hid in a dark closet until I heard from you?" she asked, a tortured expression on her face.

A smile played about his lips. "You are angry with me. Good. That means you did miss me."

"Think whatever you want." She tried to step around him into freer space. Being so close to him was tormenting her. But he placed his hands on the sink, effectively trapping her between his sinewy arms.

"Dani, I had a job to do. I barely had time to eat and sleep, otherwise you know I would have gotten word to you."

"Look . . . you don't owe me any explanations. Just because we had a couple of dates doesn't mean we are eternally bound to one another. If you'll move aside. I'll go say good-bye to your mother."

"I'll move aside but you're not going anywhere. Momma expects you to stay to lunch and has been looking forward to your visit ever since you called. Even if you don't care about me, I don't think you'd want to disappoint her," said Scott, letting go of the sink and stepping back.

"Oh, Scott, please don't put it like that," said Dani, moved by the plaintiveness in his voice.

His face softened. "You sure do look mighty pretty today. And if you don't stop looking at me like that, I'm going to kiss those rosy lips until you beg me to stop." He started toward her.

"I hope I'm not interrupting anything," said Agnes, with a broad smile, as her shining eyes danced from Scott to Dani.

"I was telling Dani how pretty she looked today, Momma," said Scott. "Did Daddy come in with you?"

"He's saddling up the palomino for Dani," said Agnes, causing Dani to look at Scott with a querulous frown.

"Didn't I tell you, sugar? I'm going to start your riding lessons today," said Scott, grinning at her.

"Oh no. I can't," Dani blurted out.

"Why not?" asked Scott.

"I'm . . . I'm not ready. I . . . I'm not dressed for it," stammered Dani.

"Aren't some of Katie's riding gear still in the closet upstairs, Momma?" asked Scott.

"Your sister left all her riding clothes here. She said she'd get new ones in California if she needed them. I don't know where your sister picked up such spendthrift habits," declared Agnes, with a rueful shake of her head. "Come along, Dani. We'll see what we can find to fit you. It shouldn't be too difficult. Katie is about your size. And Scottie . . . take a look at my new kitchen. I put the picture on the table there."

Dani dutifully followed Agnes up the stairs with trepidation in her heart, but she was determined not to display any cowardice. It was time she got over her inordinate fear of horses. After all, she was in Texas. More importantly, she would be with Scott.

It was a spacious and definitely feminine bedroom, light and airy in the palest pastel blue to contrast with the dark, rich color of the mahogany furniture.

"Look at this," said Agnes pushing back the sliding door of a large closet to reveal its contents. Black and tan riding breeches, a score of blue jeans, twenty or so blouses, plain and cowboy shirts, twelve pairs of boots in assorted leathers and hat boxes stacked neatly on the top shelf. "What a waste! Help yourself, Dani. Katie might be an inch taller than you, but you both have the same build. Come down when you're ready."

As Agnes closed the door behind her, Dani looked over the clothes and noted everything in the closet was the best money could buy. After trying on several of the pants, she decided on a dark brown form-fitting pair along with a tailored beige cotton shirt. Though all the boots were a half a size too big, a light brown pair was the most comfortable. In one of the boxes she found a light brown cowgirl hat that fit perfectly. She looked at herself in the long mirror on the front of the door to the private bathroom and smiled, thinking all she needed was a guitar and she could pass for a country-western singer.

"Well now, ain't that little lady something to see," exclaimed Tom Rowland, as Dani came into the living room.

"They fit you well, Dani, and are so becoming," added Agnes.

Dani's pride swelled under the compliments, and her glance slipped to Scott, waiting for his comment on her appearance. He said nothing, but she was pleased to see the admiration in his eyes; then, for a split second, she thought she saw something stronger than admiration, and it seared her heart.

"Come on, sugar, let's get you on a horse," said Scott, scooping his Stetson from the arm of the couch and putting his arm around her waist.

"Don't you let that little lady ride too hard," warned Tom.

"No, Daddy. Just around the ring until she gets use to it," replied Scott.

"Don't you worry none, Dani. That palomino is as gentle as the fur on a rabbit's belly," said Tom.

"I hope so." Dani was surprised when Tom used her Christian name. She was beginning to wonder if he knew it.

Dani waited outside the barn while Scott led the golden animal into the outside, fenced ring. When he began to lead the horse toward her, she held her ground, cloaking herself in all the courage she could muster.

"Hold out your hand," said Scott, reaching into his shirt pocket and withdrawing a lump of sugar. He placed it in her hand with the admonition, "Hold your hand absolutely flat and bring it to the mare's mouth."

Dani hesitated. "Will she bite me?"

"Trust me."

She slowly raised her hand to the horse's mouth and gripped her lower lip between her teeth, waiting for her hand to be taken off. Instead a warm, moist sensation tickled her palm.

"Now stroke her cheek and talk to her. Let her get to know you and your voice," instructed Scott.

"I feel foolish," she claimed.

"Try it, sugar. You won't after a few minutes."

Dani obeyed. She stroked the animal's cheek and kept repeating, "Nice girl . . . nice girl."

"Now for the moment of truth, Dani. On you go," said Scott. He helped her onto the quiet mare, handed her the reins, and gave a verbal explanation of how to handle the horse.

"It's so high up here," complained Dani. "She won't move on me, will she?"

"She most certainly will, and I'm going to be the one to make her," said Scott. He took hold of the strap around the horse's nose and slowly led her around in a circle.

After an initial spurt of terror, Dani began to regain her self-confidence and found she was enjoying the ride, even though she felt a little silly being led around in circles.

When fifteen minutes had gone by, she asked, "Couldn't we do something else for a while? This is getting monotonous."

"Sure, sugar. We can practice getting on and off until you can do it by yourself."

Practice she did, and slowly became quite good at it. She lost all fear of the animal as Scott had her ride the mare around the circle without his assistance.

"I think it's time to give it a rest and have some lunch," said Scott, his arms outstretched to receive her.

"I'll get down by myself," she said with mock haughtiness. Swelled with pride at having pretty well conquered her fear, when Scott put his arm around her waist, she boldly and unthinkingly wrapped her arm around his.

After a lunch of barbequed spareribs, hunks of savory home fries, black-eyed peas, and drop biscuits followed by apple pie, Dani announced she was going upstairs to change her clothes when Scott informed her that the riding lessons weren't over. She was too exuberant to object. She felt such utter happiness in his company. She wouldn't have objected to anything he suggested.

Back outside, Scott waited until she was safely on the golden palomino, then gracefully swung into the saddle of his powerful, well-muscled quarter horse. Side by side, they walked the horses down the lane for some distance. Dani felt the power of the creature beneath her and had the urge to do more than walk the animal. She wanted to feel the wind in her hair as she raced the horse, to feel the excitement of riding a horse hard like she had seen in so many movies.

"How do I make her go faster?" she asked Scott.

"You don't want to do that, sugar. Take it easy the first time you're out or you'll be sunning your moccasins," warned Scott.

"What does that mean?"

"It means you're liable to be thrown. The original cowmen of Texas and Mexico wore moccasins, and if they were thrown, their moccasined feet were in the air catching the rays of the sun," he explained. "I'm not about to have you break that pretty little neck of yours."

"Couldn't we go a tiny bit faster?"

He reached up and tipped the brim of his hat back, then smiled crookedly at her. "You're a strong-headed little lady." He gave an audible sigh. "Squeeze your knees ever so slightly against the mare's flanks and hold tight to the reins. Remember . . . squeeze lightly."

Dani tried it, and the horse picked up momentum until she was at a trot. After several minutes, Dani realized something was very wrong. She was coming down in the saddle when the horse was coming up. It was making her behind quite sore.

"Scott, how do I get her to go back to a walk?" she asked, the distress plain on her face.

"Pull in the reins slightly." His grin widened as he loped along beside her. "Follow me. I think you're due for a rest." He veered his horse off the lane through meadows, toward a cluster of trees that hugged the river.

Reaching the desired spot, Scott's long leg swiftly arched over the horse's back, and he was on the ground standing by the palomino, waiting for Dani to dismount. When she did, her knees buckled, and but for Scott's strong arm catching her waist, she would have slipped to the ground.

"Do you feel dizzy?" asked Scott, his sharp-planed face tight with concern.

"No. I'm not used to this type of boot, I guess," she replied, as he took the reins of the palomino, then led both horses to a tree and tethered them.

"Let's go sit under that tree over yonder," he suggested.

"Sit? I don't think I'll ever be able to sit again," she moaned, rubbing her sore bottom.

"Sitting on the ground is a different type of sitting," he said, taking her hand and leading her to the shady tree.

Gingerly, Dani lowered herself to the ground where the verdant grass sparkled golden, then darkened according to the whimsy of the tree whose leafy branches fluttered in subservience to her sister, the wind. Scott sat down next to her. Then, placing his hat on the grass, he stretched out, his hands behind his head.

"It's good to do nothing but lay back and smell the earth," said Scott. "The pace in Dallas gets a little too frenetic for my tastes at times. I'm just a plain ol' country boy, I guess. What about you, Dani? Has the Dallas whirlwind completely sucked you in?"

"I enjoy all the cultural aspects the city offers. I enjoy my work, and there's a pulse to Dallas that's hypnotic."

"Wouldn't you rather sit like this and look at the sky, the trees, the river?"

"Right now, I think it's absolutely wonderful. But I think I'd grow bored after a while. By the way, what's happened to the river?" she asked.

"Usual summer drought. Puts the poor river to a shameful muddy stream. With rain and the change of seasons, she'll be flowing again in all her glory. You should see the draws in West Texas. Dried out riverbeds of dust."

"Well, I wish that river was up a little more. I'd go and sit in it," said Dani, removing her hat and shaking her hair loose, the sun burnishing it with fiery reds and golds.

"In time you'll learn to move as one with the horse, sugar," he said consolingly, then with concern asked, "Do you really prefer Dallas to here?"

"I didn't say I preferred Dallas, Scott. Here I feel peaceful and quietly happy, yet in Dallas I feel alive," said Dani, staring at the muddy stream. She heard a sigh emanate from him, then felt the tips of his fingers through the thin cotton blouse slide up and down her spine. The sensation was beyond wonderful; it was excruciatingly tantalizing and made the intake of air in her lungs erratic. Suddenly he sat up, cupped her chin and tilted her face up toward his.

"Dani . . . a city doesn't make one feel alive, only another human being can do that," he whispered.

His lips kissed the corners of her mouth lightly, then again and again, until they had worked their way to cover her entire mouth. Her hands slipped to his neck, and one hand strayed into his thick, sandy hair as she welcomed his deepening and ardent kiss. With one arm locked about her waist and the other over her shoulders, Scott returned to his original prone position pulling her with him. The kiss increased in mercurial frenzy as Scott rolled her over onto her back, their lips never parting, their embrace loosening. Dani's fingers dug into the hard muscles of his back and she remembered the lean, sinewy figure he presented when they were on the beach at Galveston. New emotions and sensations swept through her like a brush fire out of control. But she had no time to anaylze them, for his long, lean fingers were working magic on her flesh while his tender, probing kiss was obliterating her reason. The placid stream below them turned into a roaring river in her brain, and the hot Texas sun seemed cool compared to the fire burning within her. The breeze ceased, no bird was heard. It was as though all nature conspired to be quiet and not intrude on the idyllic interlude by the river.

Dani lay curled against him, her head resting in the crook of his arm, her hand on his chest feeling the beat of his heart. A breeze blew up, pushing the summer grasses before it.

Scott tightened his hold on her and kissed the top of her head, his broad chest heaving. "Grandaddy is going to adore you, Dani. I can hardly wait to bring you out there."

"I'm beginning to get curious myself about this fabled grandfather of yours."

"Soon, sugar. After Momma's kitchen is in. I should have caught up on everything around here by then. Besides, West Texas at the height of summer is liable to parch that pretty skin of yours."

Dani pushed herself to a sitting position and stretched. She picked up the cowgirl hat and put it on her head. "Shouldn't we be getting back? Your mother and father will think we've galloped off to no-man's land."

"Momma and Daddy know very well I wanted to be alone with you."

"Then this eagerness to teach me how to ride was all a ruse?"

"No, ma'am. I really want you to learn."

"Why?" asked Dani.

"I have my reasons, sugar. And it won't be too long before you know why."

"Why can't you tell me now?"

"The time isn't right."

"Scott Rowland, you're a tease."

"Teasing you is the farthest thing from my mind, Dani." He jumped to his feet, picked up his hat, and set it low on his brow, then offered his hand. He pulled her up quickly and hard, his arms wrapping around her when she stood, his mouth vanquishing hers with a sweet, heartfelt intensity. When the kiss ended, they smiled at each other, and their eyes communed an awareness of rising emotions.

"I could sure use a tall glass of iced tea about now," said Scott, as they walked back to the horses, their arms around each other. "Want to race back to the house?"

Dani looked up at him obliquely. "Only on foot. I'm not even sure I can ride back to the house."

"Sure you can, sugar. We'll keep the horses at a slow walk."

Dani walked into her office with the strained gait of a penguin. She longed to soak in a hot tub for the rest of her life. She fervently hoped her next encounter with the palomino didn't produce such physical discomfort.

"Where have you been all day? Nick's been frantically trying to reach you," said Sandy, packing up her things to leave for the day.

"Did he say where I could reach him?" asked Dani.

"At the office. He'll be there until eight this evening. What the devil happened to you? You look like you're walking on eggs and trying not to break them."

"I tried my hand at horseback riding," explained Dani with a grimace.

"In that dress?"

"I changed into suitable clothes at the Rowlands."

"Well you'd better call Nick as soon as you can. It sounded important. I'll see you tomorrow," said Sandy, heading for the door.

"Don't worry, I'll call him. Have a good evening." Dani went to the desk and skimmed through the memo pad for the rest of the day's messages. She didn't want to call Nick, though she couldn't explain why. She felt like someone tied between two opposing worlds, and they were pulling her apart. Her emotions were telling her she was falling in love—deeply in love—yet which world did she really want?

8

"You're a busy lady, Dani," said Nick. "I've been trying to reach you all day."

"I was just about to call you," said Dani, her body relaxed from a good soak in the tub. "What's so urgent?"

"Two things. One—the most important—is the fact I got the contract for that development in Houston, and I want you to go down to Houston with me next week. I'd like you to take a look at some similar projects in the area. I'm sure your agile mind can design kitchens far superior than any existing ones there. Second—Saturday night I'm giving a party for all the subcontractors who worked on the condo here in Dallas. Naturally, I want you there, Dani. Any problem?"

"I don't believe so. What day next week are you going to Houston, so I can plan my schedule?"

"Next Wednesday. I'll pick you up at seven in the morning. By the way the party is at eight Saturday night. How have you been, Dani? It seems like ages since I've seen you," said Nick.

"I'm fine, Nick." She wasn't fine. Hearing Nick's deep voice smothered her with self-doubt. As the pendulum that governed her emotions was swinging full tilt toward Scott, Nick had a way of retarding the sway.

"I'm looking forward to seeing you Saturday night. It will give me the opportunity of showing you my condo, as the party is being held there—at the Paragon Towers. You know it, don't you?"

"Oh, yes. Who doesn't know of Paragon Towers? One of the most elaborate condominium buildings in North Dallas. I hope you don't expect me to spend more than a day in Houston. I have a lot of business to tend to here," said Dani.

"One day only. We'll leave here in the morning and fly back the same night. I'm looking forward to having you all to myself for the whole day. There's much for us to talk about. I'll firm up the plane for Houston. I've really got to go now. I'll see you Saturday, Dani."

"Yes, Nick. See you Saturday." She replaced the receiver and went downstairs to see what she could scrounge from the refrigerator.

Like a lofty monument of silver, Paragon Towers stretched skyward, reaching for the clouds, typifying the very essence of Dallas. A glorious display of man's vanity and homage to flagrant expenditure.

Dani parked her well-kept Buick, then walked the short distance to the entrance of the glistening glass structure. Inside the initial small foyer, she was stopped by an armed guard, who informed her he would have to call Mr. Hunt and ascertain her identity before he could admit her. After hanging up the telephone, he smiled and pressed a button that released the lock to the grand foyer, while giving her directions to the room where the Hunt party was being held.

The main foyer had Italian Provencale wainscoting whose scrolls were tipped with gold, while mirrors covered the wall from the wainscoting to the ceiling. In the middle of the foyer was a red velvet seat that curled in a circle like an inverted lily, while a chandelier of crystal and gold sparkled above it. Her multiple reflections in the mirrored walls had a confusing effect on Dani as she searched for the corridor the guard had told her to take. The heels of her shoes sunk noiselessly into the deep pile of the crimson carpeting as she found the corridor, then started down it. She smiled at the sight of an immaculately dressed Nicholas coming to greet her.

"Dani." he said, taking her hands in his. "You look lovely."

"Thank you. And as usual you are the epitome of sartorial elegance," said Dani.

"I'd feel underdressed without my vest and tie. Come," he urged, opening a door to a small cubicle that echoed the decor of the grand foyer, mirrors, and highly decorative wainscoting. Nick pressed a button and the elaborate elevator began to ascend.

"The guard said the party was on the main floor, the Louis XV room," said Dani, puzzled by Nick's actions.

"I want you to see my place before you join the party," he explained.

"Won't your guests miss you?"

"They're well provided for. My absence won't even be noticed. Besides, I want you to myself for a little while."

The elevator stopped on the eighth floor, and Nick led her down a long corridor, stopping before a nondescript door and opening it. Dani preceded him and marveled at the huge living room where one wall consisted entirely of glass, giving one a panoramic view of Dallas. The clusters of buildings downtown shimmered gold in the setting sun, punctuated by the globular network of lights atop Reunion Tower. The room itself was ultramodern with its plush white sofas and glass-topped tables whose chrome, tubular legs softly curled in support of the thick glass. An ornate stereo system was flanked by bookcases along one wall. Though the kitchen contained standard cabinetry, the appliances were the best money could buy. The bedroom held a king-sized bed, but still had ample room to accommodate the large dresser, nightstands, television set, and two chaise lounges.

"Well, what do you think?" asked Nick, as he led her back to the spacious living room.

"Impressive, especially the view. Did you decorate the place yourself?"

Nick shook his head. "Had a decorator do it all. I don't have the time for such nonsense. Let's go back downstairs. There is more I want to show you."

"I'm surprised you only have one bedroom," commented Dani, as they stepped into the mirrored elevator.

"Why? There's only me."

"Well, what if your family from New Jersey comes to visit?"

"I pay for the best hotel accommodations there are. I like my privacy."

"Your kitchen is a cook's dream. Do you cook much?" asked Dani.

"Not if I can help it. I eat out most of the time or have something sent into the office. Large affairs, I use the visitor's room on the first floor and have everything catered."

On the main floor he led her down a labyrinth of corridors to a brightly lighted room that was encased in mirrors, including the ceiling, which reflected a wealth of expensive exercise equipment. There was enough equipment to oblige almost everyone in the condos.

"Do you use any of this?" asked Dani, her eyes wide, as she swooped her hand around the room.

"Every morning for a half hour, then I go down here," he said, cupping her elbow and steering her down another corridor to an indoor pool where there was also a hot whirlpool tub, an ice tub and numerous saunas lining the wall. "There's a much larger pool outside."

"I didn't realize you were that athletic, Nick. You must be quite fit," remarked Dani.

"As fit as possible. I follow a very strict regimen when it comes to exercise. Would you like to try some of the exercise equipment? It's the very finest."

Dani laughed. "Not tonight, Nick. I'm not exactly dressed for it."

"Of course. How stupid of me. We'll go to the party now," said Nick, pulling her arm through his.

In the Louis XV room, a sumptuous room whose decor reflected the early eighteenth century lavish style of the French monarch, a man was seated at an exquisite and ornamental baby grand piano playing popular tunes of the day. A buffet table, laden with festive and exotic foods, was set along one wall, crowned by a bar with a uniformed bartender in attendance. A clatter of voices, underscored by occasional laughter, rose above the pianist's musical efforts. Nick introduced Dani to the majority of people there but was dragged off by a serious-looking man before he could finished the introductions.

Dani went to the buffet table, took a plate, then slowly moved along the table, selecting tempting tidbits of interest. Bits of shrimp, lobster, and crab were lined up on plastic skewers, waiting to be dipped into various sauces. Red and black caviar huddled in their respective dishes, surrounded by an assortment of crackers. Scallops wrapped in bacon were impaled on toothpicks. Small cubes of various cheeses sat complacently on a glass dish around a silver bowl of olives. Anchovies rested like crossed swords on pizzas the size of half dollars. It was a distinguished variety of hors d'oeuvres, and Dani felt as though she should sample each one. She skipped by the bar, knowing she couldn't eat and hold a glass at the same time, for there seemed to be a sparsity of chairs and tables.

"Dani . . . I just knew you'd be here," cried a bubbly Janice Gordon, as she made her way over to Dani. "Isn't this divine? And the food! Nick certainly didn't spare the green stuff tonight."

"What are you doing here, Jan? Don't tell me you got the contract to sell his condos?" asked Dani, her fine eyebrows raised in complete surprise.

"No such luck. I know one of the subcontractors, and he asked me if I'd like to come. Did you come alone?"

"Yes. I asked Sandra, but she had other plans for the evening."

"Have you thought about investing all that loot you got from this job? I have some delicious land opportunities waiting for you," said Janice.

"I really haven't decided yet."

"Don't wait too long. Someone is bound to snap them up once word gets around. I haven't openly advertised them yet. Just letting some close friends in on it for now. Let me know in the next couple of weeks, will you?"

"I will. Have you met everyone here?"

"Just about. Have you?"

"Pretty much. Nick was taking me around when he was lured away."

"I didn't think he could be lured away from you. How is the romance going? Getting serious yet?" asked Janice before taking a sip of her cocktail.

"No."

"Oh, Dani. I've seen the way Nick looks at you. Those dark eyes of his devouring you at every opportunity. It seems to me he's very taken with you, and he doesn't make a secret of it," claimed Janice.

"He's said something?"

"Of course not. But I'm not blind and neither is anyone else. I heard the whispers when he introduced you around."

"What whispers?" asked Dani.

"That Nick has been tamed at last. That he's completely under your spell. All good stuff like that. From what you've said, Dani, I can't understand why you don't grab him. The two of you seem to have everything in common. Likes and dislikes. Hard-driving business acumen. I envy you, Dani. Men like Nick aren't a dime a dozen these days. If I were you, I'd nail him down and quick."

"I'm not so sure I want to. Besides any man you have to nail down, as you put it, isn't the type of man I want," responded Dani.

"Not want to? Have you been keeping secrets from me, Dani? Is there someone else?" Janice took a sip of her cocktail and peered hard at Dani over the rim of her glass, then with a look of utter astonishment said, "The cowboy? The one Sandy told me about? Oh no, Dani. Don't tell me you've fallen for some stray cowboy who probably lives from hand to mouth. That's not your style."

"He's a very nice man," defended Dani, a little irritated by Janice's description of Scott.

"And I suppose you have a lot in common with him."

Dani shrugged. "What difference does it make?"

"Are you in love with him?"

"This conversation is wearing thin."

"Well, if you know what's good for you, you'd better drop that cowboy. I have a feeling he's a loser. Concentrate on Nick Hunt. Speaking of which . . . why hello, Nick. We were just talking about you," said Janice as Nick joined them.

"All good, I hope," said Nick.

"Of course," said Janice. "Great party, Nick. The food is absolutely divine. Come to think of it, I'll help myself to some more."

"There are still some people I'd like you to meet, Dani," said Nick slipping his arm around her waist and steering her through the horde.

As the evening wore on, Dani found the smoke and noise clogging her head even though she was having a good time. It was a little too early to go home, especially when all she needed was a few minutes of fresh air. When Nick became engrossed in a heated discussion, she slipped out one of the outside doors to find herself within several yards of the outdoor pool.

Blue lights glowed under the crystal water of the pool, making it resemble an oversized aquamarine gem. Soft amber lights dotted the cement lounge area around the pool. As though lured by an irresistible force, Dani strolled toward the pool, clearing her lungs by taking deep breaths. She lifted her head to watch the moon rise in the clear Texas sky and wondered what the sky looked like out at the Rowland ranch without all the lights of the city vying for attention. A sudden, strange longing swept through her, a desire to be by the river near the trees on the Rowland spread. So deep was she concentrating on her imagination, that when two hands came down on her shoulders, she twitched, even though Nick's cologne had preceded him.

"Why are you out here all by yourself? Bored by the party?" he asked, placing his cheek alongside hers.

"Your party is fine. I needed some fresh air, that's all."

He slowly turned her around. "I wish there wasn't a party here tonight. I like things as they are this minute. I have half a mind to go back in there and tell everyone to go home." He gripped her shoulders and the amber lights glinted flecks of gold in his dark eyes, revealing the passion mounting within him. Unerringly, his mouth came down on hers in a kiss so urgent and persuasive, Dani surrendered to its force. His hands left her shoulders to envelop her in a tight embrace, crushing her to his thick, hard body.

Dani's mind and heart numbed as sheer sensation dominated her. There was something commanding, almost manipulative, about Nick that made her resistance practically nil. Oddly enough, she felt uninvolved emotionally. It was sheer physical attraction. His appeal and amorous ways were so formidable that even the most determined woman would be hard pressed to resist.

"We'd better go in," said Dani, breaking away from him, her hands pushing against the hard muscles of his upper arms.

"As you said, the air is much better out here." He continued to hold her firmly.

"They'll be looking for us if we don't go in."

"Let them look." His lips sought hers once again, probing with a ferocity born of ardor too long subdued.

"Nick . . . please," implored Dani, when his mouth released hers for a second, her hands still pushing against his upper arms with increasing pressure.

"Hey, Nick, you out there?" called someone from inside. "Telephone."

Nick released her, then drew her arm through his, fondly patting her hand. "Next time I'll make sure there'll be nothing and no one to disturb us."

The next morning, after pouring herself another cup of coffee, Dani spread the voluminous Sunday edition of the *Dallas Morning News* over the kitchen table. Though she tried to concentrate on the words before her, her thoughts kept returning to the previous evening. Janice was right. Nick was becoming serious, and Dani felt consumed by uncertainty. It would be an ideal match. Nick was urbane, and so was she. Their cultural tastes were the same. They both thrived in and on the world of business. They lived the high and fast life and loved every minute of it. Nick was the most suitable man she had ever met, yet there was an alien tug on her heart. A tug named Scott Rowland. A man whose world was in direct contradiction to everything she knew and was comfortable with. She would have to stop thinking about him and get on with her life. Once his mother's kitchen was completed, she was sure he would drift out of her life as quickly as he drifted in. Dani had almost pushed Scott from her mind and was focusing her attention on the newspaper, when the doorbell unexpectedly chimed.

Scott Rowland stood in the doorway, his crooked smile beguiling, his broad shoulders wisping down to narrow hips, his cowboy hat tipped back on his head. He bent down and kissed her cheek.

"Good morning, sugar," his deep voice greeted.

"What are you doing here?" she asked, stepping aside to admit him. Deep down she really didn't care why he came. She was truly happy to see him, whatever the reason.

"Come to take you out to the ranch for another riding lesson," he explained.

"I have to go to a flower show this afternoon."

"Couldn't you cancel it?"

"I suppose I could make a phone call." Going to the flower show paled beside spending the day with Scott, even if she had to spend it on the back of a horse.

"Do it," he said following her into the kitchen.

"Help yourself to some coffee."

Dani went into her office to call one of the women with whom she was going to the flower show. Six of them were going in a group, and

Dani knew she wouldn't be destroying anyone's plans by not going. Why was she so anxious to submit to the torture of trying to ride a horse just to be with a particular man? Why were she and Scott such worlds apart in their personal lives? If only he and Nick could switch roles, life would be much simpler. After making the call, she returned to the kitchen to see Scott with a mug of coffee in one hand, the business section of the newspaper in his other hand.

Those bluish gray eyes looked up at her with a smile in them. "Settled?"

"All settled. But I still haven't gotten around to buying a hat and boots," said Dani.

"You can use my sister's again."

"I'll make a point of getting my own next week. I'll go change."

"Come here, sugar." He grabbed her wrist as she passed and pulled her into his lap, nestling his face against her neck. "You always smell so good. Like sweet honeysuckle on a dewy morning." With one arm around her, his hand curled gently about her neck, bringing her head to his. He kissed her long and slow, with controlled passion. His lips skipped lightly over her cheek to nibble at her earlobe, before returning to her mouth with a wide, all-consuming kiss. "You'd better go change before I forget myself," he warned in a deep, hoarse voice.

She gave him a quick kiss on the forehead and dashed upstairs to get into a pair of jeans and a blouse. She was so elated her heart was darting about like a mouse in a maze.

"I hope your mother doesn't go to any trouble about lunch," said Dani, as he helped her into the yellow pickup.

"Her and Daddy went on a vacation. They won't be back for three weeks. Momma said the men were coming to start her kitchen tomorrow, so all the cupboards out there are bare. I picked up a couple of porterhouse steaks along with the fixings. We'll have ourselves a little cookout on the patio." He started the engine, shifted into gear, and guided the vehicle casually along its course.

"Sounds good."

"What sounds good? The fact we'll be all to ourselves? Or the food?" Scott teased.

"The food." Dani smiled.

"Where were you last night? I stopped by with the intention of taking you dancing, but no one was home."

"I went to a party given by Nicholas Hunt for all the subcontractors who worked on the condominiums."

"So Hunt gave a party."

"Yes. Do you know him?" asked Dani, a little surprised.

"In a way. I hear he's quite the ladies' man. Has he captivated you, Dani?"

She glanced at his sharp profile, his eyes squinting, the corners of his mouth in downward crescents. "Nick's not an easy man for any woman to ignore."

"I hear he's showing a particular interest in you."

"Where would you hear something like that?" Dani's eyebrows gathered close in a puzzled frown. How could two men who lived such utterly different lives know anything of each other?

"In the building trade, word gets around about who is doing what. An electrician I know happened to mention that Hunt had a new ladyfriend who was a kitchen designer. One and one usually makes two."

"He's been very attentive."

"And you, Dani? How do you feel about him?"

"We have a lot of the same interests." What could she say when she really wasn't sure how she did feel? What was love anyway?

"That doesn't answer my question, sugar." He stared straight ahead, unsmiling.

"Well . . . it will have to do, Scott. To be honest, at this moment I have no idea what my true feelings are. If I did, I wouldn't hesitate to tell you," declared Dani.

"I believe you would. I suppose it's pretty obvious I'm in love with you," stated Scott.

"Nothing is obvious until it is brought out in the open." Her heart was pounding so hard she was amazed she could speak. Scott loved her! And she knew he was the kind of man who never did anything halfway.

"Would you care to make your feelings toward me obvious?"

"I wish I could. I know I enjoy being with you. But I haven't seen that much of you to really know how I feel. I've seen a lot more of Nick, and I know what he's like. But you . . . Oh, let's not talk about it anymore. We have today. Let's not go beyond it," said Dani, weary of trying to explain her emotions when she wasn't all that sure herself.

Scott looked over at her and smiled. "Sure, sugar. It's refreshing to find someone who is totally honest, with me and herself. Well, now that

I know I'm in a battle, I'll load my six-shooters and pepper you with my charm. I can be mighty persuasive when I put my mind to it. I can be every bit as much the ladies' man as your Nicholas Hunt."

Dani gave him a slant-eyed look and an impish smile. "I'm sure you can. But he is not my Nicholas Hunt, and I don't want to talk about him anymore today."

"Neither do I." He snapped on the radio, and they listened to country-western music for the rest of the way to the ranch.

Dani opened the door to the Rowland home with the key Scott gave her, then held it open as he carried the large cooler into the house. Though the thermostat of the air conditioner had been turned down, it was still much cooler in the house than it was outside.

"You go get what you need from my sister's room while I take this downstairs," said Scott.

"Downstairs?"

"Daddy had the old refrigerator moved downstairs to the game room along with the old stove. Says it'll save him from running upstairs when he wants something to eat. I'll meet you in the kitchen and you can take a look."

Dani nodded and headed upstairs. The door to Katie's room was open, and not wishing to pry, Dani grabbed the same boots and hat she used last time, then hurried back downstairs to the kitchen. It was strange to see the Rowland kitchen so bare, for she remembered it as a place of warmth and life. She sat in the chair, removed her shoes, and shoved her feet into the boots.

"Find what you needed?" asked Scott, coming into the kitchen.

"Yes. I was thinking how eerie the kitchen seems without the usual items in it."

"Think how beautiful it will be when it's completed. Momma's really looking forward to it."

"I do hope she'll like it."

"She'll love it. Are you ready to start? We have to get the horses saddled, and I'd like to get in a couple of hours before fixing lunch."

"Scott . . . why are you so set on my learning to ride? It isn't necessary, you know. I do enjoy being with you. You don't have to unearth ways to entertain me."

"Sugar, I'm not trying to entertain you. I want you to learn to ride and learn about horses. I want you to come to know my world, then you'll know more about me and just how lovable I really am."

"Are you bragging?"

"Yes, if that's what it takes. I'm going to use every weapon I can to win you. Come on. Let's get those horses." He took her hand and playfully pulled her from the chair.

The barn smelled of horses and hay. Dani found it rather pleasing to her nostrils, and was somewhat flattered when the palomino gave her a snorting nod of recognition. Dani spoke to the stalled mare softly and stroked her cheek, amazed to find out how truly beautiful the golden animal was, the very pale gold of its mane and tail giving her an aura of a fairy tale creature.

"Here . . . let me see you put these on," said Scott, handing her the bit and reins.

"Oh, I couldn't! I don't know how. Besides I'll get bit," claimed Dani, backing away.

"Take them. I'll tell you what to do and I promise you won't get bit," encouraged Scott.

Haltingly, Dani took them. Then, under Scott's explicit instructions, she got the bridle on and, to her astonishment, also put the saddle on the animal.

"How's that?" asked Dani with obvious pride.

"Sugar, you're a born horsewoman."

She held the reins of the palomino and watched Scott deftly saddle up the huge quarter horse. His tight chambray shirt made visible the heavy muscles of his back and shoulders as they bulged and slipped under his skin. After leading the horses outside, her eyes wantonly scrutinized the firm sinews of his powerful thighs as he swung into the saddle after aiding her onto her horse.

Throughout the remainder of the morning, Dani became accustomed to a speedier gait. She learned to move with the horse instead of against it, and found the experience quite rewarding.

While Dani set the small table on the patio with dishes and silverware gleaned from boxes in the basement game room, Scott began to barbeque the two large steaks.

"The game room is impressive. A full-sized pool table and a television screen that is almost as large as one in a movie theater," she observed.

"Daddy likes to watch the Dallas Cowboys on a large screen. It gives him the feeling he's there, while at the same time, he has all the comforts of home. Daddy's not much on crowds."

"I take it you're not much on crowds either."

"I can take them or leave them, sugar. I think I'd prefer to leave them, especially when I'm with you."

"Then why did you want to take me dancing last night? Those places are packed on a Saturday night."

"When I have you in my arms, there is no one else."

"Is this part of your new and undeniable charm?" She tossed him a pixieish glance.

Scott laughed. "Not yet. I was telling you the truth this time. I'll give you warning when I'm about to be charming."

This time Dani had to laugh. He was so real and open that she was totally at ease with him. She didn't have to choose her words with care, make sure her makeup and dress were perfect, or keep an interesting, intelligent-sounding conversation going. In short, she could be herself and be silly if she felt like it, not someone her companion expected or wanted her to be.

"Here we go, ma'am," said Scott, bringing the steaks to the table.

"I'll never eat all that," declared Dani, looking down at the huge slab of meat that almost covered her plate.

"You'd be surprised what riding will do for your appetite. After lunch we'll rest for a while, then I think you'll be ready to really do some heavy riding. When we're finished for the day, I'll take you back to the city for the best Oriental food you've ever tasted," said Scott.

"That is, if I don't break a leg or my neck falling off a horse," said Dani.

"You won't. The palomino is a well-trained animal. Besides, if you did, you'd have me as a personal nurse, day and night."

"That would be a novelty. No way can I picture you as a nursemaid."

"How do you picture me?" asked Scott.

"Roping. Riding, branding cattle on an empty range. An all-around cowboy who dabbles in the mundane, workaday world to make a living. For the life of me, I don't understand why you don't work here with your father."

"This is a horse ranch. There's no roping and branding here," said Scott, his crooked smile curving his lips.

"I think you're teasing me." Dani looked down at her plate to find she had eaten all her potato salad and cole slaw and ninety percent of her steak. She leaned back in the chair and sighed. "I'm full."

Scott forked the rest of her steak off the plate and put it on his own, then proceeded to finish it off. After a number of glasses of iced tea, conversation, and a suitable rest, they went to the barn to resume the riding lessons. Dani became more at ease in the saddle and found herself quickly adapting to all manner of horseback riding. At a good gallop they raced to the water-impoverished river, where Scott indicated they should cross. Coming up the bank on the other side, a vista of grassy meadow with a stand of trees not too far away greeted them. They made their way to the trees and dismounted.

"I thought the land on this side of the river belonged to a neighbor. Should we be trespassing like this?" asked Dani as she tethered the horse.

"The neighbor doesn't live here. Anyway, him and Daddy are good friends, and he wouldn't mind. Let's take a walk. For a tenderfoot, you've put a pretty long day in the saddle. You need a bit of walking to steady your legs," said Scott.

With his hands shoved in his back pockets, Scott and Dani strolled through the meadows, the now parched grasses bending like slivers of golden metal in the soft breeze. Dani drank in large gulps of clean, sweet air.

"It's truly wondrous out here. The other day I was wondering what it would be like at night in these open fields without skyscrapers obstructing the view of the sky," said Dani.

"That can be arranged. Stay the night."

She tilted her head up to look at him. "Are you propositioning me, Mr. Rowland?"

He stopped walking, turned and gazed down at her. "Darlin', I think too much of you to ever do that. The house has four separate bedrooms. Unless, of course, you . . ."

"Scott! Don't say it," she admonished. "Besides you promised me an Oriental dinner in the city, and I'm not going to let you wiggle out of it."

"Sugar, I do love you."

As his arms reached out to gather her in, Dani gladly met his embrace, raising her bright, happy face to his. Her hat fell off as his mouth conquered hers in deep exploration. His strong arms molded her body to the curve of his. They stood as one, silhouetted against the clear, blue sky like a human monument that moved and swayed to the hidden music of passion. No fabulous display of fireworks lighted the sky; no Roman candles were seen to shoot brilliant color in the heavens; no

pinwheels twirled sparkles against the firmament. But in the souls and
hearts of the two people clasping each other in the open meadow, all
manner of pyrotechnics were igniting and blazing into full and ecstatic
glory.

The decor of the Oriental restaurant was exceedingly simple. Booths
and tables were plain, complementing the stark, pale green walls. Dani
had expressed concern about the informality of her dress, but was assured by Scott that she was fine. After a quick scan of the room, she
could see most of the patrons were dressed casually.

"You're getting quite good at riding, sugar. Feel any more comfortable on the back of a horse?" asked Scott, after placing their order.

"I suppose I shouldn't tell you, but I'm beginning to enjoy it."

"Why shouldn't you tell me?"

"You might think I want you to bring me out to the ranch on a
regular basis."

"I don't think it. I intend to do just that. We'll go dancing Saturday
nights and on Sunday you can continue your riding lessons," said Scott.

"Whoa! I can't spend every weekend dancing and riding. I do have
other obligations."

"We'll see, sugar. But do reserve the first weekend in October. I'm
planning to take you to West Texas and see the family homestead.
Grandaddy's been looking forward to it." Scott leaned back in his chair
as the waitress placed covered bowls before them. Scott lifted the cover
and inhaled the savory aroma of the golden chicken stock. "Egg-and-
mushroom soup. One of my favorites."

"It is good," agreed Dani, after several spoonfuls.

Soon the table was covered with various lidded dishes and platters.
Fried rice with crab, butterfly shrimp hot to the taste, cold ginger
chicken with green peppers, chow mein with pork and snow peas,
mixed Chinese vegetables quickly stir fried before the addition of a
sweet and sour sauce.

"That wasn't a meal. It was a banquet," said Dani after refusing
Scott's offer of dessert. "And a very good one at that. Thank you for
both the lunch and dinner. I've never tasted food like we just had."

"Don't tell me you've never eaten Chinese food before."

"Chop suey . . . chow mein . . . Americanized versions of Chinese cuisine, I suspect. Nothing at all like this. So many different tastes,
each one distinctive to itself. Marvelous!" exclaimed Dani.

"I was sure you'd like it. Classic Chinese cooking is more a state of mind than filling one's belly. They pay strict attention to color, texture, flavor, and aroma. They take great care in preparation of their dishes, then cook them as little as possible. We have a tendency to do just the opposite. There is an old Chinese proverb that states all man's diseases enter his mouth, while all his mistakes fly out of it. The world has become so busy producing beautiful and wonderful things, people no longer have the time to enjoy them, especially what they eat," said Scott.

"Stop and smell the roses and all that. You don't seem to practice what you preach," countered Dani.

"Ah . . . but I do. I work hard when life demands it, but I play with keen attention to all around me. You'll find a different world in West Texas. Right now you're under the steamrolling effects of Dallas."

It was late when they left the restaurant. Scott's good-night kiss lingered on her lips long into the night as she lay in bed. Was the opulence, affluence, and optimism of Dallas overpowering her? Were her true values being smothered by the glitter and heady upbeat of Dallas? She felt as though she were looking at the scales of justice, with Scott on one end and Nick on the other in perfect balance. Would the trip to West Texas cause the scale to tip one way or the other?

9

"Cowboy boots and a hat! Really, Dani—aren't you carrying the Texian image a bit too far? After all, this is Dallas, and you should be thinking more along the line of a new Saint Laurent or a Roberto Fabris design," declared Janice, as they sat in a small coffee shop at the Galleria Shopping Mall.

"Who is Roberto Fabris?" asked Dani.

"Who is Roberto Fabris?" echoed Janice. "What rock did you crawl under? He's a new French designer. His designs are so luxurious and unexpected. He has leather creations that would knock your eyes out. Tweeds and knits that are absolutely fabulous. His fall collection has the most scrumptious designs this side of the Seine. You should give up the boots and saddle bit and come back to reality, Dani."

"I'm not being whimsical, Jan. I'm really beginning to enjoy riding. It's a whole different world, a world of freedom and nature. I really need a hat to keep the sun from melting my brains and good riding boots so the pointed toe will slide quickly and easily into the stirrup and a high heel to keep my foot from slipping right through," explained Dani.

"Three hundred dollars' worth? A bit much for a plain old pair of boots," claimed Janice.

"French calf leather lined with soft sheepskin doesn't come cheap. Scott said to get the best and I did."

"You still seeing that cowboy?"

Dani nodded.

"Is that why you haven't been seen at the garden club for a while?"

"In a way."

"Playing cowgirl is not for you, Dani. This is not the old West. This Scott of yours is nothing more than a figure representing the romantic, hard-riding, he-man cowboy of the stagecoach era. He's not real—he's an image, and that's not your style, Dani."

"You shouldn't knock horseback riding until you've tried it," said Dani defensively, while wondering if there was a grain of truth in what Janice said. Was she romanticizing Scott? Seeing him as some great hero of the West and not as a twentieth-century man?

"I have no intention of saying 'giddyap' to anything but my BMW. I feel much safer sitting on velour with four wheels under me, not four legs. I can see you've totally ignored my advice regarding that cowboy of yours. Well . . . you're over twenty-one. And I suppose with my track record in the romance department, I should keep my mouth shut. I just don't want to see you make a terrible mistake and bring a cloud of unhappiness down on your head, Dani," said Janice, her pale brown eyes flickering with true concern.

"You're sweet, Jan. I know you have my best interests at heart. If it was anyone but you, I'd tell them to mind their own business."

"Does Sandy make any comment?"

Dani smiled broadly. "You know Sandy. She's so wrapped up in her own personal affairs, she doesn't notice anything else. I'll say one thing, though. Whatever difficulties she may have in her personal life, it doesn't show in her work. She gets more competent every day. I sometimes think I could go away for a month or more and everything would be running like clockwork when I came back," said Dani.

"You'd better give her a raise. Good people are hard to find. Who should know better than I?" Janice sighed.

"I did better than that. Every quarter she'll get a percentage of the business we've done for that quarter. I thought that would be a far better incentive than a weekly raise. It gives her a tangible interest in the business. Sounds like you're having problems with your staff. Anything serious?" asked Dani.

"Nothing I can't handle. But it gets so damn irritating. Petty squabbles over listings, delayed closings, agents psychologically mishandling clients or stealing potential clients from each other. All trivial matters but highly annoying. I suppose I'll live through it. By the way, how was your trip to Houston with Nick?" asked Janice.

"Fine. There's construction everywhere, especially on the outskirts of the city. Nick owns a Lear jet, and we were down there in no time. Took a look at the sites where he is to erect the buildings, had lunch, then went through several similar projects that had been completed last year. All very interesting," said Dani.

"And Nick? Was he interesting?"

"Nick's always interesting."

"Rumors are floating hot and heavy about you two."

"Oh? What kind of rumors?" asked Dani, slightly concerned.

"That wedding bells are about to ring forth. You're the first woman Nick has seen on a steady and exclusive basis. A ripple of surprise echoed through the building community when he took you to Houston. He never takes a woman on his business trips," said Janice. "Has he asked you to marry him yet?"

"No. And I don't think he will," replied Dani.

"Want to bet?"

"Don't be silly, Jan," said Dani good-naturedly. "Nick is a perennial bachelor. I can't imagine him with a wife and family." Yet she could picture Scott as a family man, even though he also appeared to be a man who prized his independence. So did she, for that matter, and maybe that is why she was so attracted to both men, Dani thought.

"Sometimes the perennial bachelors make the best husbands and fathers. But enough of men. I'm ready to do more shopping," said Janice.

A few days later, a large bouquet of long-stemmed yellow roses arrived at Dani's house with the note, "Have tickets for the opera tomorrow night. *La Boheme.* How can you resist? Nick."

"Aren't they lovely," remarked Sandy, as she watched Dani arrange them in a vase on the kitchen table. "That Nick Hunt is such a thoughtful man, a real gentleman."

"Yes, he is," agreed Dani with some reservations. Whenever he kissed her or held her, true gentleness seemed to be lacking. A savage urgency always seemed to be furtively hovering beneath the surface of his affection. At times Dani found it quite disquieting.

"Oh . . . while you were out this morning, a messenger brought the final payment on the Rowland kitchen, and we received deposits for four more kitchens to be remodeled. When do you think you'll be field measuring the condos and houses for the Houston project?"

"By the end of October at the latest. I'll be seeing Nick tomorrow night, and I'll ask him how close they are. All I need is to have the rough plumbing in. I don't expect too much deviation, if any. The condos we did for him were right on the money with regard to the architect's plans."

"I think it pays to check though. An inch or two in a wall or a pipe can be a costly mistake for us," said Sandy seriously.

Dani smiled. Since she had initiated the percentage system with Sandy, she had taken on a far more conscientous attitude, as if she now had a real vested interest in the business. And in a way, she had.

"Have you heard from Mrs. Rowland?" asked Sandy.

"No. Why?"

"I was wondering how she likes the kitchen."

"I'll have to phone her," replied Dani. Little bubbles of anticipation formed in her stomach at the thought of going to West Texas with Scott. He had said they would go right after his mother's kitchen was finished.

Without any more questions, Sandy went back to the office and the ringing telephone. Dani cupped a rose between her hands and smelled it. Then, with a faint smile, she went back to her drawing board to begin work on the watercolor renderings of the four new kitchen remodelings.

The gown Dani chose to wear to the opera was an exquisite combination of deep purple taffeta and pale lavender tulle, the latter cascading in full folds around the sheath skirt of taffeta. The sleeveless bodice of taffeta was snug, while tuffs of the pale tulle edged the deeply scooped neckline in front. In the back it ran down to her waist line in a vee. Dani was pleased with her appearance and decided against a wrap of any kind, for it was unusually hot for the end of September.

Nick had a sly grin on his face when she opened the door.

"You look lovely, Dani," said Nick in a somewhat off-hand manner. "Are you ready to go? I have a surprise for you."

"Yes," replied Dani, snatching her small envelope purse from the table in the foyer.

He took her arm after she locked the door behind her. Then, with a flourishing wave of his hand, exclaimed, "Voilà, mademoiselle! The fruits of labor."

"Oh, Nick, that's quite a machine." praised Dani, as she gazed upon the brand-new ruby-red Porsche with its black leather interior sitting in her driveway.

"Isn't she a beauty? I had it special ordered with all sorts of custom devices on it. After a two-month wait, it finally came in," he said, opening the door of the sleek sports car, then snapping it shut with a solid thud.

When he took his seat behind the wheel and started the car, Dani asked, "Did you trade in your Cadillac?"

"No. It's at home. I'll use it for site inspection and save this for special occasions, like tonight. Some of those sites can be pretty muddy or dusty."

Dani could see that Nick was full of pride over his new automobile and, from the look of the plush interior, he had every right to be. While he went into detail concerning the purchase of the car, Dani studied his handsome profile with fascination and perplexity. If only there was a definitive criteria that discerned love from superficial attraction, she thought. A list explaining, in detail, each emotion that characterizes love—real love. A handbook that would give reliable, unfailing, and precise insights into the various aspects of the emotional human condition. How can one separate superficial passion from a passion born of true love? Dani didn't have any answers. She had always believed that love hit one like a thunderbolt, and that she would never have to stop and analyze her feelings. Perhaps all her speculation was for naught. Perhaps she wasn't in love with either man. The right one may not have come along yet. But deep down she knew that excuse was feeble. Oh, why didn't that thunderbolt strike?

Everyone at the opera looked so "Dallas." Opulent, dazzling gowns were flaunted by bejeweled women. The cut of the tuxedos worn by the men rivaled, and in some cases surpassed, the fashionable world of the wealthy in London, Paris, and Rome. Dallas was a city well on its way to having an international flair, submerging any image of an old Texas cowtown and slowly destroying "Bubba," the personification of a Texan good ole boy—as polarized from the yuppie as the Artic is from the Antarctic.

The musical performance and interpretation of Puccini's *La Boheme* was spectacular. Both Dani and Nick applauded long and vigorously, Dani stopping once or twice to wipe a stray tear induced by the plaintive ending. In the lobby they spent almost half an hour talking to acquaintances. They were persuaded by a few couples to have a late-night drink with them. It was close to midnight when the Porsche sped northward on the Central Expressway.

"I have a brillant idea," said Nick. "It's such a warm night, why don't we take a swim in the pool at my place. It'll be deserted now, and we'll have it all to ourselves."

"I don't make it a habit to carry my swim suit around with me," said Dani amiably.

"We'll stop and pick it up at your place. It'll only take a minute. It'll be the pièce de résistance of an excellent evening. Don't say no, Dani. I seldom do anything on the spur of the moment, and tonight I feel quite daring. What do you say?" He gave her a quick, imploring glance.

"Why not? It would be a novelty. I've never been swimming at midnight." Dani wasn't sure if it was the wise thing to do, but she was in a gay, frivolous mood and didn't feel like being wise or overly cautious. After all, she was a grown woman and could handle herself in any situation.

Dashing into the house, she ran upstairs and stuffed a bikini, a beach robe, a large towel, and a hairbrush into her canvas tote bag, while Nick waited in the car.

"That was quick," commented Nick, turning the key in the ignition as Dani slid into the black bucket seat.

"Didn't need much. Will we be able to swim in the outdoor pool?"

"That's the one I had in mind. If you like, we could use the hot tub, then jump into the ice tub," suggested Nick.

"I like to swim, not shock my system. Have you ever done it?"

"Yes. Many times. I find it extraordinarily stimulating. Perhaps by the time we've had our swim, I can talk you into it. You shouldn't knock anything until you've tried it."

"Well . . . we'll see," said Dani, wondering if she had the physical courage to jump into an ice tub, then remembering she had said almost the same words to Janice regarding horseback riding.

Seeing Nick, the night guard automatically pushed a series of buttons which caused the doors to swing open and admit them to the opulent foyer. With Nick's hand under her elbow, Dani was ushered into the mirrored elevator, and they went up to his floor wordlessly.

"I'll only be a minute," said Nick, once they were in his apartment. "Make yourself at home," he called, as he disappeared into the bedroom.

Dani nodded and tossed her tote bag on the sofa before walking over to the wall of glass to stare out into the night. The lights of downtown Dallas still shimmered golden against the dark sky, rivaling the stars for attention. She peered down into the courtyard and saw that the amber lights around the pool were still forming a halo of pale sienna. The pool appeared much smaller from that height, and the underwater lights made it seem like a multi-faceted jewel that had been inadvertently dropped in haste.

"I'm all set. You can use the bedroom to change," said Nick.

Dani turned from the window and drew in a sharp, inaudible breath at the sight of Nick in short black trunks, a white towel around his neck. His stocky physique was all muscle, taut, and thick. Black hair tufted across his deep chest and echoed on the hefty sinews of his arms and legs. He was perfectly proportioned for a man of his stature.

"I'm sorry if I startled you. You must have been deep in thought," said Nick smiling.

"I'm afraid I was. I'll go change now." Dani quickly regained her composure and smothered the ripple of excitement that was beginning to rush to her nerve endings.

Nick's bedroom was immaculate. Dani put her tote bag on the deep blue satin bedcover. Her hands went to her back to unzip her gown while her eyes strayed to the door. She instantly dropped her hands and went to the door. With a twist of a small button on the knob, she locked it, knowing if it had been Scott out there, she wouldn't have bothered. There was something about Nick that didn't command her full confidence. A latent need to dominate all those with whom he came in contact seemed to be a strong characteristic of Nick's, one she wasn't comfortable with. In short, she didn't trust him. She laid her gown neatly on the bed, slipped into her bikini, and beach robe, grabbed the tote bag, and left the bedroom. Nick was in the kitchen sipping on a scotch and water.

"Want a drink before you go down?" he asked, his dark eyes skimming over her youthful form with obvious pleasure and desire.

"No, thank you."

"Then we'll get downstairs." He drained the remainder of his drink, and they went down to the main floor.

After going through the chandeliered foyer and the mirrored exercise room, Nick stopped before the glass doors of the indoor pool, tubs, and saunas. He pushed the door open and signaled for Dani to come in.

"I thought we were going to swim in the outdoor pool," she said

"We are in a few minutes. I want you to try the heated Jacuzzi with me." He tossed his towel to one side and reached for her hand.

"Just a minute." Dani removed her beach robe, folded it and put it in her tote bag, which she placed against the wall. She took his hand and let him lead her down the steps into the warm swirling water. "This is marvelous, Nick. I'm surprised you don't spend all your time here," she remarked, letting the soothing water play its delightful energies over her body.

"Don't have the time. I do indulge myself on a particularly strenuous day once in a while. It's quite helpful when I've had a bad day, then have to attend an important function in the evening. I spend about fifteen or twenty minutes in here, then jump into the ice tub. Invigorating to say the least."

"Invigorating? I should think it would be conducive to a heart attack," said Dani, her eyes sparkling merrily.

"I don't suppose I could talk you into trying it."

She shook her head, "No way."

"Coward." He grinned. Suddenly his expression became serious. "I want you to come to Houston with me again. I've got the contract to build more condos down there."

"There's not much use in my going down to Houston if the ground isn't broken yet. I can work from blueprints for the estimate."

"For the new ones, yes. But I also secured a contract to finish up a hundred condos that are almost ready for kitchens. The previous contractor was past schedule, hitting too many cost overruns, and was having labor problems. They let him go and I got it. I have to bring it in within three months."

"I need six weeks, you know."

"I realize it will be tight. That's why I want to get you down there as soon as possible. I can't afford unnecessary delays," said Nick solemnly.

"When did you want to leave?"

"I have a jet that is set to leave tomorrow at eight in the morning," he replied.

"What?" Dani's eyes widened. "Why didn't you tell me this earlier? I would have gone straight home and to bed. What time is it now?"

"A little past one."

Dani slid her body over to the small set of steps and grabbed the chrome curved handles and hauled herself from the warm, bubbling water. "You'd better take me right home if you expect me to be coherent tomorrow."

"Two laps around the pool and I'll let you sleep on the plane," said Nick, jumping out to stand beside her. "At this point, an hour isn't going to make that much difference."

Dani's shoulders sagged. "I suppose you're right. Besides, right now, I'm wide awake. Maybe a few good laps will tire me out."

She grabbed her tote bag and they headed for the amber-lighted pool. Dani dove in first, with Nick splashing in shortly after, quickly overtaking her with sure, steady strokes. With arms moving rhythmically, they swam side by side for a number of laps, pushing off the cement ends of the pool for swift turns. After half an hour, Dani climbed the chrome ladder feeling exhilarated, even though her energies were spent. She plucked the large towel from her tote bag and began to towel herself off.

As she vigorously rubbed her short hair, a pair of hands clasped her upper arms from behind and lips greedily nibbled at her shoulder. She stiffened but didn't resist when he spun her around. Nick's somber eyes gazed at her for a fleeting second before his mouth impacted itself on hers. Insistent arms went around her and their flesh met, sending shock waves to ripple under Dani's skin. His hands moved over her as though she was a piano whose every note had to be played. His kiss was as powerful as his body pressing against hers, his naked thighs persistently nuzzling hers. His breathing was deep and rapid as his chest rose and fell on her breasts. Dani's heart and brain had no effect in stemming the sensuality he was causing to rise in her. Before she was pulled into the whirlpool from which she might not return, she placed her hands on the hard muscles of his upper arms and wrenched her lips from his. But his powerful arms held her fast.

"Dani," he whispered huskily, his dark eyes glazed. "Stay here tonight. We can leave together in the morning."

The suggestion brought Dani to her senses, her brain and heart fully alert. "No." With newfound strength, she pulled herself free, picked up the towel that had fallen to the cement apron of the pool, and shoved it in her bag. "Please take me home now."

"Dani . . . don't turn your back on something that could be wonderful for both of us. Why do you think I suggested we come here? You're not that naive. I know you want me as much as I want you. Don't play the tease—it doesn't become you," said Nick, grabbing her arm.

"I'm sorry, Nick. I shouldn't have given you that impression. It was wrong of me. I apologize. I like you, Nick, and I didn't mean for you to think I was leading you on. I'd like to go home or, if you prefer, call a cab for me," she said, yanking her arm free, then headed for the door of the building.

"Dani . . ." he called as he rushed to catch up with her. "Look, I'll marry you if you want."

Her eyes flashed with indignation and she was about to blurt out, "Don't do me any favors." Instead she looked at him and suddenly realized he was sincere in his offer; he was making the greatest sacrifice he knew to win her favor. She was flattered and, without sarcasm, said, "That's sweet of you, Nick. But I don't think so. I don't love you." There . . . she had said it aloud and the thunderbolt struck. She loved one man and only one man. Scott Rowland, the cowboy, the drifter.

"You only think you don't. It will take a little time for you to realize how much you really do love me. We've got everything going for us, Dani. Our tastes in music and literature coincide. We both enjoy our work. And we are physically attracted to one another. Don't deny it. I can see it in your eyes, taste it in your kiss, feel the tremors in your body when I hold you close. The air is charged with electricity whenever we're together. Admit it, you want me as much as I want you. Don't fight it, Dani. We're destined for one another." He put his arms around her as he stood behind her.

"I'd like to go home," she said softly.

He sighed heavily, put one arm around her shoulders, and led her to the elevators.

He drove her home in silence, a brooding scowl on his handsome face. When he stopped the Porsche in front of her house, he snapped the radio off and half turned in the bucket seat to face her.

"Are you still going with me to Houston tomorrow?"

"Is there any reason why I shouldn't? You did intend it to be a business trip, didn't you?"

"Of course. Regardless of any deep personal relationship between us, or lack of, I still hold your professionalism in high esteem. You've proven your abilities to me, and I'm not one to cut off my nose to spite my face."

"Neither am I. I like the work and the money. I'd hate to lose them because . . . well . . . you know what I mean," said Dani.

Nick nodded while holding up a staying hand. "You don't have to explain. I want to make sure you'll continue to design and supply kitchens for me."

"I will, Nick." She smiled warmly at him. "What time will you be picking me up?"

"Close to seven . . . and Dani, remember what I said. You will come to love me. All I ask is that you don't fight it when it does come." He took her hand in his and kissed it.

She smiled weakly and went into the house.

After setting her alarm, she crawled into bed. It does come like a thunderbolt, she kept saying to herself, and finding it all so wondrous. A happiness she never knew before swelled within her, and she tried to push images of Scott into her mind, but sleep smothered all thought.

10

Dressed in a dove-gray linen suit and rust-colored blouse, Dani boarded the Lear jet with Nick coming up the steps behind her. On the way to the plane from her house, Nick had pointedly kept the conversation on a business level. Yet, on the plane, Dani noticed he gave her an occasional glance that had nothing to do with business. As always, Nick was well organized and a car was waiting for them at Houston's airport.

Adjacent to the giant, futuristic city, a sprawling suburbia, complete with shopping malls, fast-food places, and elegant restaurants bubbled out of Houston like ripples on a pond after a pebble has been tossed in.

Construction was all around them as Nick parked the car and they entered the first unlandscaped condominium. While Nick studied what remained to be completed, Dani opened her briefcase, took out her layout pad, pencil, and retractable metal ruler and immediately went to work. With professional deftness and speed, she moved from one condo to the next and had a third of them measured by noon. After a quick lunch with Nick, she went back to finish measuring the kitchens while Nick went to check out the site for new construction.

It was quite late in the afternoon when Nick and Dani reboarded the Lear jet. Once airborne, Dani took out her layout pad, with all the measurements, and had every intention of working out the cabinetry but her eyes absently strayed to the window. She looked with puzzlement at the lowering sun. Something was wrong.

"Nick . . ." she began causing him to lift his head from a sheaf of papers, ". . . the sun sets in the west, doesn't it?"

"Always has. Why?"

"Well, we're heading west and Dallas is north of here."

"My, you are observant. You worked pretty hard today so I thought I'd surprise you with a leisurely, well-deserved dinner in San Antonio. It's a little more laid back than Dallas or Houston. We can sit by the river and relax while we eat. How does that sound?"

"Delightful. I trust you intend to be back in Dallas before midnight."

"Are you worried about it?" asked Nick, one black eyebrow raised, a hint of a smile on his lips.

She looked at him steadily. "Should I be?"

"A little sightseeing, dinner, then home to Dallas," he replied.

After the plane landed, a taxi whisked them to the heart of the city and deposited them in the Alamo Plaza, a small park across the street from the historic mission, San Antonio de Valero, later to become famous as the Alamo. They entered a little over half an hour before the shrine was due to close and walked around the large, cool room of the mission house, reading plaques and peering at the historic artifacts encased in glass.

"Five thousand," murmured Dani aloud.

"What?" asked Nick bringing his head to her shoulder.

"One hundred and eighty-eight men fought off the Mexican Army of five thousand for thirteen days. Seems incredible," said Dani.

"Texas is incredible," said Nick drily. "Let's go outside. This place smells of death."

Dani looked at him quizzically. This was a side of Nick she knew nothing about—his aversions and quirks. Suddenly she had the feeling that there was a whole other Nick hiding somewhere inside that splendid body, a deep, dark side that he purposely kept submerged. She wondered if she wanted to know this other side of him.

Outside they strolled the paths that wound around the beautifully landscaped gardens within the walled fence which surrounded the grounds of the shrine. Time being short, they shunned the souvenir shop and went directly to the Long Barrack Museum, which, during its mission days served as a kitchen, dining hall, and living quarters for the priests. It had been refurbished to house visual aid machines that recreated, with sound and sight, the final hours of the siege of the Alamo, along with sabers, guns, clothes, and miscellaneous items relating to the area in the mid-nineteenth century and pertaining to the Alamo.

Their curiosity sated, they left the landmark, walked back through the small park, and crossed another street to find themselves at one of the many entrances to the Paseo del Rio. They walked down the stone steps to the walkway one level below the bustling streets of downtown San Antonio. Dani felt as though she had entered another world, as they strolled beneath live oak and pecan trees, giant cypress and palms, accented by flowering shrubs and tropical foliage. It was nature at its lush and colorful best, thriving in the very heart of a modern, busy city. Rimming around both sides of the San Antonio River were restaurants, sidewalk cafes, art and gift shops, hotels, boutiques, and cabarets while paddle boats and wide flatboats, the latter carrying tourists, plied the dark green waters.

Dani eagerly observed everything, the charming arched bridges that spanned the river at various points, offering access to the other side, or the bustling traffic of the streets above.

When they came to an unusually wide set of steps that doubled as seats for an audience to view the outdoor theater on the other side of the slow-moving river, hardly wider than a city street and no deeper than a swimming pool, Nick and Dani found themselves in what appeared to be a restored Mexican village where narrow streets, authentic adobe houses, and shaded patios transported one back to another era. The restored houses were shops where artists and craftsmen displayed their wares, all indigenous to the area.

"I'm getting hungry. How about you?" asked Nick after they had browsed for some time.

"Starved. Seems like I've been walking all day," said Dani with a smile.

They went back to the riverwalk and studied the many posted menus before deciding on a restaurant that suited both their tastes, even though it was extremely expensive.

The tablecloth and napkins were of the finest linen, the glassware of crystal, and the dishes of delicate china. The waiter was a professional of the highest order, charming and genuinely friendly.

Platters of raw oysters on the half shell and cooked, peeled shrimp resting on crushed ice was placed on their table, along with small dishes of sliced lemons and a tomato horseradish sauce. A buttery cream-of-tomato soup, lightly laced with chili peppers, was followed by a succulent and tender chateaubriand for two. Nick declined dessert but Dani couldn't resist a slice of the raspberry torte splashed with real whipped cream.

"Full?" He looked at her with a warm smile after taking a sip of his coffee.

"I should say so," replied Dani with a sigh. "I'm glad you suggested this side trip. I've never been in San Antonio, and it is a marvelous city. And you're right. The pace here is a lot more leisurely than Dallas or Houston. The dinner was excellent, especially when I can look out the window and see all that lovely vegetation and the river. Quite serene and beautiful."

"Putting you in a good frame of mind?"

"Yes. Why?" asked Dani, a little startled by his question.

"I want to talk about last night."

"Let's forget it."

"I can't. It's been preying on my mind. I was crude, unthinking, and generally made a mess of it." He held up a staying hand when he saw Dani was about to speak. "No . . . let me finish what I have to say. Last night I wanted you desperately. I mentioned marriage without too much thought behind it. But I was up most of the night seriously thinking about it, and realized it wasn't an offhanded remark. I had meant it, even though I had phrased it very poorly. I do want you to marry me,

Dani. We work well together and I deeply admire you for your business acumen and ability to get things done. I think we'd make a great team. I don't want you to answer me right away. Think about it for a while. And think of all the possibilities of us as man and wife." Nick's handsome face was set with only a trace of eagerness in his dark eyes, the latter searching her face for a clue to her emotions.

Dani was impressed by his sincerity, if not by the air of romance with which he proposed. It was more like a contract proposal than one of marriage. "I'm very flattered, Nick—"

"I want you to think about it, Dani," he interrupted. "I don't want your answer today. It's been a long day, and you must be tired. Give your mind a chance to work on it when you're relaxed and clearheaded. More coffee?"

She shook her head. Her mind was clear now. She had to admit she had been greatly attracted to Nick, but it was the cowboy with the soft Texas drawl she loved. It was true she had a lot of things in common with Nick, and they did work well together, but her heart would always yearn for and belong to Scott Rowland.

When the small jet landed in Dallas, Nick drove his new Porsche to her house and fervently recounted his plans for the Houston project. He did not mention his proposal of marriage again that night.

"How was Houston?" asked Sandra Parks, as she came into the game room to begin the day's work.

"We'll have a lot of orders to fill from there. Nick has a staggering amount of projects to do there," replied Dani, her ruler and pencil quickly moving over the layout pad on her drawing table.

"Have we got the contract?"

"I'm pretty sure we do. I have to finish these right away so we can draw up the contract and get it signed today. The order to the factory should go in today if possible. They're almost ready for kitchens in one group of condos. We have a little more lead time on the others. Were there any calls while I was away yesterday?" asked Dani, never lifting her head from the drawing board.

"Three," replied Sandy, picking up the message pad from the desk. "A Mrs. Julia Blair and a Mrs. Ethel Mitchell. Evidently both women have seen Mrs. Rowland's kitchen and now want their kitchens remodeled. Sounds like they're willing to spend big bucks."

"Did you make appointments for me to go and see both women?"

"Yes. Both later this week. They seemed anxious, and I thought you'd better see them as soon as possible, before they changed their minds. I tried calling you last night, but there was no answer," claimed Sandy, sitting down at the desk.

"When we finished in Houston, Nick took me to San Antonio for a little sightseeing and dinner. Have you ever been there, Sandy?"

"No. I've never left the Dallas–Fort Worth area. How was it down there?"

"Beautiful. There doesn't seem to be the frenetic energy swamping the city like there is here. I had the feeling that at any minute everyone would stop working and have a fiesta—mariachis, swirling skirts, and stomping feet. After measuring kitchens all day long, it was a real treat. And I finally got to see the Alamo. You ought to go down there sometime, Sandy."

"Maybe I will on my next vacation."

Dani concentrated on her layouts, drawing one kitchen after another with a well-practiced hand. Suddenly she looked up. "Sandy . . . you said there were three calls. What was the third one about?"

"Oh—Scottie called, looking for you. I told him you were in Houston. He said he'd call you later at night, but I guess you weren't home then either."

"Did he say what he wanted?" asked Dani anxiously as she looked up from the drawing board.

"No."

"Do you have his home phone number there?"

Sandy flipped through her Rolodex. "Yes."

"Would you please try and reach him for me?"

Sandy dialed the phone and, after several seconds, put the receiver back. "No answer."

Dani found it difficult to concentrate on her layouts. She hadn't heard from him since his mother's kitchen was finished. Her heart pounded at the thought of him. In her mind, images of his handsome face, with its quick and boyish grin, haunted her. She knew she would never be able to reach the roving cowboy by phone. She would have to wait until he called her.

When all the layouts had been completed, cabinetry and counters priced, Dani made out the contract. She sent Sandy over to the Hunt offices to get the contract signed. She did so for two reasons. One, she wasn't in the mood to get into a long conversation with Nick. Two, she wanted to be home in case Scott called.

The phone rang, and Dani almost knocked over her drawing table in her rush to grab the receiver on the desk.

"Hello?" she asked with breathless expectancy.

"Are you free for lunch?"

"Oh, it's you, Jan."

"Well, don't sound so overjoyed."

"I was expecting a call from someone else."

"Nick?"

"No."

"What about lunch?"

"I don't know. I'm up to my eyeballs in kitchens. I think I'll take a raincheck," said Dani. "Besides, Sandy isn't here to cover the phone."

"Where is she off to this time of day?" asked Janice.

"She took the contract over to Nick's office," explained Dani.

"I'm surprised you didn't take it yourself. Don't tell me you had a spat with the formidable Nicholas Hunt."

"No. Nothing like that. As I said, I'm loaded with work."

"Look . . . I'll drop by about one o'clock. Maybe by then you will need a break."

"Okay. Sandy should be back by then. Bye for now."

"Catch you later."

Dani went back to her drawing board. Every fifteen minutes, her head would lift to let her eyes glance at the telephone, as if she could will it to ring. She gave up and focused her efforts on the kitchens before her. When her mind was totally absorbed, the perverse telephone rang.

"Why did you send Sandy over with the contract? Why didn't you come yourself?" asked Nick, his tone a mixture of hurt and anger.

"I'm swamped with work, Nick."

"Are you sure you're not avoiding me?"

"Oh Nick. I really am trying to get a handle on this work load."

"Why don't you hire extra help?"

"Someday. Right now there seems to be a deluge. It'll ease up soon."

"You need a vacation, Dani. Perhaps we both do. A honeymoon would be a good excuse to take one." There was a quiet urgency in his voice.

"Is Sandy still there?" asked Dani, purposely ignoring his suggestion.

"No. She left some time ago with the signed contracts. Look . . . I have another call I have to take. I'll call you back later and we'll make arrangements to go to dinner this week."

The line went dead before Dani could protest or say goodbye. Before she could get back to the drawing board, the phone rang again, and Dani wondered how Sandy ever got any work done.

"Oh Dani . . . the kitchen is absolutely beautiful," said Agnes Rowland. "I've been cooking up a storm. Tom is real proud of it. The microwave oven fascinates him. He's been trying out all sorts of things in it. He likes the way it cooks bacon in three minutes. Scottie will have to bring you out to lunch or dinner, or both, real soon."

"I'm glad you're pleased with it, Agnes. Mrs. Blair and Mrs. Mitchell called and want their kitchens remodeled," said Dani.

"I know. You should have seen their eyes bulge when they stepped into my kitchen. Pea-green with envy, they were. Even Scottie was impressed."

"That's good." Dani hesitated a minute then rushed on. "I haven't seen Scott since your kitchen was finished, so I'm glad to know he approves. He did call yesterday, but I wasn't here."

"He probably wanted to tell you he wouldn't be around for a while. Tom and Scottie went to Tulsa early this morning," explained Agnes.

"Oh? When will they be back?"

"One never knows with those two. Sometimes it's only for a day. Other times they're gone for a week. They always try to get some time with each other. Man talk, or so they tell me. Well . . . I just wanted to let you know I adore the kitchen and you have a standing invitation to visit anytime."

"Thank you, Agnes. And thank you for the endorsement. I appreciate the business."

"Don't you go working too hard now. Take care," said Agnes before she hung up the phone.

Dani stared at the receiver for several minutes before she put it back in the cradle. She felt empty inside. Her heart was obliterating all common sense. But a shadow of reason lingered in a small corner of her brain to cause her to wonder if Scott wasn't an erratic, unreliable drifter who followed the whims of his nature. He picked up jobs here and there, whatever took his fancy at the time. Went off fishing, or some such thing, whenever the mood struck him. Lived out of a sleeping bag, yet forked over big bucks for a kitchen. It wasn't beyond the realm of possibility that he had that kind of money, for he lived quite frugally and drove an old, sad pickup truck. But she had the feeling his father had come up with most of the cash. Could she endure such a lifestyle? Would and could love conquer a haphazard way of life?

She walked over to her drawing table, looked down at it, and sighed. There was no sense in trying to work. Her heart wasn't in it. She went into the kitchen and started the coffee maker.

"Hi! Anyone home?" called a familiar voice.

"I'm in the kitchen, Jan," said Dani as Janice Gordon strolled into the kitchen. "You're early, aren't you?"

"I had to get out of the office before I went bananas," said Janice, throwing her hands in the air dramatically. "Children! I'm running a damn nursery school!"

"What happened?" asked Dani with a smile.

"I keep telling them it's an agency. We all work together for the good of the agency. The more the agency makes, the more they make. But what do they do? Squabble over listings and clients. One of my agents was out sick the other day. So when her client walked in, another agent did some showings. The client bought, and when the agent came back, she was furious and wailed to me how her client was stolen from under her nose. And on and on it goes. Talk about artists being temperamental! Let's go out to lunch now. I need some reward for putting up with all the nonsense this morning."

"Sandy isn't back yet. Why don't I rustle up something here? I have a few goodies in the refer," suggested Dani.

"Sandy's not back? What's up?"

"I don't know. Nick called a while ago and said she had left with the signed contract. It's not rush hour. I haven't the foggiest notion what's keeping her."

"Maybe you should call the police. That doesn't sound like Sandy at all," declared Janice with deep concern.

"No. I have a feeling it's something personal. I'm sure she'll explain when she comes back."

"What have you got for goodies?" asked Janice.

Dani opened the refrigerator and rattled off the contents. "Ham. Cold chicken. Fixings for a salad. Swiss cheese. Potato salad."

"Cold chicken, potato salad and a tossed salad. I'll do the salad while you get the rest ready," declared Janice.

The two women worked in silence. The table set, the food on serving platters, they sat down to their lunch as though they were at some posh restaurant, totally unmindful of their surroundings as they chatted amicably.

"Now that you've listened to all my trials and tribulations, how goes your battle?" asked Janice.

"Nick asked me to marry him."

"That's great, Dani. I hope you said yes. Men like Nick don't come along that often."

"He refused to hear my answer. Wants me to think it over thoroughly before I reply."

Janice narrowed her eyes suspiciously. "I have a feeling you're going to be stupid and turn him down. Don't do it, Dani. You two go together like apple pie and vanilla ice cream. Besides he has money oozing from every pore. You'd be a fool to pass it up."

Dani shrugged. "I'll admit I like Nick and we get along quite well—"

"But," interrupted Janice "that roving cowboy is standing in the way. Oh, Dani. Don't waste your time on a man who will bring you nothing but grief. From what you've told me, this cowboy lives like a gypsy, constantly breaking camp to move on. He doesn't even know how to dress. Can you see yourself arriving at the opera or ballet in an old pickup truck draped on the arm of a man dressed in worn Levi's and a sports shirt? Think about it, Dani. Don't throw your life away for an infatuation."

"I'm afraid it's more than an infatuation. I can't stop thinking about him, wanting to be with him," confessed Dani.

"You'll get over it, believe me. I've been through it a dozen or more times. No big deal," declared Janice. "Believe me, being married to the dynamic Nicholas Hunt would make any woman forget some drifter in a snap. I know it would me. Do you realize how lucky you are?"

Dani sighed, knowing she'd never make Janice understand how the heart could rule the head entirely. Janice was far too pragmatic. "Anyone new in your life?" she finally asked.

"Okay . . . okay," said Janice, putting up her hands defensively. "Don't take my advice. Waste your life mooning over a nomadic cowboy. Now me . . . I've found Mr. Right at last. He's—" Janice's words were cut off by the slamming of the front door. Both women turned their heads toward the noise to see Sandra Parks come stomping into the kitchen. Instead of her usual conservative, inexpensive attire, she wore a stylish Albert Nipon outfit with expensive costume jewelry. Her shoes and purse were Etienne Aigner originals. Janice and Dani looked at each other in shock, then turned their attention to the fashion plate approaching the table.

"Breaking out of the cocoon, Sandy?" asked Janice with a broad and admiring smile.

"Damn right I am," spewed Sandy angrily as she took a seat at the table.

"Coffee or iced tea?" asked Dani, a little surprised by the depth of Sandy's anger. She was quite placid as a rule, not easily ruffled.

"Coffee. And black," declared Sandy.

"I know you're dying to tell someone, Sandy. Now's as good a time as any," said Janice, as Dani got a mug and poured coffee into it.

"Some men!" grumbled Sandy as she took the mug from Dani, the latter reseating herself at the table.

"Do you have the contract?" asked Dani.

"Yes. Right here," replied Sandy, patting the briefcase by her feet.

"Now what's this all about?" asked Janice.

"You both know I've been going with Jim Mansfield for two years now. Going with him? I practically supported him! I paid the rent, the utilities, and bought the food. The other day he said he had the deal of the century. It would put us on top for the rest of our lives. All he needed was a loan of twenty-five hundred dollars. After I finished at Nick's, I went to the bank and got a certified check, made out to cash, for the amount. Not wanting to carry around that large a check, I decided to stop at the apartment and put it away." Sandy took a swallow of the hot coffee then stared down into the mug as though it contained an alien liquid. "There he was with another woman in my bed . . . my bed!" she emphasized.

"What did you do?" asked Janice, on the edge of her seat.

"I told him to pack his things and get out, and if he wasn't gone by three o'clock, I'd call the police and have him thrown out. Do you mind if I leave at quarter to three, Dani? Naturally I'll call all the orders in to the factory first," said Sandy.

"Sure. Why three o'clock?" asked Dani.

"I'm having a locksmith come at three and change all the locks."

"And the new image?" asked Janice.

"I've decided I come first from now on. There's no doubt in my mind he was going to take the money from me and blow. If it's going to be spent on anyone, it's going to be me."

"You spent all twenty-five hundred?" Dani's eyes were wide with disbelief as her delicate eyebrows arched.

"No. I redeposited the check in the bank, then, went on a quick shopping spree with my charge card. That's why I'm so late. I had to get rid of a little steam," replied Sandy. "I hope you don't mind, Dani. I'll work late tomorrow and make it up to you."

Dani shook her head. "No need to do that Sandy. Let's call it a sick day. You never take any sick time off. In fact, why don't you take the rest of the day off?"

"I'd rather stay and work. It'll keep my mind busy," said Sandy.

"Aren't you afraid he'll walk off with everything in the apartment?" asked Janice.

"There's nothing of value in the apartment. Besides, I told him if he touched anything I'd call the police and charge him with burglary."

"Friday night I'm having a party. Why don't you come, Sandy? You too, Dani," said Janice.

"I'd be delighted. What time, Jan?" asked Sandy.

"Eightish. You know my place, don't you?" asked Janice to an assenting nod from Sandy. "What about you, Dani? Can you make it? Or do you have other plans?"

"I have other plans," replied Dani, secretly hoping Scott would be back from Tulsa by the weekend.

The conversation turned to clothes. In half an hour, Dani and Sandy returned to work and Janice left.

Over the next few days, Sandy worked quietly with efficient speed. When Friday came, Dani noticed she had brightened a bit.

It was late in the day and Sandy was preparing to leave when Dani asked, "Are you looking forward to tonight at Jan's?"

"Yes, I am. I accepted out of anger, but now I find I'm excited about going. Even bought a new dress and shoes for the occasion."

"I hope you're getting over Jim without too much pain," said Dani soothingly.

"I'm surprised how painless it can be. Once in a while I find myself missing him, but I've also found there are other things in life," said Sandy.

"I'm thinking of taking on more help on a permanent basis. What do you think?"

"With all the business coming in, it sounds like a good idea. Marge graduated in June. She's working at one of the banks and doesn't much like it," said Sandy.

"I'll call her Monday morning and see if she can come over after work. She'd be a good choice. She's a good, steady worker and already knows a little about the kitchen business. We'll talk about it Monday. I don't want to hold you up. Have a good time tonight."

"I intend to."

After Sandy left, Dani went back to finish some layouts for remodeling older kitchens. The house seemed inordinately quiet. She turned on the radio. She always worked better when there was some soft music in the background. It was almost seven in the evening when she decided to call it a day and get herself some supper. She had just finished loading her dirty dishes in the dishwasher when the telephone rang.

"Hi, sugar. Miss me?"

"Scott! How was Tulsa?" Her whole body smiled and her heart danced.

"Boring. Everything is boring when you aren't there with me. Am I still in the running or has Nick Hunt roped, hog-tied and branded you for his own?" His voice was lighthearted and somber at the same time.

"Nobody brands and hog-ties me," she replied, delighted that he cared.

"Then you're free this weekend?"

"Yes. Are you in Dallas?"

"Yes ma'am. Getting ready to curl into my sleeping bag. But I had to hear your voice to make my dreams sweet. I tried to call you before I left, but your gal Sandy told me you went to Houston with that Hunt fellow. Sure had me worried, especially when I called at night and you weren't back."

"Got in around eleven. What's this about the weekend?"

"Grandaddy's expecting us. Called him from Tulsa to set it up. He's like a steer gone wild waiting to meet you. Can you make it for the weekend?"

"Yes," she replied eagerly. "What should I pack?"

"Riding clothes and a pretty dancing dress. I'll pick you up around six in the morning. Okay?"

"Fine. I'll see you then."

"Sugar . . . I do love you. Until tomorrow."

When she hung up the phone, she wanted to laugh, sing, and cry with joy. All she had to do was hear Scott's voice, and all Janice's words of wisdom had no meaning for her. Nick had no meaning for her. She was hopelessly in love. She refused to even let the word "infatuation" enter her brain.

11

The single-engine plane bumped over the dry ground of the empty field, leaving a trail of dust to rise behind it. Scott taxied the craft down to the far end, where three horses and a man waited.

Dani peered through the window of the cockpit trying to make out the face of the man with the horses, while waiting for Scott to come around to her side of the plane. The door swung open and arms reached up to aid her. She never tired of looking at Scott's smiling face.

"Who's the man with the horses?" asked Dani, as her feet touched the ground.

"Grandaddy. I knew he wouldn't wait at the house," Scott replied, putting his arm around her waist and starting to walk toward the patiently waiting man.

"What about my suitcase?"

"Someone will fetch it from the plane. Don't worry, sugar. Can you see why I told you to wear your riding clothes and boots? I had a feeling Grandaddy would be bringing the horses instead of the pickup." He gave her waist a squeeze before he removed his hand and went to greet the tall, lean, gray-haired man.

The two men embraced, slapping each other's backs with gusto. Dani looked at the older man and smiled. She could see Scott in him. The sparkling gray eyes that were a little watery as they squinted against the sun, the worn cowboy hat pushed back on his head. He had the same sharp-boned face, only the taut skin had become heavily and deeply lined, like fissures on a dried stream. His denim pants were fairly tight of leg with the points of his tooled boots peeking out. Underneath his light leather jacket was a plaid flannel shirt. When the men had finished their exuberant greetings, the older man turned his attention to Dani.

"So this is Dani," said Scott's grandfather taking Dani's outstretched hand in his, then covering the clasped hands with his large, free one. "You're sure one pretty little lady. My grandson has as good an eye as his old grandaddy. Hope you can ride."

"Yes, I can, Mr.?" Dani's eyes went to Scott with a plea. He hadn't told her his grandfather's name, and she couldn't very well call him Grandaddy.

"That grandson of mine was so excited about you seeing our little spread, he plumb forgot to tell you my name. No sense of manners, that boy," chided the older man shaking his gray head ruefully as he pulled Dani's arm through his and patted her hand. "We'll strike a bargain, little lady. You call me Angus, and I'll call you Dani. How's that?"

"Fine with me, Angus," said Dani.

As they approached the horses, Dani's eyes widened with terror. The horse was no dainty palomino. It was huge, muscular, and frightening to her. Her eyes quickly shifted to Scott. His eyes told her she could do it. She bit her lower lip and was surprised at how smoothly she mounted the creature. She gave a short sigh of relief, then tossed Scott a smile of confidence. Those blue-gray eyes squinted at her as he pulled the brim of his hat down and gave her a crooked smile. With the two Texans, tall in the saddle, flanking her, Dani rode the horse carefully, remembering everything Scott had taught her.

"Now you'll get to see the real Texas, won't she, Scottie?" asked Angus.

"Sure will," responded Scott, glancing at Dani fondly.

"No steel and glass shimmering into the sky around here," continued Angus. "Nope. We got floods, drought, lizards, dust, hot wind, rattlers, sky, and land that never ends. Marvelous country, West Texas. Love it! Keep your Dallas and Houston. Ulcer makers. Wait till you've been here a couple of days, then go back to Dallas. You'll know what I mean, Dani. At night the sky is so clear you can see from horizon to horizon without some newfangled high rise poking up and obscuring the stars as if steel could ever compete with nature. Wait until you've seen the sun pop up over the flat prairie blazing its rays over the land like some gigantic eye of fire. You'll feel really alive. The land, little lady, the land is all. It makes you or breaks you."

"Grandaddy, I don't think Dani wants a lecture on your philosophy of life," said Scott.

The watery gray eyes of Angus turned to Dani with a questioning look. She smiled. "Don't listen to him, Angus. I'm enjoying your talk of Texas. Scott tells me you're quite an authority on the Indians."

"Now you've done it, sugar. I'll never have you to myself," declared Scott good-naturedly.

"Dani's right. One doesn't understand Texas without knowing the Indians and the Mexicans. It's all part and parcel of Texas," said Angus.

She knew Angus wasn't kidding her about the heat, dust, and wind. Her face was beginning to feel like a prune and her mouth like the Sahara Desert. She wasn't sure which would come first, her body shriveling to nothing or dying of thirst. Just when she was sure there was no end to the flat prairie, a golden structure rose in the distance like a mirage.

"Is that your house, Angus?" she asked, unable to hide a twinge of relief in her voice.

"Sure is. My daddy and I were both born in that house. And a good, solid home it is. I wish Scott had been born there. But I suppose a woman has to go with her husband. Anyway, my Agnes picked a good man in Tom Rowland. My Agnes thinks quite highly of you, Dani. Says you did a real nice job with her kitchen and at a reasonable price. Like working for a living, do you?" asked Angus.

"I like what I do. I'm not so sure I'd like working for a living if I had to pick cotton all day long," she replied honestly.

"And she's damn good at what she does, Grandaddy," added Scott.

"I like a woman who can fend for herself in this world. That's what made this land. Women with backbone who can work alongside their men to forge a good life. Amy, my wife, was a strong woman who could ride and rope with the best of them. Why, she could shoot the eye out of a rattler while riding herd on a stampede."

"Aren't you stretching it a bit, Grandaddy? I remember Grandma making biscuits, cooking ribs, and knitting afghans," said Scott with a wry smile.

"You didn't know your Grandma in her prime. She was a feisty little lady. Could ride herd as hard as a man, yet made the lightest, fluffiest biscuits you ever sunk a tooth into. She mellowed and stayed more to home in her golden years. Seems so long ago now. Well . . . there's the house. I'll bet you could use a tall, cold drink about now, Dani," said Angus.

"I sure could," said Dani, her tongue ready to turn to dust.

As the three of them reined in their horses before the boxshaped wooden structure where a wide porch guarded the front of the house, Dani was introduced to the young man who took their horses. Angus led the way into the house, the screen door unceremoniously banging shut after Scott. Dani whipped her hat off and shook her damp hair loose.

"Rosa . . . Rosa," called Angus.

A short plump woman with dark eyes, dark hair, and clear olive skin came plodding to greet them. She nodded to Dani with a smile when they were introduced, then left to get the iced tea Angus requested.

They sat in the living room, which was notably cooler than outside, even though it lacked air-conditioning. Though the room was simply furnished, it was evident one could consider most of the pieces antiques of the early west. The whole house spoke of the hard, sober days of early settlement. Plain, sturdy furniture, some with dull green or red coverings. The wallpaper was old and faded as it met the wainscoting, the latter now scarred by time. Though the house had electricity, oil lamps were placed about the room as if to remind the inhabitants that it had survived through generations without it. For all its age, the house was immaculate.

Angus sat in a large leather chair whose spidery cracks revealed its age. Dani and Scott sat across from him on a faded, chintz-covered couch, an old oak coffee table in front of them. Rosa bustled in, carrying a large tray with a sizable pitcher of iced tea and glasses filled with ice. She placed it on the low table, then went to a cabinet, opened it, and brought a decanter of whiskey to the table.

"Thank you, Rosa," said Angus, then turned to Dani, "My medicine. Can't stand the taste of that danged iced tea." He poured some of the whiskey over the ice in his glass then filled all three glasses to the brim with iced tea.

Dani took her glass eagerly and drained almost half of it. "That tastes so good. I could drink gallons of it."

"Once you've been out here a while you get use to the dry heat and your thirst adjusts itself," said Scott, half-turned on the couch to face her. "When you've had enough iced tea, I'll show you your room, then give you a tour of the ranch."

"On horseback?" asked Dani.

"On foot," replied Scott.

"You going to hog Dani all to yourself while you're here, Scottie?" grumbled Angus. "I thought you'd ride out to the herd and let me do the honors for our visitor. I don't get too many pretty girls all to my-self."

"Now, Grandaddy, you know how you enjoy riding out to see the herd."

"That's when I don't have such pretty company. Besides you haven't been around much lately. It's time you got your hand in before you forget how," warned Angus.

"Why do you have to ride out to the herd?" asked Dani.

"Roundup and cutting time," replied Angus.

"Cutting? You cut the animals?" Dani was astonished, but Angus and Scott laughed.

"We call separating the bulls, cows, and calves 'cutting,' " explained Scott.

"Couldn't we all go? I'd like to see that. You can give me the tour of the ranch later," suggested Dani, her large blue eyes looking from one face to the other.

Scott looked at his grandfather and smiled as if to say I told you she was smart.

Angus drained his glass, then asked, "Shall we go?"

"I'd like to freshen up first," said Dani as she stood.

"Sure, sugar. I'll show you to your room."

Scott led her upstairs and opened a door to a very austere bedroom. Her valise was resting on the bed. The two windows let light stream through the old-fashioned lace curtains. A large chifferobe took the place of a closet. A bed, bureau, and a nightstand were the only other furniture in the rather small room. The wallpaper danced dizzily around the walls, displaying large, green, unrecognizable flowers, while a faded, muted green rug lay complacently on the floor.

"Very nice," said Dani, more impressed with the spotlessness of the room than anything else.

"You don't have to be considerate of anyone's feelings, especially mine, regarding this house. This room, like most of the others, is stark and a little crude. Grandma may have been feisty but she was also quite frugal. Like my great-grandma, she was a mail order bride straight from

Scotland. Didn't believe in buying anything new just because what she had was out-of-date. If it was servicable, it stayed," said Scott.

"Does the house have plumbing?" Dani asked anxiously.

Scott smiled down at her. "Sure have. That was one improvement Grandma had no objection to. It's down at the end of the hall, shower and tub included. I'll go down and tell grandaddy he's not to make any passes at my girl."

As soon as Scott left, she opened her valise, grabbed her brush and a jar of moisturizer, then headed for the bathroom where she thoroughly washed her face, removing any vestige of makeup. The clean face made her feel like a new woman. She applied a thin film of the moisturizer on her skin, which felt as though fine sand had entered every pore. She brushed her short hair and hoped she got all the dust out. Finished, she put her things back and rushed downstairs to the two men waiting for her.

The three horses, with riders, moved along at a fairly good gallop over the flat landscape, their hooves kicking up the dust of the arid ground as the sun rippled heat waves in the distance.

"Getting tired, sugar?" asked Scott after they had been in the saddle almost an hour.

"A little," replied Dani. "This is the longest I've spent on a horse at this pace."

"It won't be long now," said Scott soothingly. "Then all you'll have to do is sit back and watch."

"If I'm still capable of sitting, you mean," retorted Dani.

"Aren't you a full-fledged horsewoman?" asked Angus.

"No, Angus. Scott has given me some lessons but I'm still somewhat of a novice. I confess I'm getting a bit sore."

Angus laughed heartily. "What you need, Dani, are some good hard calluses. We'll try to give them to you this weekend. In fact why don't you stay for the week? I could use my grandson around here for a while, and with you here, he certainly wouldn't be running around Texas like some itinerant farm hand."

"I'd like to, Angus. But I have a business to run and a living to make. Thanks for the offer anyway."

"We could go to Inveraray. You'd . . ."

"Grandaddy . . . Dani is a very successful kitchen designer and doesn't want to jeopardize her position in the field. I promised to have her back Sunday night, and I don't break my promises," interjected

Scott, his rugged face stern, as his eyes tossed his grandfather a warning.

"What in heaven's name are those?" asked Dani, staring wideeyed at odd, stationary creatures sitting atop old posts with their huge wings spread ominously.

"Turkey vultures," Angus informed her.

"Why are their wings out like that when they don't look like they are about to fly anywhere?" she asked.

"Sunning themselves," said Scott.

"They're ugly. That naked red head . . . weird," commented Dani.

"They have their use. They're valuable scavengers. Keep West Texas clean," said Scott.

"There they are," exclaimed Angus putting his heels to the horse, spurring the creature to an all-out sprint.

"The old boy can still ride a horse," said Scott, warmly gazing after Angus as he kept his own pace at a lope to match Dani's.

"You're very fond of him, aren't you?"

Scott pushed his hat back, looked at her, and smiled. "Grandaddy is an exceptional man. Never saw him lose his temper, regardless of what happened. For all his bluster and apparent toughness, he's a very gentle man. And shrewd. He has an intuitive judgment when it comes to sizing up people. He seldom misjudges a person's character, a talent that has done well by him."

They rode up to the group of smiling, dusty men where Dani was promptly introduced all around, shaking their hands with a grip equal to their own.

"Where are your horses?" she directed the question to the group.

"The only thing we saddle up around here is our pickup or jeep," replied one of the men with a grin.

"Then I'm not going to see a roundup?" Dani asked Scott.

"Sure you are, sugar."

"With riding and roping?"

Scott laughed as he put his arm around her waist and steered her to one of the large fenced-in pens. "Not exactly. A plane gathers most of them from the prairie, then the boys go out and drive the cattle up toward the pens here."

"Suppose there are strays?"

"The plane spots them from the air, then radios their position to the men in the trucks, all of whom have radios," said Scott, as automotive engines started up. Soon all vehicles were gone, and Angus sauntered over to Scott and Dani.

"It won't be long now," drawled Angus.

"Scott tells me there won't be any roping. Don't you have to chase the calves by horse to rope and brand them?" asked Dani.

"Branding is done in the spring, Dani. And we don't rope them anymore. They're driven into a pen, then forced, one by one, into a squeeze box, which is nothing more than a slatted, wooden box whose sides can be thrust together to hold the calf absolutely still. The critter is branded and given his inoculation at the same time. A lot quicker and easier than roping and hog-tying them," explained Angus.

"Don't the men ever ride horses?" She was a little disappointed by the intrusion of modernity. She had hoped to see and, in a way, be part of a wild-west show.

"Sure do, sugar. Sometimes the cattle get into mountainous terrain where the jeeps and trucks are useless. We resort to the old methods then," said Scott.

"Cowboys on horses to ride herd are so much more romantic," declared Dani.

"Cow punching isn't very romantic when a norther comes thumping over the prairie. A hard, fierce wind driving dust in such large particles you can hardly see the sky, as those sandy particles choke your throat, fill your nostrils and ears and make it almost impossible to open your eyes, as the temperature suddenly drops. Sometimes there was more sand in my chili than beans," said Angus. "Then there's the words no cowboy likes to hear. 'Tie your hats to the saddle horn boys. The herd's broke.' You can lose men, horses, and cattle in a stampede. It's a long hard ride. You don't eat. You don't sleep. It may look romantic on the big, silver screen, but when you have to live it, you get a different perspective. Why, I remember when we were driving a herd to . . ." His voice was drowned out by the lowing of cattle moving fast on the horizon.

Scott moved quickly to open the gates on the three huge holding pens, then mounted his horse, one long leg easily and swiftly rising, his foot coming to rest firmly in the other stirrup.

Dani watched Scott put his horse through its paces as the cattle approached the pens. For the first time she truly knew what the phrase "tall in the saddle" meant and her heart filled with pride and love as she continued to stare at him, totally unaware that Angus was staring at her.

Her attention was soon diverted by the noise, dust, and energy of the cattle as they began to fill the pens. Engines were being turned off and wide-brimmed hats were being slapped against cattle hides as the men urged the few remaining beasts into the pens.

"What now, Angus?" shouted Dani over the lowering of the cattle, her face and throat coated with the ever-rising dust.

"We cut out what isn't going to market, turn them loose, then load the rest on trucks to be taken to pens where they'll be fattened up a little more before market," answered Angus.

"I don't see Scott. Where's he gone to?"

"Lost on the prairie, I hope. It's about time I had me a pretty and young woman all to myself. That grandson of mine hasn't let me have a minute alone with you," said Angus flashing a smile that was so familiar to her. "Why don't we ride back to the house and leave him here?"

"I couldn't," said Dani with a impish grin.

"And why not?"

She masked her face with a certain seriousness. "I don't know if I could control myself if I was alone with you. You're a very attractive man."

"Are you trying to tease an old man?"

"Yes."

"Why?" asked Angus with an amused look.

"Because without the old man, there never would have been a grandson with such character of face," she said.

"I get the impression you'd much rather be with my unsettled grandson than with me."

"I'd much rather have something cold to drink than be with either of you."

Angus laughed loudly and strongly. "Nothing I like better than a gal that speaks her mind. Don't worry, Dani. The chuck wagon will be here soon. It'll have all the cold drink you want."

"With ice?" Her blue eyes widened.

"With ice," he assured her. "A far cry from the old days when the mess wagon jolted and bounced along, creaking itself ahead of the moving herd so Cookie could have the noon meal ready when we caught up to it. Fires of mesquite heating the black cast-iron pot held by a tripod, an old enameled coffee pot resting on the coals. Beans with dollops of salt pork, hot biscuits . . . I can almost smell it now."

"Is that what we are going to have for lunch?"

"Our mobil chuck wagon is a rolling cafeteria these days. Tacos, enchiladas, burritos, empanadeas, hamburgers, sandwiches, hot tea and coffee, iced tea, soda. It's geared to everyone's taste," replied Angus, as Scott dashed up, reining in his horse so quickly the horse reared.

"Dani . . . get on your horse. We're off to rescue a dogie," said Scott enthusiastically.

"Dogie?"

"A motherless calf," explained Angus, then to Scott, "What the devil do you need her for? Go get the critter yourself. I'm having me a fine time with Dani. Go get your own ladyfriend."

"I've got the only ladyfriend I want, Grandaddy. And no old buckeroo is going to steal her from me. Get in the saddle, Dani, before this old coot tries to steal you away from me," said Scott smiling.

"And don't you think I couldn't, young fella. You'd better go with him, Dani, before he starts bucking like a bronc that's gone loco. I'll see you at lunch."

As Dani and Scott kept their horses at an easy gait over the range, she asked, "Why didn't one of the pickups go out for the calf?"

"Simple. I wanted to be alone with you for a minute or two. Grandaddy has an afternoon of sightseeing planned for us. He wants you to see the Rio Grande and Big Bend National Park."

"That's quite a ways from here, isn't it?"

"Not by plane."

"You seem to have a special relationship with your grandfather."

"What makes you say that?"

"Oh, the banter between you two a little while ago."

"He enjoys it. Makes him feel more than just a grandaddy. More like a very good friend and companion. What do you think of him?"

"He amazes me. His mind is as clear as a bell and physically, he seems to be a forty-year-old instead of an octogenarian. I think the world would pay a small fortune to learn his secret of health and longevity. Do you know what it is?"

"I asked him once and he said, 'Hard work, a good woman, and chili peppers.' His stomach must be a raging inferno, for he's a champion at eating chili peppers. When I was fifteen, he challenged me to a chili pepper eating contest. I matched him pepper for pepper until tears were

streaming from my eyes. I no longer felt my mouth, fire had destroyed
my stomach, and there was Grandaddy sitting there grinning at me as
though he was eating ice cream," said Scott with a wistful smile.

"Who won?"

"Is there any doubt? Grandaddy, of course."

"Your grandfather seems to have been very much in love with his
wife. How long has she been gone?" asked Dani.

"She's been dead a long time now. Maybe twenty years. And he was
deeply in love with her," replied Scott.

"Twenty years? And he never remarried?"

"You'll find the men in our family are strictly one-woman men. It
might take us a mite longer than others to find the right woman, but
when we do, it's for life."

"I thought your grandmother was a mail-order bride. How could
your grandfather know she was the one for him?"

"Some distant relatives in Scotland sent her picture. Grandaddy
wrote to her and they exchanged letters for over a year before he could
convince her to come to Texas. As Grandaddy tells it, on the day she
arrived at the railroad station, they took one look at each other, and
were married the next day."

"Sounds like a whirlwind courtship."

"When we see what we want, we don't hesitate to go after it." He
looked over at her and smiled that familiar crooked grin. A weak, raspy
bawl caught his attention. "There she is. You stay here, Dani."

She watched him swing from the saddle gracefully, then tether his
horse to a small mesquite tree. Talking low in his soft Texas drawl,
Scott uttered soothing words to the bewildered calf. There was a mountain of warmth and love in Dani's eyes when she saw him gently lift the
frightened animal. Scott's ample muscles tightened and bulged under
the weight of the calf as he placed it in front of his saddle, gangly legs
dangling over either side of the patient horse. Gathering the reins from
the mesquite, Scott mounted, holding them in one hand while placing a
staying hand on the calf. They turned their horses and slowly went back
to the corrals.

"I see you got the dogie all right," said Angus, as one of the men took
the calf from Scott's horse.

"Did you think for one minute I wouldn't?"

"Had my doubts for a while. Thought you'd take Dani off when you saw how attractive she found me," said Angus with a quick wink at Dani.

"Almost did, Grandaddy, almost did." Scott dismounted then went to hold his arms up to catch Dani as she dismounted.

In the distance a silver box shimmered in the ground heat waves like a ghostly spectre in a mirage. Wide grins spread over the faces of the mechanized cowboys. They knew what the undulating image was. The chuck wagon.

Dani had been to innumerable cocktail and garden parties and fancy luncheons, but never had she experienced anything like a chow line on the range. There was no desultory conversation, no sentences with double-edged meanings, no idle gossip, no ponderous business discussions, no inane banter to be polite. Instead there was stories of various experiences, real and imagined, related with bravado, as they all sat around munching on their chosen lunch. The men included Dani in their talk as if it was the most natural thing in the world, and she was surprised to find she was actually enjoying herself in an open, natural way.

When the meal was over, the men went back to work. Angus watched Dani and Scott mount their horses almost in unison, smiled, then followed suit.

At the house they exchanged the horses for a pickup truck. Scott drove and Dani sat between him and Angus as they headed to the field where the plane awaited them. Angus gave a running account of his boyhood escapades as the pickup bumped its way over the rutted, well-worn dirt road. They settled in the plane and Dani was a little surprised how matter-of-fact Angus accepted his airborne existence. She had expected a land-bound man, used to horses and trucks, to be a bit squeamish about going up in a light aircraft. But he seemed to be comfortable and at home as Scott took the plane aloft and headed south.

Dani looked down at the flat, barren land that had the appearance of the aftermath of an atomic blast. Nothing but empty and desolate country which God had seemingly forgotten about. Then she saw them. Huge green discs like giant plates filled with spinach surrounded by ochre-colored parched earth.

"What are those down there?" she asked.

"Circles of wheat or alfalfa, each about one hundred and thirty-five acres," answered Angus, who was seated behind Scott and Dani. "A sprinkler working off a center pivot keeps them watered. An expensive way to farm. Sometimes the crop doesn't bring as much on the market as it costs to raise it."

"There's Big Bend up ahead," announced Scott.

Dani narrowed her eyes but could barely discern the gray mountains. Not until they were flying directly over them did she get an opportunity to admire the stark beauty of the cragged mountains, sloping plains, mesas, and hills of the desert's rugged terrain. The pale green—at times gray—Rio Grande had sliced through the rock to create deep, majestic canyons.

"When the Spanish came to Big Bend in the mid-sixteenth century, they called it El Despoblado—the uninhabited land," Angus informed them. "Hot, dry summers are long. Even the critters stay in the shade. They have a lot more sense than the tourists."

"I can see trees and grass down there," said Dani.

"There are some flood plains. And the vegetation is starting to come back," said Scott.

"Come back? What happened to it?" asked Dani.

"Sections of the Park were ranchland around the turn of the century. Herds of cattle, horses, goats, and sheep overgrazed the land, stripping it bare, leaving no roots to regenerate," explained Angus. "It became a National Park in 1944. It's beauty is slowly returning."

"It's also one of the last havens for the mountain lion and peregrine falcon," added Scott. After a few more passes over the enormous park called Big Bend, Scott veered the plane northward.

"Going home already?" asked Angus. "I haven't showed Dani all the park yet."

"Gas, Grandaddy, gas. I've got just enough to get back," said Scott. "Besides Dani and I have big plans for tonight, don't we sugar?"

Dani looked at him quizzically. But the angled planes of his handsome face melted any questions in her mind. She knew she'd go anywhere with the man seated beside her, his blue-gray eyes squinting into the endless sky.

12

Dani sat on the wooden swing with Angus, its movement slight, while Scott half sat on the porch railing facing them. The lowering sun cast a rosy glow over the land, house, and porch. If the pickup truck hadn't been parked so close to the house, one would think the scene was taking place in the eighteenth century. Dani's loose, white, off-the-shoulder blouse and full skirt of calico cotton emphasized her femininity as she sat talking to the two lean men dressed in hard-used denims, boots, and shirts.

"That was a marvelous meal. Rosa is a fine cook," said Dani.

"Rosa was mighty pleased you like it. Doesn't get much praise from me," said Angus. "Has Scottie subjected you to his brand of cooking yet?"

"Yes. He's quite the chef. I almost needed the Dallas Fire Department after eating his chili," said Dani, her eyes and lips smiling as she turned to glance at Scott, before her attention went back to Angus. "Do you cook too, Angus?"

"Can't even brew coffee," he replied. "Scottie takes after his great-grandaddy. Now there was a man who could cook. He could make a feast out of thin air on the prairie. His rabbit stew would set your mouth to watering at the first sniff."

"Did he make chili too?" asked Dani.

"Did he make chili? Why little lady, does a gopher dig holes? The entire Gulf of Mexico couldn't put out the fire in your belly after a spoonful of his chili. And his rice and beans would keep a man straight in the saddle all day long."

"Didn't your mother cook at all?" asked Dani.

"Momma died when I was eight. Daddy became mother and father."

"How sad for you." Dani was genuinely moved.

"Don't feel sorry for me, Dani. Daddy and I had a fine life, not to say

I didn't love Momma. I did. But she suffered a good deal, and God taking her was for the best. Daddy did get a housekeeper to ride rough-shod over me," said Angus. "You're quiet tonight, Scottie. Am I too much competition for you?"

"I'm just loosening the reins so you can have the lead. My turn will come later." Scott smiled that crooked, confident smile of his as his eyes shifted from his grandfather to Dani.

"Later? It's getting on time to turn in. Don't forget we get up around five out here," said Angus.

"Five?" queried Dani with astonishment.

"Not you, sugar. Only Grandaddy and I. You can sleep as late as you wish," said Scott.

"I hope you're not going to keep her out all night," said Angus.

"I might," retorted Scott. "After all, it's Saturday night, Grandaddy."

"I suppose you're taking her to Queenie's," surmised Angus.

"One's got to do a little stomping on a Saturday night," said Scott, his mirth obvious.

"Queenie's?" Dani's head was swiveling from one man to the other as though at a tennis match.

"A saloon," said Angus grimly. "You know I don't approve, Scottie."

Scott laughed. "Oh, Grandaddy, when will you realize the women of Texas are not the women of yesteryear. Saloons today are cafés where virtuous women can participate as openly as men."

"Still . . . they have a tendency to become a bit rowdy down at Queenie's. I wouldn't want Dani to get the wrong impression of us here in West Texas," argued Angus.

"You know I wouldn't take Dani anywhere that wasn't suitable. It was back in your day when Queenie's was rowdy. It's quite subdued nowadays," said Scott before looking down at his watch. "I think we'd better get going, sugar, if we're going to get a good night's dancing in."

"I'm ready whenever you are," said Dani, rising from the swing.

Angus also left the swing and put his hands on Dani's shoulders. "I'll say my goodnight now. I'll be asleep by the time you come back." He kissed her lightly on the cheek.

"Now, Grandaddy, don't you be taking privileges you aren't entitled to," said Scott good-naturedly.

"Never saw a man so jealous," said Angus shaking his head. "Good-night, Dani. Good to have you here."

"Goodnight, Angus," said Dani, as Scott came to stand beside her and slip his arm around her waist before he led her to the pickup.

Queenie's was a fairly large hall with a bar at the far end and a small raised stage at the other. A good-sized dance floor spread its bare wood before the stage. Between the dance floor and the bar were numerous tables and chairs, bare of any decoration. The hall was dim and hazy with smoke. The smell of leather and hay mingled with that of whisky and beer. Shouts of greeting hailed Scott as they entered. He ushered her to a table and they sat down. A short, burly man, carrying a tray, materialized and deposited the contents of the tray on their table— nachos, pretzels, a pitcher of iced tea, and two glasses.

"Long time no see, Scottie. Visiting Angus, are you?" asked the man, his words heavy with a Texan drawl.

"Have to keep the ole boy on his toes every so often. Queenie, I'd like you to meet Dani," said Scott.

"Howdy, Dani."

"Hello, Queenie," greeted Dani with a question in her tone.

"My real name is Roy. I bought the place from Queenie a long time ago, but the boys think it's real cute calling me Queenie. Would you care for something other than tea, Dani?" asked Roy.

"No, thank you. Iced tea is fine."

"If you want anything else, Scottie, just yell. Nice to have met you, Dani." He quickly moved away to answer a yell of Queenie.

"He seems to know you and your tastes quite well," said Dani, reaching for a pretzel.

"There was a time I spent a few years at the ranch and used to come here every Saturday night. No one ever forgets someone who drinks only iced tea when there is a bar handy," said Scott as he poured the iced tea.

"Did you bring a ladyfriend with you?"

"Jealous?"

"No. Curious."

"Sometimes. If I didn't have the time to make a date, there was always a spare woman around here."

"Don't tell me you didn't have a steady girl when you stayed here during those years."

"Only went with a girl once, when I was in my early twenties. Didn't know any better, I guess."

"Oh? A tale of unrequited love?" asked Dani.

"No. I dumped her."

"Would it be too personal if I asked you why?"

He shrugged indifferently. "She kept pushing marriage at me. Guess I wasn't ready to be hog-tied and branded."

"Do you ever think about her?" For some reason, Dani prayed the answer would be no.

"Nope. I've found the one I want, the one I care for and love." He reached across the table and took her hand in his.

"Would it bother you to see me with another man?" teased Dani, holding tight to his hand.

"I'd strap on my six-shooter and gun him down. Let's dance."

With their arms around each other, their bodies molded as one, they moved around the dance floor to the sad tune of a lost love. Her arms soon circled his neck, and she laid her head against his chest. She felt his cheek come to rest on the top of her head and it seemed his arms wrapped almost twice around her waist. The hard sinews of his thighs pressed against hers, his heartbeat strong and solid, his arms forceful and protective. Her heart swelled with love for the man, and the very existence of Dallas vanished from her mind. She noticed their feet moving less and less as their clasped bodies found swaying to the music far more sweet.

Scott's head lifted, and he whispered, "Dani."

She raised her face to his and smiled. His lips touched hers briefly, then again and again, until their mouths clung with a lusty appetite. An undulating heat rose within her and her nerve endings danced in a wild frenzy, even though she was almost standing still. She pulled her lips from his and stared into his half-closed eyes peering down at her.

"I think we'd better go back to the table and wait until they play something a little faster," she said hoarsely.

He smiled, his lips angular, and led her back to the table. People came to the table, chatted amiably for a while, then left to be supplanted by others. In between visits, they danced every fast dance the small western band played. Scott seemed to be deliberately avoiding the slow tunes, for which Dani was grateful. Being locked so close in his arms was a strain on her self-control, and she sensed it wasn't that easy for Scott either. It was after eleven at night before they left.

"That's more of a workout than a health spa," commented Dani when they were in the pickup.

"You're getting so you stomp pretty good. Keeps one in shape." He quickly glanced at her then turned his eyes back to the road. "I've told you about my past. What about you? Ever have any serious relationship with a man?"

"Do you mean have I ever been in love?"

"I guess so."

"Once."

"Did you love him very much?" asked Scott, his face a somber mask.

"Very."

"What happened?"

"I moved on."

"You left him behind in Iowa?"

"Yes."

"Do you still love him?"

"I'll always love him." Dani smiled furtively when she saw the hard set of his jaw, his eyes narrowing.

"Want to talk about it?"

"I'd love to," said Dani, deciding not to continue teasing him. "I was nine years old and he was a history teacher in his thirties, married and with a family. I thought he was the handsomest man I ever saw and so knowledgeable. I fell in love instantly. Unfortunately, I spent most of my time in class mooning over him instead of learning history." She noticed Scott visibly relax, a smile creeping to his lips and into his eyes.

"No one since?"

"No. Who could measure up to a nine-year-old's vision of an ideal man?"

"I could make a suggestion." He glanced over at her and gave a broad smile, his white, even teeth visible in the dark cab of the pickup.

It wasn't long before he was parking the truck by the old farmhouse. As Dani headed for the porch, Scott took hold of her arm and tucked it in his.

"I want to show you something," he said, leading her in the opposite direction.

"At this time of night? I thought you had to get up early in the morning."

"I'll manage. There's something you said you wanted to see, and there's no time like the present."

He led her across the yard to a hay wagon and lifted her onto it before climbing up himself.

"Don't tell me we're going on a hay ride." She gave him a puzzled smile.

"Nope. Look up."

A canopy of dark velvet was proudly displaying its twinkling lights like a jeweler flaunting perfect diamonds. The absence of a full moon enhanced the clarity of the stars. Scott lay back in the hay, his hands folded under his head.

"No city lights. No mountains or trees on the horizon to obscure the full panorama of the sky. Isn't that what you wanted?" asked Scott.

"It's beautiful!" exclaimed Dani.

"Lie back so that pretty little neck of yours doesn't get a crick."

Dani lay back and, enraptured by the beauty of the night sky, said nothing for a while.

"Over toward the east is the constellation Orion." He took one of his hands from behind his head and pointed. "You can always spot Orion by the three bright stars in a row. They are supposed to be the hunter-god's belt and the bright star, Betelgeuse, on the northern end, while kitty-cornered from it is Orion's other bright star, Rigel. Over there . . ." his pointed finger moved in an arc ". . . is the Little Dipper. The last visible star in it's handle is Polaris or the North Star. Can you make it out?" asked Scott.

Dani hesitated, then gleefully announced, "Yes . . . yes . . . now I see it!"

"Go back to Orion."

Her eyes shifted.

"Can you find it?"

"I think so. There . . . the three stars together."

"Right! Move your eyes a little to the west. That bright star is Aldebaran, the brightest star in the constellation Taurus. And if you keep moving your eyes west, you'll see a tight cluster of stars—Pleiades." He continued to spot the constellations and their brightest stars for her with phenomenal expertise.

"You amaze me, Scott," said Dani, truly stunned by this side of him she never dreamed existed. "Where did you learn all that?"

"Sitting alone on the prairie at night with only the stars to look at started me wondering about them. Got me some books on astronomy, a small telescope, and I was in business."

"Have you ever seen the rings of Saturn?"

"Sure. The first time I saw them, I let out a whoop that scared the skin off the coyotes. I think that was one of the biggest thrills of my life," said Scott.

"What were some of the others?"

"Getting my first horse. Riding herd with Grandaddy. And last, but certainly not least, meeting you." He rolled onto his side and gazed down at her. "What were yours?"

"My first long evening gown. Getting my driver's license, and receiving that condo contract from Nick Hunt," replied Dani.

"Is that all?"

She looked at him and smiled. "Well . . . maybe learning to dance slow, Texas style, with a cowboy I know."

"Oh, Dani," he murmured softly.

His lips came to nibble at hers and one arm gathered her close as they lay in the soft hay. His hand traced over her cheek and jawbone as his lips began a more serious and passionate exploration of her mouth. He rubbed her jawbone between his thumb and forefinger before his hand worked its way through her hair to hold her head to his, while he savored the sweet depths of her mouth with tenderness.

Dani's hand swept around his neck, the other sliding across the broad expanse of his well-muscled back. She held him to her, delighting in the warmth and firmness of his body. Even the scent of him filled her nostrils with a rare pleasure. No man had ever made her feel like this. Her whole body tingled with joy as she eagerly joined his serpentine kiss with one of her own, releasing any remnant of inhibition that might still claim her. She arched her body, molding it to his as his lips played along her slender neck and his hands fired her senses to new and raging flames.

"Oh, Dani . . . how I love every part of you," whispered Scott between kisses. "Your blue eyes, your hair that sparkles red and gold in the sun, your soft lips, your fingers, the way you smile. I feel alive when you're in my arms and live in the glory of it."

"Oh, Scott . . . Scott. I . . ."

His mouth covered hers, and Dani let her hands, her body, her lips, express the deep emotions that were possessing her. His fingers worked magic on her flesh as they caressed with tender warmth, gently exploring her femininity. His lips moved over hers knowingly, and she nuzzled his neck with kisses of her own. She never realized love could be like this. So wondrous. So provocative. So stirring and electrifying. The tremulous glory of it all rushed through her body as Orion chased

Pleiades across the night sky. The shimmering stars now became gleeful spectators as they watched the two lovers in the hay wagon on the moonless prairie. They glittered and winked like crystal shards sharing a most delightful secret. When the passion below reached fruition, the stars applauded with barely visible meteor showers and a minor nova or two as the dusty Milky Way twirled through the heavens with approval.

Dani stirred as the bright morning sun spilled into the dated bedroom, the smile never leaving her lips. She moaned aloud and stretched in the large bed. Her eyes fluttered open and still she smiled. She reached for her watch on the nightstand, blinked her morning-misted eyes to focus on the tiny dial. Seven-thirty. She sat up and shook her head to clear it of the sleepy cobwebs. After a quick shower, she dressed, then dashed downstairs, eager to see Scott.

The house appeared to be empty. Dani found her way to the kitchen, where a smiling Rosa was preparing breakfast.

"Good morning, Rosa. Where is everyone?" Dani asked brightly.

"Good morning, Miss Wexford. They went out early to tend to the loading of the cattle. They'll be here in a few minutes to get their breakfast. Is there anything I can do for you?" asked Rosa.

"No thank you, Rosa. I'll go out on the porch and wait for them."

"Miss Wexford . . . how big a steak do you want?"

"Steak?" Dani's expression was one of disbelief.

"The men like chicken-fried steak with their breakfast along with grits, eggs, toast, and coffee," explained Rosa.

"Just grits, eggs, and toast will be fine for me, Rosa, no steak."

Rosa smiled and nodded. Dani left the kitchen and went to wait on the porch. She leaned against one of the columns that flanked the steps. Her eyes strayed to the horse barn and corral, then moved to gaze over the vast, empty prairie. She had never felt so alive in her life, never so satisfied with the world around her. She no longer cared that Scott Rowland was not of that dazzling world of Dallas. She no longer cared that she was a professional career woman and he was a plain cowboy. She was a woman and he was a man, all man. And she loved him, his cattle and his battered yellow pickup truck. She breathed deeply of the cool, crisp morning air, her lungs expanding with the joy of it.

In the distance she spied two tall men on horseback, Angus and Scott. She waved with exuberance and one horse broke into a frenzied gallop. Scott's horse skidded to a halt before the porch with Scott half off of it before it full stopped. Dani dashed down the steps into his open arms. He lifted her high in the air and twirled her about and then planted a solid kiss on her lips.

"You smell real good, sugar," said Scott as they held onto one another.

"And you smell of sweat and cattle."

"Object?"

"I love it." She smiled up at him.

"Is this a private admiration society or can anyone get a small token of recognition?" asked Angus as he slowly dismounted.

"Good morning, Angus," greeted Dani, her smile large enough for the whole world.

"How about a morning kiss for an old man who wouldn't presume to lift you into the air?" said Angus.

"On the cheek now, sugar," warned Scott. "Can't take a chance on his blood pressure rising."

On tiptoe, her hands on his shoulders, Dani kissed Angus lightly on the cheek. Angus swept his arm around her waist and led her into the house, saying, "There's nothing I like better than to be leading a pretty gal into my house early in the morning."

Dani went into the dining room and slowly sipped her orange juice while the men washed up. She cast a knowing smile at Scott when the men took their seats at the table. The smile was returned tenfold. Rosa served breakfast with a loving look in her eyes, a look that swung from Dani to Scott.

"No steak, Dani?" asked Angus.

"No. I haven't been out doing a day's work."

"And only one egg?" continued Angus.

"I seldom eat a large breakfast."

"She's only a slip of a gal, Grandaddy," defended Scott.

"Still . . . she should eat," grumbled Angus, while Scott gave Dani a smile and a wink.

With breakfast finished and more coffee served, Dani was casually looking around the dining room when her eyes rested on a ten-foot-long spear whose shaft was wrapped with multicolored beads. Great tufts of eagle feathers decorated it, while at the end, was a majestic plume.

"What is that over the fireplace?" asked Dani.

"A coup stick," replied Angus. "It is to the Indians what a scepter is to a monarch—a symbol of power, of a chief. That one, over the mantle, is said to have belonged to the great Comanche chief, Quanah Parker."

"Parker? Isn't that a peculiar name for an Indian?" asked Dani.

"Now there's a story . . ." began Angus.

"Now you've done it, sugar. Grandaddy's about to launch into one of his long-winded Indian tales."

"Really Scott, I'd like to hear it. I'm quite curious as to why an Indian had an English name. Please Angus, tell me about it," urged Dani.

"You have to understand the situation at the time, Dani. When Texas became independent of Mexico, the Comanches wanted peace, but they also wanted a large section of Texas to call their own. Now the Texas lawmakers weren't about to have any of that. They believed that any land not already settled by a white man was free to be settled by another white man. This made the Comanches meaner than rot-gut whiskey, and they just went looking for trouble.

"John Parker had a family of three dozen or so, including relatives and children. They settled a little east of what we now call Waco, and their settlement at that time, 1836, was considered border territories. Now the Comanches and the Kiowas were warned not to bother these frontier settlements, settlements the Indians believed were on their land. Well, that really put the hot juice on their feathers. They swooped down on John Parker's little fort, killed some of the defenders, and took five women captives. Some of the women were ransomed and told tales of such horror, the name Comanche became synonymous with cruelty.

"A female child, somewhere between nine and thirteen, did not return. One Cynthia Ann Parker. She became the wife of Nokoni, chief of the Nokoni Comanche. She bore him several children, and when her brother came to the village to take her away, she refused to leave. Many years later, she was forced to leave the Comanche camp along with her infant child. She and the baby died soon afterward. Her fifteen-year-old son stayed behind with his father. He became known as Quanah Parker, one of the greatest of the Comanche chiefs," concluded Angus.

"That's a fascinating story, Angus," exclaimed Dani. "Do you know any more like that?"

"That tale was only a spit in the river, sugar. Grandaddy could go on endlessly," said Scott.

"Was it a true story?" asked Dani.

"Of course it is a true story, Dani," said Angus. "Between the Comanche, Apache and Kiowas, the stories are many, and some of them so terrible it would make a snake lose its rattle. Why, for years along the Santa Fe Trail the cry of Kiowa struck terror into the hearts of men, women, and children. Tonight we'll sit around the fire, and I'll tell you tales that'll curl your fingernails."

"I'd really love to but I have to be back at work Monday morning. Scott said we would be leaving right after dinner."

"Why don't you call your office and tell them you won't be back for a few days?" suggested Angus.

"I'd really like to, but I can't. I have to interview a young lady for a position with my company," said Dani.

"You're hiring additional help, or is Sandy leaving?" asked Scott.

"Additional help. With the addition of multiple units, along with all the remodeling, it's becoming a handful for just Sandy and me. I intend to start teaching Sandy how to field measure. I'm beginning to find out I can't be everywhere at once," explained Dani.

"Dani," began Angus slowly. "A good businessman—or woman— always keeps his, or her, finger on the pulse of the business, but delegates the action and the legwork to subordinates. It keeps the mind clear of trivia, a vital necessity to get anywhere in your chosen field."

Dani looked at the old man as though she was seeing him for the first time. But his previously solemn demeanor slyly slipped back to one of ingenuousness. Yet his words stirred the business acumen in Dani. She suddenly realized there was more to this old man than herding cattle.

"Grandaddy, did you have any particular plans for today?" asked Scott.

"Sure did. Want to show Dani our spread here," replied Angus. "Why do you ask?"

"I thought I might fly Dani down to Padre Island for a swim."

Both men turned their attention to Dani as though she was the deciding factor. She looked from one face to the other, then said, "As long as we're here, why not take a look around. I had an airplane ride yesterday and will be flying back to Dallas tonight. I think that's enough flying for one weekend."

"Good. That settles it," declared Angus beaming broadly. He pushed his chair back and stood. "I'll go get one of the boys to saddle up the horses."

"Now why did you go and say that, sugar? Down on Padre Island I could have you all to myself," Scott said when Angus had left.

"I couldn't go off and leave him. He seems so tickled to have you here. It must get lonesome for him out here. Why doesn't he move to Dallas and be nearer his family?"

"You'd never pry Grandaddy from Inver . . . from the old homestead. If he couldn't hear and smell cattle, then he would be lonely." Scott braced his hands on the table and pushed himself up. "Let's go, sugar."

"Where will we be riding to?"

"Probably to the old family cemetery, then on to what was once a thriving old west town." Scott put his arm around her waist when they reached the porch. "The old town is deserted now, but Grandaddy keeps it up a bit. Never let's it get too run down. He feels there should be some authentic relic remaining in its original surroundings. He hates the way everything is moved to museums."

"And you? What do you think of museums?" asked Dani.

"I think they have their purpose in the scheme of things."

"I really have no idea of what you like and dislike, Scott. What kind of music do you like? art? literature?"

"You."

"Be serious."

"I am. Right now I can't think of anything else," said Scott as they approached Angus and the horses.

Dani was fascinated by the gravestones, with their antiquated and cryptic eulogies to those resting beneath. When they arrived at the abandoned town, she felt as though she had walked onto a movie set. They stopped back at the house for a long lunch, then got back on the horses and rode in the other direction.

Throughout the morning and afternoon, with Angus being quite garrulous, a new sense of herself began to pervade Dani. With a strange suddenness, she began to realize material things weren't half as important as she had thought. People, land, and the creatures that inhabit it were the true values in life. As they slowly headed back to the house, she glanced over at Scott, so tall and straight in the saddle, his sharp-boned, handsome profile set as his eyes squinted toward the horizon.

For dinner Scott grilled thick porterhouse steaks, Rosa supplying a large dish of home fries, an ample salad, and a deep bowl of fried peppers and onions.

When it was time for Scott and Dani to leave, Angus took them out in one of the battered pickups to the field that passed for an airstrip. He kissed Dani on the cheek and told her to come back again soon. There was a lot more for her to see.

The sun was low on the horizon when Scott landed the plane at Dallas. The yellow pickup reached Dani's house moments before the sky darkened.

"Want to come in for some coffee or iced tea?" asked Dani, as she put the key in the lock.

"Another time, sugar. I have a mountain of work to do over the next few days, and want to get an early jump on things," replied Scott, standing alongside her.

"I had a lovely weekend and your grandfather is a character—but a nice one."

"He's a good man . . . like his grandson. Look, sugar, I have to be gone for a few days. I'll call you the minute I get back." He bent down and kissed her lightly, almost indifferently, on the cheek.

"Thanks again for the weekend," she called, as he quickly went back to the truck.

Those were the words she spoke, but other words beat in her heart, words of love and longing. But she couldn't bring herself to say them when she sensed his sudden preoccupation. If only he had held her in his arms and kissed her with warm passion, her thoughts of love and desire would have tumbled aloud from her lips for him and all the world to hear. But his kiss was cool with a trace of disinterest, and his physical presence at her door was so fleeting, she was suddenly submerged in doubt. Had the night under the stars changed his feeling for her?

13

"Now that I've explained what your duties would be, do you think you'd like the job, Marge?" asked Dani.

"Oh yes," replied the nineteen-year-old, with obvious enthusiasm.

"When would you like to start?"

"I'll have to give the bank at least a week's notice. Would a week from today be all right?"

"Fine," replied Dani. After the happy young woman left, Dani turned to Sandy. "I think it will work out well for all of us. What do you think, Sandy?"

"She's real good with figures. That's why she went to the bank first. I think she'll pick up things around here quickly. The bookkeeping system is simple enough," replied Sandy.

"Well . . . I'll leave her in your hands for the first week, then I'll start taking you with me so you can grasp the essentials of field measuring. You're used to the cabinetry nomenclature, so learning to do layouts won't take you long to digest."

"I'll never be able to do the watercolors of the projected kitchens like you do," said Sandy.

Dani gave a small laugh. "I'll have to do something around here to earn my keep. Besides, I enjoy doing them. That reminds me, I have those two to deliver. I'd better get going. I won't be back before you leave for the day. After I deliver the paintings, I have another kitchen to measure, then I'm meeting Jan for dinner. Make sure you lock up."

"Always do."

Dani was late in arriving at the restaurant. After profuse apologies to Janice, they were shown to a table and promptly placed their orders.

"Where have you been all weekend?" asked Janice.

"I went to West Texas with Scott to meet his grandfather," replied Dani.

"Oh? First the mother and father. Now the grandfather. I get the nauseating feeling that all this is becoming serious between you and this cowboy. Is it?"

"You know, it's funny," began Dani smiling weakly. "Nick has never mentioned love, yet he's asked me to marry him. Scott is always declaring his love for me, but never mentions marriage. I don't know quite what to make of it."

"He's not going to, Dani. You'd better get it through your head that this Scott of yours is not about to be tied down by any woman. He probably declares his love for any woman who poses no threat to his freedom. But the minute it looks like the woman might make a claim on him, he cuts loose. Stay away from him, Dani. He sounds like a real heartbreaker. What have you told Nick?"

"Nothing."

"Isn't he pressing you for an answer to his proposal?"

"No. But I really haven't seen that much of him lately," replied Dani.

"Take my advice. Nail him down and quick. A man like Nick doesn't come along with a proposal every day. How's Sandy doing without Mr. Parasite?"

"From what I can see—good. It's certainly improved her wardrobe and general appearance. She now goes to the beauty parlor on a regular basis to have her hair done. Her clothes are still on the conservative side, but are more fashionable and expensive. She seems a lot surer of herself."

"Watch it! As her confidence grows, she might want a better position, one where she can be top banana," warned Janice. "Look at me! Started out as another real estate agent almost lost in the shuffle of a big firm. Now I have my own agency. Sandy might want her own kitchen business."

"I don't think so. She has all the importance and freedom where she is and also a piece of the action now. She's not the type to take on the headaches of running one's own business."

"Still, I think you might dangle a larger carrot before her."

"I already have. I hired Marge on a permanent basis to take over most of Sandy's duties while I teach Sandy my side of the business. The fieldwork and layouts are getting quite hectic for me to keep up with. I've realized I can't stay on top of everything myself."

"Especially if you're running off to West Texas every weekend."

Dani chose to ignore the trace of sarcasm in Janice's comment. "Going to West Texas did one thing for me. I'm beginning to see things in a different light."

"The world through rose-colored glasses?"

"Jan . . . I know you don't like Scott because he's not a mover and shaker of the high-powered world of finance and business. But please don't make fun of him."

"Oh Dani. The last thing in the world I want is to hurt your feelings. I don't want to see you get hurt, that's all. I won't make another disparaging remark about the cowboy. But do try to at least consider my thoughts on the man. Promise and I'll say no more."

"I promise."

"Now what do you see in a different light?"

"Land. I want you to find me a nice piece of land in the country," said Dani.

"Around Dallas?"

"Not necessarily."

"Good. Land values within a certain circumference of Dallas have become way overinflated. Give me a radius and I'll see what I can do," said Janice.

"No more than a five-hour drive one way."

"You'll have to give me the figure you want to spend."

"I'll have to go over my accounts. I'll call you tomorrow and let you know. Now what about the men in your life?" asked Dani.

"Regarding the tales of the men in my life, I can outstrip Scheherazade. Lately I've been seeing Jeffrey Matthews, a banker and a widower. Quite a hunk for a man in his late fifties." Janice went on to relate all the man's attributes in glowing terms.

Almost two weeks went by, and when Dani hadn't received any word from Scott, Janice's words came back to haunt her. The casualness he displayed at their parting had all the makings of a permanent parting. He had said a few days. After two weeks he could have made some effort to contact her if he really wanted to. The more she thought about it, the more she dwelled on Janice's words. Her cowboy had rode off into the sunset without her. The fact she hadn't heard from Nick in the same period of time never entered her head until he called.

"Nick! I haven't heard from you in a while. What's up?" she asked, as she switched the receiver from one ear to the other.

"I've been down in Houston going over architectural plans and arranging funding at the bank," replied Nick.

"Any problem?"

"No. Everything went as smooth as glass. I have some duplicate plans for you. You can pick them up anytime. But that isn't why I'm calling. Are you free Saturday?" asked Nick.

"All day?"

"No. From about five o'clock on."

"Sure. What's on?"

"Auctions, dinner, and a charity ball. It's a big affair. The elite of Dallas will be there," explained Nick.

"Formal?" asked Dani.

"Definitely."

"What are they going to auction off?"

"Nineteenth-century French art and horses."

Dani laughed. "That's an odd mixture. I certainly hope it's not going to be in the same room."

"Hardly," replied Nick with some amusement. "I'll pick you up around four-thirty. Saturday-night traffic can be a bit tricky, and I'd like to be there on time."

"Considering buying anything?"

"There's a couple of items I have my eye on. Do you have a catalog?"

"No. But I don't think I'll be buying anything. I've seen how high some artwork can go in Dallas."

"I'll send a messenger over with a catalog anyway. I may as well send the plans with him too. The catalog will give you an idea of what they're offering. See you Saturday."

Though she really wasn't in the mood to shop for a new gown, she knew Nick would expect her to wear an exceptional and dazzling gown. She spent all of Saturday morning and a fair part of the afternoon shopping for the gown and accessories. She spent more than she had intended, but she was glad she did when she saw the results in the mirror.

The gold lamé gown had huge but short puffed sleeves that rested off her shoulders and ended in the middle of her arm. The gold lamé wrapped tightly around her waist and diaphragm to flute upward in stiff pleats to cover her breasts, then billowed out in a generous full skirt that barely revealed the tips of her gold shoes. The envelope purse was of the same gold lamé material. A matching stole lined with gold silk completed the ensemble.

As always, Nick was prompt. When she opened the door for him, she could see the blatant look of admiration on his face.

"You are exquisite, Dani, positively exquisite. Tomorrow morning you'll be the talk of Dallas," claimed Nick, as they walked to the car. He opened the door of his Porsche, slammed it shut, then walked around to the other side and slipped into the bucket seat. After starting the car, he asked, "Did you see anything in the catalog that appealed to you?"

Dani couldn't help but laugh. "Oh, come, Nick. Nineteenth-century French impressionists? I couldn't afford the frame on one of those. Believe me, I'm not going to twitch a muscle at that auction. What interests you?"

"A small Degas drawing and a pen drawing by Van Gogh."

"Well, I hope you get them."

One would think a worldwide coronation was being held in the large building. The jewels and gowns worn by the women more than rivaled the crown jewels and the gem-encrusted brocades and silks of royalty. No two gowns were alike, as people milled about in the vast foyer waiting for the auctions to begin. The fashion houses of Dallas knew they would be finished if two women wore the same gown to the affair. Diamonds, rubies, and emeralds glittered at the throats, ears, wrists and fingers. By comparison, Dani's plain, gold chain choker and gold stud earrings were like penhens to peacocks. Still she felt as grand as the other ladies present. Coiffures ranged from elaborate to bizarre to simple, Dani's being among the latter. The drawl of native Texan voices flooded the room and seemingly bounced off the great crystal chandelier which hung stately from the high mirrored ceiling.

"Which is going to be held first? The horse or art auction?" asked Dani, slyly noting the furtive glances of awe and envy being cast at her and the elegant, handsome Nicholas Hunt.

"They'll be held simultaneously."

"Suppose one wants to attend both?"

"Horses they have to see in the flesh, while there are excellent photographs of the art work. All they have to do is decide what they want, set a limit, then have a proxy bid for them. Oh . . . I see someone I want to have a word with. Would you mind waiting here for a minute, Dani? I won't be long. Then we'll go directly into the auction room," said Nick.

"Go ahead. I'll be fine right here. Besides, it'll give me a chance to study the latest Dallas fashions," replied Dani.

Only a second or two passed when several women from the Garden Club joined Dani, all chatting amiably about clothes, jewels, and the latest in horticultural news. Dani was startled, and turned suddenly when a hand touched her shoulder.

"Agnes!" exclaimed Dani.

"Dani . . . how good to see you. I wasn't sure it was you at first. I never expected to see you here, and you look positively enchanting. Are you going to the art or horse auction?"

"The art auction. Is that why you're here?"

"Gracious, no. Tom has two horses in the auction. Will you be staying for the dinner and charity ball?"

"Yes."

"Oh, good. The children's wing at the hospital is one of my favorite charities. Scottie will be so happy to know you are here."

Dani felt as though a steel rod filled with dry ice had been shoved down her spine. Scott was back in Dallas and never called her. Her heart was thrown into the street for all to trample on. "Scott's in Dallas?"

"For now. The poor boy has been running around like a steer gone loco these past weeks. I sure hope he decides to stay in one place pretty soon. Tom and I can hardly wait for him to bring you out to the ranch again. We had such nice visits. We miss you, Dani," said Agnes, taking Dani's hand in hers. Suddenly Agnes's eyes slipped past Dani. "Oh . . . there's Tom now. I guess the auction is about to begin. He's making those funny little signs. Promise you'll come out and visit us soon."

Dani gave a weak nod and a feeble smile then stared vacantly as Agnes walked off. The thought that Scott was in Dallas and hadn't bothered to contact her numbed her senses. Slowly, it dawned on her that Janice was right. Scott was through with her. He made her fall in love with him, and when he saw that love growing in her, he bolted like a wild stallion that would never stand the bit between his teeth. Though her world was crumbling around her, she knew she had a long evening ahead of her, and she had to maintain a certain semblance of gaiety and sanity. Sanity would be the hard part. She prayed Scott wasn't at the auction. She wouldn't be able to bear seeing him, especially if he was with someone else. She wished she had never come to Dallas, never gone to Galveston or West Texas. But she quickly squashed the impulse to go home to Iowa. She was not one to run away from a situation. Besides, she had worked too hard to get where she was to let some itinerant cowboy topple her growing business. When Nick returned, she clutched his arm as though it were the only safe harbor in a growing storm.

"I see you know a few people here," said Nick, as he began to steer her through the spacious foyer toward the corridor that led to the auction gallery.

"Some of the ladies from the garden club," she informed him.

Before they could turn down the corridor, a tall, rangy figure cut them off. He was formally attired in an expensive, well-cut tuxedo which stressed his wide shoulders. The superb tailoring also enhanced his lithe hips and towering form. The tips of his black leather boots poked out from under the narrow pants. His sandy hair had the healthy glow of being carefully brushed, yet there was a casualness to it that was appealing, as it emphasized his widow's peak and broad forehead. He exuded a tremendous aura of male elegance and power that caused Dani to take a deep breath. It was Scott, but it was a Scott Rowland she had never seen, never knew existed. Still, those blue-gray eyes squinting down at her were too familiar, and she knew that beneath that polished exterior was the man who had captured her heart, then cruelly stomped on it.

"Hello, Scottie," greeted Nick. "Haven't seen you around in quite some time, especially at a function like this."

"Daddy has a couple of horses in the auction," replied Scott, his eyes never leaving Dani.

"Forgive me. This is Dani Wexford. Dani . . . Scottie Rowland," introduced Nick.

Dani's voice had fled. She was catatonic as Scott cooly surveyed her.

"Miss Wexford and I have met," said Scott.

"You'll have to excuse us, Scottie. There are a few items I intend to bid on, and I don't want to miss the start of the auction. Maybe we'll see you around later," said Nick, ushering a mute Dani past Scott to melt into the crowd moving down the corridor.

Like an automaton, Dani sat down. She stared straight ahead, not a muscle moving. Pictures and voices blurred in her brain. The brief encounter with Scott had had a devastating effect on her, sending her back to grassy fields outside Dallas and to the stark vistas of West Texas. She could feel the powerful magnetism that Scott engendered in her. It was as if he were sitting next to her, his arms tight and possessive as they embraced her. Once or twice Nick said something to her, and she nodded instinctively without being cognizant of the words spoken. Nick was concentrating so deeply on the works of art he never noticed Dani's state of mind.

"Well, that's it," said Nick standing, his smile broad and confident as he offered Dani his hand.

The din of chairs scraping and the increased babble of voices brought Dani out of her stupor. "Did you get the drawings you wanted, Nick?"

"Yes. In fact, I procured *two* Van Gogh drawings. They didn't command the high prices I thought they would. Did you enjoy the auction?" asked Nick as they walked out of the room.

"Oh, yes. Very much."

A thought that had lain dormant in Dani's brain during the art auction now began to blossom with urgency. Nick knew Scott. And seemed to know him quite well. Had Scott worked for Nick at one time? She could hardly wait to ask Nick, but with people coming to talk to them and Nick stopping to chat occasionally, it was next to impossible. She would have to wait until they sat down to dinner. Her demeanor was calm, her conversation amiable, but a volcano was erupting inside her. It was with an enormous sense of relief she let Nick put his hand on her waist to guide her into the vast dining room that boasted a bandstand and spacious dance floor. Dismay crept over her when she saw most of the tables were set for groups of six. She wanted to be alone with Nick to question him about Scott. The fates were on her side, for they were shown to one of the many tables for two marching around the room.

"Where are your newly acquired treasures, Nick?" asked Dani, as the waiter held her chair.

"They'll be sent directly to my apartment tomorrow. I couldn't see lugging them around all evening." Then, noticing the waiter standing patiently by the table, Nick asked, "Do you want something to drink, Dani?"

"Yes. A double vodka martini," she replied. She had to have something to stop her knees from trembling and her heart from fluttering.

"Scotch on the rocks for me," said Nick to the waiter, who quickly and wordlessly departed.

"There's no menu," observed Dani.

"No. Everyone is being served the same thing. I believe it starts with shrimp scampi and deviled crab, oxtail soup, salad, then rib roast, potato, and vegetable. I forgot what the dessert was. Did you see anything at the art auction that struck your fancy?"

"Not really. I think the paintings I favor most from that period are hanging in museums and are probably priceless."

"I know what you mean. Some of the oils went for a fabulous sum. Where did you meet Scottie Rowland?" asked Nick as the waiter placed their drinks on the table.

"He dropped into the office one day wanting a new kitchen for his mother," answered Dani, happy that Nick brought up the topic first. In her mind she had been trying to find the right words to bring up the subject of Scott.

"Oh. Then he did take my recommendation."

"Your recommendation?" asked Dani.

"He asked me if I knew of a good kitchen man. I had just gone over your layouts and prices on the condos. Of course I hadn't met you yet, and I told Scottie you seemed to know what you were doing and the price was right. I guess he took me at my word," explained Nick.

"How long have you known him?"

"Ever since I first came to Texas. He gave me my first condo to build."

"Scott?" Her eyes widened to their fullest.

"Why so incredulous?" Nick was smiling.

"I didn't know he was in the building business."

"Back then you would have. Scottie was the champion of playboys in Texas."

"Playboy?" She was beginning to wonder if there was something wrong with her hearing.

"I take it you have a totally different conception of Scottie Rowland."

"I thought he was a cowboy, an itinerant worker of some sort."

Nick laughed softly, then said, "Angus McPherson Rowland an itinerant laborer? Hardly, Dani. His grandfather, Angus McPherson, is one of the largest cattle and oil men in all of Texas. Why old Angus practically owns the city of Midland, not to mention acres that are probably counted in the millions. The old boy is quite a real estate holder too. Sizable pieces of property in Houston, Galveston, and Corpus Christi. He owns a lot of the tracts we are building homes and condos on in Houston, besides many of the office buildings there.

"Scottie decided to have a race with Angus. He was determined he would build up Dallas the way his grandfather expanded Houston. From what I heard, he bought up property like a wild man in and around Dallas. That was before I came. Well . . . you can see the results," said Nick.

"But I briefly saw his apartment one day. It was almost bare, and he was using a sleeping bag for a bed."

"Scottie's changed a lot in the past seven years. As far as the condo goes, he uses any empty condo in his buildings to bunk down in rather than driving all the way home. That way he's never too far from his offices in downtown Dallas."

"But the way he dresses and that old pickup truck he rides around in." Dani's mind persisted in her image of Scott Rowland. The man Nick was talking about was totally alien to her.

"Like I said, Scottie's changed a lot. Used to be suits from Savile

Row, big expensive cars—first class all the way. But around seven years ago, he dropped out of the high society of Dallas. In fact it was quite a surprise to see him here tonight. Come to think of it, this must be the first social function he's attended since he became Mr. Anonymous. I wonder if he plans to come out of his cocoon now," mused Nick.

Dani spooned the hot soup into her mouth without tasting it. She thought she had eaten some shrimp and crab too, but barely remembered it.

"His parents seem to be regular. They don't act as if they were all that wealthy. Their home is quite modest." Dani was finding it more than difficult to digest Nick's words.

"Tom Rowland? He's one of the top geologists in the country. And he also owns quite a number of oil wells in Oklahoma. I'd say the McPherson-Rowland clan are beyond being wealthy. I wouldn't be surprised if even they didn't know how much they are worth," said Nick.

Dani shook her head ruefully. "They live so frugally."

"Not really. I understand they have a beautiful old home in Galveston, a small mansion in Corpus Christi. But from what I hear, West Texas takes the cake. Old Angus had a castle from Scotland shipped there, stone by stone, and reconstructed the castle in all its authenticity. I hear it's quite a place, or should I say palace. Olympic-size swimming pool, tennis courts—all the little luxuries no millionaire should be without."

"I'm surprised Scott Rowland isn't married. He's what? Thirty or so?" Dani put her fork in her mouth mechanically as an anger started to grow within her. Scott had been playing her for a fool.

"He's about two years younger than me. I'd say he's around thirty-six. The matrons of Dallas have been trying to snag Scottie for their debutante daughters for years now. I guess you could say he is one of the most eligible bachelors in all of Texas. Maybe that's why he's making his reappearance in society, looking for a bride to carry on the family name. Speaking of marriage, I think I've given you a substantial amount of time to consider my offer, Dani."

"I know, Nick. You've been very patient. I . . . ."

Her well-thought-out refusal was interrupted by an announcement from the bandstand. Some one rattled off the amount the charity ball had taken in for the children's wing at the hospital. A few speeches were made, followed by the proclamation the ball was officially underway. The music started, and Dani realized she had eaten the entire meal without ever tasting it. Neither was she aware that Scott was swiftly making his way toward their table until he was standing so close she could feel the power emanating from his formidable physique. A pulse in her neck began to throb uncontrollably as he placed one hand on the back of her chair and, with his other hand braced on the table, lowered his face to meet hers. For a moment his eyes searched hers, sending spasmodic tremors along her spine.

"Would you care to dance, Miss Wexford?" asked Scott, his tone more of a command than a request, a warning in his eyes that, if she refused, he wouldn't hesitate to make a scene.

Forcing an imperious smile to her lips, she turned to Nick and asked, "Would you mind, Nick?"

"Not at all, Dani." Nick replied.

On the dance floor, Scott did not hold her the way he did in the cafés he had taken her to. It was all very proper. His hand lightly at her waist, her hand in his as they did a fox trot.

"What are you doing here with Nick Hunt?" asked Scott, a chill falling on each word.

"Having a good time." Her anger superseded all other emotions. By what right did he dare question her? "I wasn't aware my actions concerned you, Mr. Angus McPherson Rowland."

"I see Nick's been shooting his mouth off."

"At least he's honest with me."

"I've always been honest with you, Dani."

"Have you now?"

"Honest in the things that count."

" 'I'll call you in a few days, sugar,' " she mocked.

"Dani . . . let me explain," he began.

"You don't owe me any explanations, Scott. As far as I'm concerned you can come and go as you please. Just leave me alone." She tried to pull away, but his hand gripped hers, and his arm tightened around her waist.

"I tried to call you all morning and this afternoon. There was no answer."

"And what about the two weeks in between? The telephone system ceased to exist? Or were all your fingers broken? And why couldn't you have been honest with me and told me who you really are instead of letting me think you were some poor cowboy who hadn't found his niche in life?" she sputtered.

"You're angry . . ."

"Angry?" There was almost laughter in her voice. "Anger is hardly the word for what I feel. I feel like I've been taken on a roller coaster ride where the cars are spit off the highest point like a marble coming out of a shute and I don't like it one bit."

"Oh, sugar, right now you're upset. If you'll . . ."

"Don't you 'sugar' me, Scott Rowland. I've had enough of you and your insidious deceptions. I'd like to go back to my table now, if you don't mind."

"I can see there's no talking to you while you're in this mood."

"It's not a mood. It's a permanent state of mind."

"I'll be over first thing in the morning and cook breakfast for you, then we'll discuss this like two rational human beings."

"There's nothing further to discuss," she said coldly.

"There's more to discuss than you can imagine." He released her, cupped her elbow and led her back to the table where Nick was standing, engaged in a conversation with another man. "Tomorrow morning, Dani," Scott whispered in her ear then left.

After introducing her to the man with him, and some desultory conversation, Nick took her to the dance floor, where they danced until the band took a break.

"How come Scottie asked you to dance? That young, pretty woman at his table didn't seem too happy about it," said Nick after ordering another round of drinks for them.

"He wanted to tell me how much his mother likes the kitchen."

When the opportunity presented itself, her curiosity caused her to glance furtively around the room to locate Scott's table. There were Scott's parents, another older couple, and a lovely young woman sitting next to Scott. Suddenly his eyes caught hers and—across the wide, busy ballroom, and through all the laughter and conversation of the crowded room—conveyed a deep but incomprehensible meaning. It was though their eyes were irresistible magnets that no power could stop. Scott started to rise, but the young woman put a detaining hand on his arm, breaking the galvanizing field between Scott and Dani.

Dani and Nick danced often and ended up sitting at a table with a group of acquaintances. Earlier on, it didn't escape Dani's notice that the Rowland table was empty but none of its former occupants were on the dance floor. They had left the charity ball.

"How about dinner tomorrow night, Dani?" asked Nick as he walked her to the door. "We didn't get much chance to talk tonight. And I'll warn you right now, I'll expect an answer from you one way or the other."

"You'll have it, Nick. I'd ask you in, but I'm really bushed," said Dani. She wanted to be alone. Her head was a muddle of disconnected thoughts.

"It has been a long night." He leaned over and kissed her cheek. "We'll have a nice quiet dinner tomorrow."

14

Her hand flailed out trying to curb the incessant screech of the alarm clock. It was futile. She had to open her eyes and find the blasted thing. Why had she set it in the first place? It was Sunday morning. Her eyes flew open and she got out of bed immediately. Scott was coming for breakfast. A quick, cool shower washed the remnants of sleep from her. After dressing she started the coffee maker, then retrieved the Sunday paper from her step.

She poured her coffee, sat down at the table, and scooped out the society section first to see if there was a piece on the auction and ball last night. There was a large picture of Agnes and Tom Rowland standing in front of a horse which was said to have brought the highest bid of the evening. Dani sat back in her chair and sighed. Maybe she had been too rash. A man of Scott's wealth and position must be harassed by women wanting to marry him. Perhaps he assumed the role of plain cowboy to avoid money- or status-hungry women. Maybe he had a legitimate excuse for not calling her. This morning she was thinking clearer. She would listen to him with an open mind.

After the society page, she read the current world news, then the local news. She read the comics, the Arts and Entertainment section, the television schedule, the real estate ads. She scanned the advertisements, and with the exception of the sports page, every other part of the enormous *Dallas Morning News*. Having exhausted every aspect of the paper, she started to work the giant crossword puzzle with glances at her watch becoming more and more frequent.

The dial of her watch showed it to be a little past ten by the time she finished the crossword puzzle and three cups of coffee. She couldn't sit at the kitchen table any longer. She went into the living room and snapped the television set on. She didn't notice her foot was tapping impatiently as she blankly stared at the colorful screen. An anger, no— a rage, was building in her, a storm-tossed sea of raw emotions that seethed and blustered, ready to erupt at any moment. Scott was totally oblivious to her feelings. He thought nothing of blocking out her time, then never showing up. No telephone call. Nothing.

At lunch she dawdled with her potato salad and ham slices. Her stomach churned and her mind filled with all sorts of vilifications to hurl at Scott. She suddenly realized she was working herself into a fury over a man who evidently thought very little of her. She went to the telephone and dialed.

"Sandy . . . are you still going to the movies this afternoon?" asked Dani.

"Why, yes. But if you want me to come over and help you with something, it can wait," said Sandy.

"Never on Sunday, remember? I was wondering if you'd like some company."

"I'd love it."

"Good. I'll be right over."

Going to the movies with Sandy was the best idea she had had all day. By the time she returned home, she was considerably calmer, and not having much time to get ready before Nick picked her up for dinner gave her little time to dwell on Scott's unforgivable behavior. She had just put the finishing touches to her makeup when the door chimed. Nick's losing his touch, she thought. He's a few minutes early. On her way to the door, she grabbed her purse and was ready to leave without delay. With a smile, she flung the door open. The smile vanished and once more her heart swelled with rage.

"Scott!" Her eyes flashed tempestuously.

"Look, sugar, about this morning . . ."

"Go away and don't ever come here again," she ordered, her voice low and menacing.

"Please, Dani . . . let me come in. There's so much for us to talk about."

"On the contrary, there is nothing for us to talk about. Now if you'll excuse me, I'm expecting someone."

"Hunt again?"

"What if it is?" She thrust her chin forward in defiance.

"He's not for you, Dani, and you damn well know it," fumed Scott.

"I'll be the judge of who is for me and who isn't. And I would categorize you in the latter column. Nick's asked me to marry him, and I think we'd make a good team. I'm to give him my answer tonight, so will you please leave. He'll be here any minute."

"You can't marry Nick."

"Oh no? Well you just watch me. After all, you have your little society friends. I'm not in your league, so go away and let me get on with my life," she cried furiously.

"Listen to me, Dani . . ." began Scott but his sentence was cut off by the slam of a car door. He turned around to see the elegant and handsome Nicholas Hunt striding toward them.

"Hello, Scottie," said Nick with an amused smile, as he looked the man up and down. "You look like you've been playing in the oil field again."

Scott looked down at his oil-stained blue chambray shirt and tight, well-worn jeans. Automatically, his hand tried to brush the soaked stains away. He looked up, his eyes sliding past Nick. "New car, Nick?"

"Yes. She's a beauty, isn't she?" asked Nick, turning to look at his shiny Porsche.

Scott's gaze returned to Dani. "She sure is."

"You ought to get yourself one," said Nick.

"I've had every kind of sports car there is. I'll stick to my pickup."

"To each his own. Well, are you ready, Dani? I have reservations," said Nick.

"Quite ready." Dani slid her hand through Nick's crooked arm and, without a backward glance, walked to the Porsche.

It was a few days later when Dani met Janice for dinner at a comfortable but not posh restaurant. Since Sunday her mood was one of despair and hurt. And what made matters worse was the fact she knew she would never stop loving Scott. She had thought he would try and see her again, but he didn't, not a word or a note from him.

"You looked absolutely fabulous at the charity ball a few nights ago," remarked Janice, as she and Dani took their seats in the restaurant.

"I didn't know you were there, Jan."

"We left right after the dinner. I didn't get a chance to talk to you."

"We? Still the widowed banker?"

"Strangely enough, yes," replied Janice.

"Don't tell me you've finally found the right man."

"Whether he is the right man or not, we get along exceptionally well. Quite frankly I'm happy with that. What about you? You and Nick made a dazzling couple. The very symbol of all that is great about Dallas. Have you two set a date yet?"

"Sunday night he took me to dinner and I turned him down. It was all quite civilized and friendly."

"Oh Dani . . . why did you go and do that?"

"I don't love him. It's as simple as that."

"What has love got to do with it? Life isn't some romance novel or fairy tale where everyone gets to live happily ever after. Call Nick and tell him you've changed your mind before it's too late. Don't be foolish, Dani. Don't cling to some idyllic notion that one can live on love. Believe me, after a while you'll come to resent that a loafer like your cowboy is living off of you. He'll pull you down and break your heart," said Janice with deep sincerity.

Dani smiled. Janice knew she was irrevocably in love with Scott Rowland. But poor Janice didn't know who Scott really was, and Dani felt now was neither the time nor place to tell her. Besides, she needed time for the scars to heal before she could talk about Scott freely.

After a long, hard look at Dani, Janice decided to change the subject. "How's Marge working out?"

"Great. She reminds me of myself when I first got into the kitchen business. Her enthusiasm is infectious. And what is even more amazing, Sandy is developing a sense of humor."

"That's a minor miracle. By the way I'm still looking for a piece of land for you but haven't come across anything yet. A lot of people are pricing themselves right out of the market," declared Janice.

"Well . . . I can wait."

As the week drew to a close, Dani was pleased with both Sandy's and Marge's progress. Marge had an aptitude for the work and seemed to enjoy it. Sandy was becoming quite adept at field measuring the kitchens and it gave Dani more time to work on her drawings and layouts.

She spent most of her time working in the office, occasionally going out to measure a custom remodeling job.

It was almost the end of the day. Sandy was out in the field and wasn't expected back until Monday morning. Marge, seated at the desk, stretched her arms and let out a contented sigh before standing.

"Well the books are in tip-top shape," said Marge.

"You're doing a fine job, Marge," commented Dani looking up from her drawing board and putting her pencil down. "How do things look?"

"Well . . . the projected profits from the next quarter look like they are going to be quite sizable."

"In that case I think it's time you gave yourself a raise. Say twenty dollars a week. How does that sound?"

"Great!" exclaimed a smiling Marge, as she gathered up her things. She looked out the window and remarked absently, "I hope the rain holds off for a while. Why does it always seem to rain on a weekend?" She paused, an expression of wonder lighting her face. "Do you know anyone with a white Rolls-Royce, Dani? A chauffuered one at that."

"No." Dani left her drawing board and joined Marge at the window. Her eyes widened as a tall, lean man emerged from the sleek automobile. He wore a tailored gray suit, a white shirt with a black string tie, and a gray Stetson. "Good Lord! It's Angus!" exclaimed Dani, then made a dash for the door, reaching it as the bell chimed. "Hello, Angus. Won't you come in?"

"I sure will, little lady." He had a mischievous grin on his face which broadened when he saw Marge.

After brief introductions, Marge left, and Dani ushered Angus into the living room. "Can I get you something, Angus?"

"Nope. Don't have a lot of time. I want to have a talk with you, Dani."

Dani sat down on the couch and waved a hand in the air, motioning toward a chair. "Please sit down."

"Not here. Too many interruptions," declared Angus as he steadily stared at her.

"I don't understand."

"I want you to come to West Texas with me. You've never seen my real home, Inveraray. I want to show it to you."

"Now?"

"Yes."

"It's pretty short notice. I don't think . . ."

"Please humor an old man. And I don't say please to many people," said Angus grimly.

Dani gazed into those gray eyes and saw a sadness in them. It moved her. What harm would it do to humor an old man? Besides there was an urgent plea in those eyes. She didn't have the heart to refuse him. She could see it was very important to him that she go with him.

"Give me a minute to change out of these work clothes."

He nodded, and she went upstairs with the distinct feeling it all had something to do with Scott. Yes. That was it. Angus was taking her to see Scott and was trying to be clever about it. Scott probably told him that she would never come if she knew he would be there. A chill ran through her. The prospect of seeing Scott made her weak, as her thumping heart filled with elation. The old man was playing matchmaker. But was it with Scott's permission? Did Scott want to see her? She had been pretty curt with him at their last meeting. And to walk off with Nick, leaving him standing on her door step, was quite insulting. Maybe she was wrong. Maybe it had nothing to do with Scott. Secretly and unconsciously she prayed it did.

She slipped out of her slacks and blouse, stained by traces of watercolors, then washed her hands and face. After donning a pale yellow dress and buckling the white belt, she brushed her hair quickly, shoving her feet into yellow-strapped sandals. Grabbing her purse, she dashed downstairs to find Angus going through the portfolio of her watercolors which were not kitchen related.

"Hope you don't mind," said Angus, seeing her enter the living room.

"Not at all."

"You're quite good, Dani, quite good. In fact, I'd say you're very talented." He closed the portfolio and put it back where he found it. "Ready?"

"All set."

The Rolls-Royce cruised effortlessly down the Central Expressway to the LBJ Freeway and west, finally coming to a halt at the Dallas-Fort Worth Airport, where they boarded a private jet. The interior of the plane stunned Dani. It was like a plush living room with every modern convenience. Angus showed her where to sit and buckle up until they were airborne.

Once airborne Angus showed Dani around the plane with a certain amount of pride. There was a beautifully appointed bedroom and an adequate kitchen where Dani fixed herself and Angus a large glass of iced tea each. Back in the living area, Angus flavored his tea with his customary whiskey, then took a seat on the deep-cushioned sofa, with Dani sitting on a twin sofa opposite him. Angus regaled her with numerous tales of the various Southwest Indian tribes. Some caused horror to rise within her, others were rather amusing. Both of them refrained from mentioning Scott's name, for which Dani was grateful. Angus was an experienced raconteur. He seemed bent on keeping her entertained, and she had a suspicion it was to deflect her thoughts from anything too serious. For the most part, he succeeded.

After they landed, she followed Angus out of the plane and they walked across the tarmac of what could be described as a miniature municipal airport. Angus assisted her into the waiting car, his tales of the Old West never ceasing as the chauffeur drove the long, sleek car in silence.

When Angus finally fell silent, Dani glanced at his profile and trembled slightly at the familiar sharp planes. She quickly looked away, concentrating all her attention on the landscape. Then she saw it. A gray Scottish castle looming on the treed horizon shimmered in ghostly undulations on the heated prairie. As they drew closer, she perceived the battlements, the turrets, the parapets rising loftily in the clear blue sky. The mullioned windows toyed with the rays of the sun, then reflectively cast them back like glittering prisms. It was an awesome and glorious sight as the distance shortened. The great castle had all the qualities of a fairy tale structure that tried, in vain, to deny the fact it was bolted to the land of West Texas.

Angus led her up the aged, but solid and sturdy stone steps, and the great oaken door opened as though they had crossed a hidden beam. In reality, it was a human hand that caused the magical opening of the door. A fully liveried butler greeted them with a crisp English accent, then ushered them in. Dani's head swiveled slowly as her eyes took in the wonder of it all. The marble floors, the richly carved mahogany staircase and paneling. Statues cloaked in armor stood guard on either side of the entrance. Paintings which Dani recognized as museum pieces graced the walls. Electrified brass sconces marched around the foyer in measured distances. What she saw was opulence without ostentation, and she felt as though she had entered a bygone world.

"This way, Dani," said Angus, cupping her elbow and conducting her to a pair of heavy sliding doors. Effortlessly, Angus slid them open. "Go in, Dani. I'll be with you shortly. I have to see about dinner."

She walked in slowly, not quite knowing what to expect. Her vision fixed on the huge fireplace with its ornate mantel. Light swirled into the vast room through orieled windows at either end of the room. Thickly padded furniture was dispersed in a manner to please the eye and still be functional. She spun around when she heard the soft click of the sliding doors as Angus shut them. When she turned to face the fireplace again, there was Scott, standing as though he had materialized out of thin air. She realized he must have been sitting in the huge leather chair before the fireplace. She had only noticed the tall back of the chair. As she gazed at him, a powerful aura of masculinity emanated from him, as he stood there dressed in a white shirt, opened at the neck, the sleeves rolled to his elbows. The fawn colored pants clung to his sinewy legs, while dark brown lizard boots poked their pointed toes from under the cuffs of the pants.

In a way she knew he would be here, but the sight of him made her feel like a patient undergoing acupuncture, with the doctor using spears instead of fine needles. He smiled that crooked smile of his, and there was a trace of triumph about his lips. A confident arrogance glinted in his blue-gray eyes as they surveyed her. The proud and imperious expression on his face stirred in her all the pride and desire, pain and longing, anger and love that her emotions could conceive. She wanted to run to him, beat him on the chest, then fall lovingly into his arms. Instead she stood there mute.

"Aren't you going to say hello?" asked Scott.

"Hello."

"Why don't you sit down?"

A short, quick sigh escaped her lips, and with an air of weary resignation, she walked to the large sofa and sat down. "Why this elaborate subterfuge, Scott?"

"After Sunday's fiasco, I felt if I called you'd hang up, and if I came to the house, you'd probably shut the door in my face. I don't suppose I'd blame you if you did. I seemed to have gone about this all wrong. You still have that look of anger in your eyes."

"Why did you have your grandfather drag me all the way out here?"

"Would you have come with me?"

She looked down at her hands, clutching her purse in her lap, and she wondered if she would have. She knew one thing though. If he had told

her to make plans to come here and then didn't show, it truly would
have been over between them.

"No. I don't think you would have. You'd probably think I'd only
stand you up again," said Scott. "I wanted to talk to you some place
where you couldn't walk away from me, where there would be no interruptions from unexpected guests or the telephone. Here we have absolute privacy. Will you hear me out, Dani?"

"Do I have a choice?"

His wide shoulders lifted as he took a deep breath and rested his arm
on the mantel. "Do you want one?"

She looked up at him and stood. She felt he had once again tricked
her, and it made her perverse. "Yes. I want to go back to Dallas right
now."

He left the fireplace and came to stand in front of her. With a bent
forefinger, he lifted her chin to gaze steadily into her blue eyes. "I'll see
to it you get back to Dallas immediately if you can look me in the eye
and tell me you don't love me and never want to see me again."

She stared into those blue-gray eyes and the world with all its realities
vanished like blown dust. There was only Scott and he was touching
her. Pride and the need for explanations of his erratic behavior dis-
solved, and she was left floating in the limbo of pure love. Her lips
trembled as the words struggled out of her heart.

"I've been so miserable without you these past weeks."

"Oh Dani." He clasped her to him, cradling her head against his
chest as he rushed kisses over her hair. "I'll never forget the day when
you walked into your office, and I saw you for the first time. My heart
collapsed into my boots. I knew in that moment you were the only
woman in the world for me. Oh sugar, I love you so much . . . so
much. The thought that I might lose you was making me loco. Ever
since Sunday I haven't been able to work or sleep. I kept trying to think
of a way to win you back. I came here to think. When Grandaddy
found me here, he knew something was wrong, and he bullied me into
telling him. This afternoon he got dressed and told me he had business
in Dallas. He had the pilot call from the plane to tell me he was bringing you home to Inveraray, and if I didn't settle things between us, he
would."

She moved her head from his chest and looked up at him. "Why,
Scott? Why couldn't you have told me about yourself instead of letting
me hear it from someone else?"

He bent down and lightly kissed her on the lips, then led her to the sofa, where she sat curled in his arms.

"When I was in my early twenties, I was pretty wild, spent money like it was tumbleweed. Big cars, nightclubs. Had all sorts of debutantes being shoved in my path, not only from Dallas, but from Boston, Houston, New York—all the cities where moneyed society functioned. My ego was unbounded. Beautiful, wealthy young women were falling all over me. Women from prestigious colleges, finishing schools, their tour of Europe behind them, were now on the prowl for a husband who could keep them in a lifestyle to which they were accustomed. Bubble-headed beauties whose main contribution to any marriage was the art of spending money. I don't think any one of them knew me as a human being. I was rich, eligible, and of the social elite. That was all they needed to know about Scott Rowland, Texas millionaire.

"Then Grandaddy called and said he needed me on the ranch here. He said he was too sick to run it. He can be a consummate actor when he wants to be. Anyway I came out here and stayed at the old homestead. Looking for strays in mountainous terrain is a lonely job. I had a lot of time to think and watch the stars. One has to experience it to know the feeling it can instill on one. I stayed two years. It changed my way of thinking, my way of life. The Scott Rowland you know is the real one. The one I wanted you to know, not some playboy dripping with money that might color your view of me. I wanted you to love me with or without money. Can you understand what I'm saying, Dani?"

"To be loved for one's self is what everyone in this world wants. Of course I know what you're saying and how you feel." She gave a small laugh.

"You're amused. Why?"

"I used to say to myself that I was making enough money now to support the two of us."

He hugged her. "That's my sugar. I knew you'd never try to make me a jet-setter, a mogul of society. Those years on the prairie taught me it's the simple things in life that bring real happiness."

"And after those two years of self examination?"

"I went back to Dallas, sold all my fancy cars, and bought the yellow pickup. I also bought land, all the property in and around Dallas I could lay my hands on. Nick Hunt built my first condo," said Scott, his hand gently rubbing her arm.

"I know. Nick told me. By the way, how do you know I'm not already engaged to him?" She smiled mischievously.

"I called him Monday. I had to know for sure."

"For sure?"

"I knew you loved me and weren't the kind to marry someone you didn't love."

"How did you know I truly loved you?" she teased.

"By your kiss, your touch, and the fact there was a spark of jealousy in your eyes when you told me to go back to my society playmate. But there was an even stronger reason for me to know you loved me. Grandaddy. When we were out on the range that day, he told me he saw the love in your eyes whenever you looked at me. His judgment is infallible."

"I'll remember that." She snuggled close to him. "I can understand your disguising the fact you're a wealthy man. But I'll never understand why you never phoned me to let me know what was happening. I would have waited all day Sunday for you if you had called and asked me."

He kissed her forehead. "Half the time there was no phone. I did a lot of the trouble-shooting on the oil rigs. Sunday I got a call about three o'clock in the morning informing me there was trouble at one of the rigs in Oklahoma. I didn't think you wanted me calling you at that time of the morning. Besides, I thought I'd have it fixed and be back early. But it took longer than I expected. I didn't want to waste time by driving into town and calling you. I wanted to get the job done so I could be with you.

"As far as my long absences go, I have been very busy consolidating the business. Daddy and I went to Tulsa to make arrangements to have those offices moved to Dallas. I've been interviewing people to take over the trouble-shooting on the oil rigs. I wanted to be able to work everything out of Dallas so I could come home to my wife every single night."

"Wife? Is this a proposal, Mr. Rowland?"

"Sure is, sugar. I wanted to ask you that night in the hay wagon, but the ring wasn't ready yet. I wanted everything to be perfect and proper." He disentangled himself and went to the fireplace, where he took a small black velvet box from the mantel, then went back to the sofa and sat next to her. "Will you marry me, Dani?"

"I wouldn't dream of marrying anyone else. Oh, Scott, you know I will."

He flipped the lid open and removed the diamond solitaire, then slipped it on her finger. "I guess you know you'll be mine for life."

"Oh Scott! It's beautiful! It must have cost a small fortune," exclaimed Dani, as her blue eyes reflected their disbelief at the fabulous gem.

"They had to send to New York for it. I thought one carat was too small and three carats too showy. I told them I wanted a perfect two-carat diamond set in platinum. It took longer than I thought. Isn't it customary for you to throw your arms around me and give me a great big kiss about now?"

Dani didn't need any prompting. Her arms slid around his neck and their lips met in a hungry kiss, as he swung her across his lap, deepening the heated kiss. Love deafened them. They never heard the sliding doors open. Startled they looked up when a voice boomed through the room.

"I hope you children have settled your spat. I'm hungry." Angus bounced the sliding doors shut, an impish grin on his face.

"We'd better join him," said Dani.

"Not yet. I've waited too long to hold you like this. Besides, now that I have you in my power, I have a favor to ask you."

"Anything my lord wants."

"I'd like to move in with you after we're married."

"I had every intention of us living together. Didn't you?" she asked, trying to keep a straight face.

"Sugar, it's all I think about."

"I'll get a regular office so we can have the house to ourselves."

"No need. I thought we could live there while our house is being built."

"House? Where?" asked Dani.

"Remember that property I showed you across the river from Daddy's spread?" She nodded. "Right there. We can ride to work together and I can pick you up at the end of the day. That is, if you want to work."

"I wouldn't know what to do all day if I didn't. We'd better join your grandfather now."

"He'd be the first to approve of what I'm about to do."

His mouth covered hers and moved with renewed warmth and passion as they clung to each other in remembrance of a night under the stars over Texas.